Rogue Wave

A Blue Portal Novel

V.A. Purcell

ROYAL OAKS
PUBLISHING

Cover Design: Clarissa Yeo

ISBN-978-0-9940489-5-0

A division of Value Improvement Associates (Canada) Ltd.

DEDICATION

To my amazing children and step-children

Nathan, Alanna, Meagan, Zachary, and Meghan

THE BLUE PORTAL NOVELS

These stories can be read in any order.

Tendrils

Rogue Wave

Torn Feathers

OTHER BOOKS BY V.A. PURCELL

Kindling Friendships: A Memoir

ACKNOWLEDGMENTS

So many people have played a part in making this book a reality.

To Donald Perry for taking me out on his lobster boat. Not only did he show me the beautiful coastline of Nova Scotia but he taught me all about the ins and outs of lobster fishing – complete with a hands on demonstration of how to put bands on lobster claws.

To Spurgeon Crouse, contractor and storyteller extraordinaire, for his patience with my renovation demands and his stories about lobster fishing. Thank you for taking time out of your day to share tales about lobster fishing on the South Shore. As a "come from away", any errors are my failure to understand.

To my advance reading team of Pat Barr, Karen Loranger, Linda O'Toole, Geraldine Tuck and Lynnette Werner. I couldn't ask for better friends. You made this a much more polished book. Any mistakes that remain are totally mine.

And to my husband Gerry. You are my rock. Thank you for always believing in me, even when I didn't. This book is a result of your unending support – both emotional and financial.

Thank you to each and every one of you for helping me tell this story. I am lucky to have you all in my life.

Veronica

1 CHAPTER ONE

Alone, at night, in the middle of nowhere.

I was too ambitious for my own good. The safe and prudent choice would've been to stay at the top of the cliff, but I had the bright idea to take the photograph of the lighthouse from down on the beach. It made for a more dramatic picture.

It felt more like November than May. The dampness seeped through my jacket, into my bones. The sharp wind whipped the string from my hood, stinging my face. My breath hung in the air like fog. Below me, the waves crashed into the rocks huddled directly below the lighthouse.

My eyes strained to make sense of the unfamiliar terrain. The beam from my flashlight only illuminated a small area. The twisted bushes outside the pool of light looked like animals or strange beings from the underworld lying in wait for me. The path was easy to see in daylight, but it was a whole different thing at night.

It was foolish to continue down to the beach, but I had the perfect shot pictured in my head—the moonlight reflecting off the turbulent waves making a dancing path of light all the way to the horizon, the serene silhouette of the lighthouse a

1

shadow off to the side. Would the photograph be good enough from where I stood? I turned and gazed up at the lighthouse. Not quite. If I didn't get this shot, then it would be more proof that I'd made the wrong choice—not only about tonight, but about my life.

The full moon poked through the cloud cover and bathed the rocky path in soft, yellow light. *Alma Sinclair, you can do this!* I straightened my shoulders and inhaled a lungful of air heavy with the pungent scent of dried seaweed. Gripping my flashlight tighter, I took another step down the path toward the beach. My foot slipped on the wet rocks and my arms waved wildly as I fought to regain my balance. Watching the beam of my flashlight ricochet crazily over the jagged rocks, it occurred to me that the light could be mistaken for a distress signal. Maybe I was in over my head. My heart beat faster as I half-slid and half-stumbled down the dark cliff onto the beach.

Once my feet were safely planted on sand, my heartbeat slowed. My ponytail had loosened and strands of hair tickled my face. I put the flashlight down, pulled off the elastic, and recaptured the errant strands, twisting the elastic more tightly around my hair. The sound of the waves was much louder. I picked up the flashlight and pointed the beam toward the water. The angry ocean churned like a pot of boiling water. The waves were so high they frightened me. My shoulders tightened with each crash.

I peered at the LCD screen of the camera. The shot was almost perfect. A couple of steps closer to the water and I'd get the shot I'd imagined—maybe even better. I took a tentative step backward and felt the icy water swirl around my foot. Another wave surged around my ankles. Something hit my boot. Moonlight glinted off glass. When the object re-surfaced, I reached out and grabbed it before the next wave could snatch it away.

It was an old bottle shaped like a flask, surprisingly heavy for its size. *Maybe there was a message, or perhaps a love letter hidden inside.* Bits of sand clung to the surface like grains of dried rice on a dinner plate. I brushed off the sand and raised the bottle up to the light. Twisting it this way and that, I tried to see inside. The thick, cloudy glass sucked up all the bits of light. The beam from my flashlight illuminated the glass enough to read the embossing on the front of the bottle. *PRESCRIBED BY R.V. PIERSE, M.D. BUFFALO N.Y.* The neck was long and the rim was chipped. There was no stopper. My shoulders dropped. If there had been a message, it was long gone. Still, I turned the bottle over and shook it. Nothing. Not even a few drops of sea water. My hand stiffened from holding the bottle too tight, and a tingling sensation crawled up my skin. I shoved it into my pocket and waved my arm around loosely. Almost immediately, the pins and needles sensation stopped and the tension in my hand eased.

I was about to take a final glance at the LCD screen when a shrill cry cut through the air. I stiffened. The high-pitched sound cut like a knife through the crash of the waves. I held my breath. There it was again. Someone was calling for help. I abandoned my attempt to take the picture. The weight of the bottle pulled my jacket down on one side, and it banged against my leg as I rushed off in the direction of the cries.

Boulders loomed up out of the darkness. The hungry waves licked at my boots and my feet slid on the tiny pebbles strewn on the sandy shore. My heart pounded in my ears, my shoulders heaved each time my lungs filled with air, and I regretted not keeping up with my gym membership. Would I be too late to help? A bead of sweat trickled down the side of my face. As I stopped to wipe it away, someone moaned nearby.

I ran in the direction of the sound. "Where are you?"

I came to an abrupt halt when the beam from my flashlight caught a figure perched on an outcrop of boulders. The reflective tape from their life jacket made an eerie design. The figure was slight—perhaps a woman. They were doubled over, and strands of long, wet hair covered their face. They glanced up when they saw my light and tried to stand, but quickly slumped back down onto the boulder.

Holding my flashlight up, I saw it was a young woman,

maybe in her early twenties. A tiny diamond embedded into the side of one nostril twinkled like a star then disappeared as my light moved over her face. She had a gash on her forehead. She didn't appear to notice the trickle of blood running down the side of her face.

I dug a crumpled, clean tissue out of my pocket and dabbed at her cut. "Hey, are you okay?" My flashlight caught the hills and valleys of the sodden clothing that clung to her small frame. The life vest covered much of her torso, but her jeans and thin jacket showed no rips or tears. No broken bones protruded at odd angles from underneath her clothes.

Her fingers brushed against my arm. "Help...help me...please!"

"What happened?"

She didn't answer.

My life-saving skills were limited to what I'd seen on television and in movies. With more confidence than I felt, I said, "Don't worry. Everything's going to be all right." I crouched down in front of her. "My name's Alma. What's yours?"

The words sounded stilted and impersonal, so I gave her a warm smile. She stayed silent so long I wondered if she had a concussion. Slowly, she sat up straighter.

"Joan. Joan Naugler."

"Joan, do you think you can walk back up to the lighthouse? There's a phone in my car. We can call for help."

She nodded.

"Okay. Let's get you up. Slowly now."

Joan shivered. I helped her out of her life vest then took off my jacket and wrapped it around her. She looked up at me and smiled her thanks. It was slow going, but we got to the car. Once she was safely tucked in the passenger seat with the heat blasting, I pulled my phone out of the glove compartment. Before I could dial, Joan grabbed my wrist with surprising strength.

"I'm all right. Don't call for help."

"You've got a cut on your forehead and you're trembling."

The tissue was glued to her forehead with dried blood and I was reluctant to replace it with a new one. "You're in shock. Who knows what other injuries you might have? Please, let me call for help."

Joan pulled her hand away quickly, as if she'd touched a hot stove. "Sorry," she mumbled. She folded her hands in her lap and intertwined her fingers so tightly the knuckles whitened. "You don't need to call for help," she repeated. "I'll be all right, like, in a few minutes."

It didn't make any sense. However, I wasn't going to argue with her. Instead, I changed topics. "What happened?"

Her trembling worsened, and I had to wait a few minutes until she'd stopped shaking long enough to answer.

"The wave. A rogue wave came out of nowhere. One moment w— I was on the boat, and the next minute I was in the water." She sobbed. Tears slid down her face and fell onto her lap like fat raindrops. She didn't have the energy to brush them away.

I was certain that she almost said we. "You were out in a boat by yourself? On a night like this?"

"I do it all the time." Her jaw jutted forward. "The ocean was calm when I left." Her eyes challenged me to disagree with her, then she quickly turned and stared out the window. "It was a stupid idea. Now I'm paying for it. I guess I'm lucky you were there." It sounded like she hated to admit it. Her shaking had subsided. She glanced up at me, her eyes pleading. "It was dumb, like, to go out in the boat..." She hesitated for a moment before adding, "Alone. I don't want anyone to know. Please, don't say anything."

I gripped the steering wheel and stared at the lighthouse. The beam cast a long path out over the water and I could see the white-tipped waves raise their heads as they charged toward the beach. I sighed. She was right. There'd be a big to-do. And she looked better.

"Do you live close by?"

"Nope."

"Is there someone I could call?"

Joan shook her head and slumped down in her seat. She chewed on her thumbnail and stared out the window while I debated. After a few moments, I turned to her and smiled. "Tell you what. I don't live too far from here. How about I drive you home and get you some dry clothes and something hot to drink? Then we can decide what to do. Okay?"

Joan smiled. "Great. Thanks."

When she turned to reach for the seatbelt, the bottle slipped out of my jacket pocket. I caught it before it could get wedged between the seat and the door. A shock ran through me. Quickly, I dropped it onto the floor behind my seat.

Joan glanced back at the bottle. "Looks kinda old."

I nodded. "I found it washed up on the beach right before I heard you call for help. Pulling out of the parking lot, my headlights caught the figure of someone near the lighthouse. I slammed on the brakes.

Joan jerked forward and gasped. Rubbing where the seat belt crossed her chest, she asked, "What's the matter?"

"Did you see that?"

She glanced over at me. "See what?"

I pointed across the parking lot. "A man was standing beside the lighthouse. He was tall and thin, wearing a sailor's cap. It was too dark to see his face."

Driving the car to the edge of the gravel and almost onto the lawn, I switched on the high beams. The solitary shape of the tall, white building stood out against the night sky. Its walls reflected the light back in my eyes. I turned to ask Joan if she could see anyone, but her eyes were closed. Her face was pale again. It seemed like a good idea to get her back to my place as soon as possible.

We didn't pass any other cars on the drive back. My headlights bounced off the trees lining the edge of the dark, two-lane road. They looked like soldiers standing at attention, their branches whipping back and forth in salute as we passed. Joan's breathing became more even. The silence gave me a chance to reflect on the evening's events. Was Joan telling the truth? Had she been alone in the boat? And if not, why would she lie?

* * *

The deep blue wood siding of my home appeared black in the darkness. The only light was the one above the front door. Moths bounced against the glowing fixture like stones being skimmed across ripples in a lake. Joan leaned heavily on the railing as she climbed the few steps onto the porch. An old rocking chair filled one corner. Joan sat on the edge of the seat, making the chair tip forward. I noticed her glance at the glass starfish in the front window as I unlocked the door. Once inside, Joan followed me into the kitchen. She shrugged off my jacket and hung it on the back of a chair.

"Are you okay on your own for a minute? I want to run upstairs and grab you some dry clothes."

Joan nodded and sat down wearily.

I rummaged through my bottom dresser drawer searching for something that was a couple of sizes too small. My wish that one day they'd fit again was unlikely to be granted. When I bustled into the room Joan's head jerked up as if she'd been asleep.

Handing her the clothes, I nodded in the direction of the front hall. "The washroom is upstairs, second door on your left. Feel free to run a hot bath while I make some tea."

She gave a slight shake of her head. "No, I'm okay. Tea's great. Thanks."

Joan slipped back into the room a few minutes later. Even my smallest clothes hung on her slender frame. The neck of the shirt fell down below her collarbone, showing the word "Confuses" tattooed in elaborate, dark blue lettering etched into her white skin. Although I'd just met her, *confused* was not a word I'd use to describe Joan. It made me curious to know if there was more to the tattoo. I tried not to stare at it as I asked her how she'd like her tea.

"Milk, two sugars." She paused. "Please."

I placed the mug on the table and sat across from her.

"How are you feeling? Does anything hurt?"

Joan bent over her mug rather than raising it to her lips and took a few sips before she answered. "I'm okay. Just tired."

"Is there anyone I can call?" I slid the plate of cookies toward her. "I'm sure they must be worried."

"Nope." Her eyes narrowed, and she gripped her mug tighter. "You'd wake them up. Besides, I'm used to taking care of myself." Then, as if a switch had been flipped, the tension in her body eased. Joan loosened her grip on the mug and sat back in her chair, brushing the damp, stringy strands of blond hair from her face. Her eyes slid around the room. "You've got a nice place."

I grinned with pride. "Thank you. It's not much, but I love this little cottage. It used to be my grandmother's."

Her eyes flashed. "You're lucky. It may be small, but, like, at least it's yours." Her voice had an edge to it.

"Oh, no." Warmth flooded my cheeks. "I'm not complaining. I realize how lucky I am." I gave a shrill laugh. "Well, sort of…" Joan frowned. "My grandmother left me this place on condition that at least one of my paintings is sold in a recognized art gallery. So far, I haven't been very lucky."

"Recognized? Who decides that? Is it one of those places that waits until you're dead and then gets rich off you?"

I frowned. "I certainly hope I don't have to wait until I'm dead for my paintings to sell."

Joan shrugged. "It's a hard life, being an artist." She said it in such a way that it gave me the impression she knew what she was talking about. "But at least you get to do what you love, right?"

I nodded. "That's what I thought. Now I'm not so sure." The words slipped out before I could stop them. For a few moments, we sipped our tea in uncomfortable silence. The only sound was the grandfather clock in the front hall as it chimed midnight.

I carried our mugs over to the sink. "You might have a concussion or something. You shouldn't be alone. I'd feel terrible if something happened to you. Leaning against the counter and folding my arms across my chest, I said, "Why don't you stay here tonight?"

Joan shook her head. "No, I want to go home." I retrieved a plastic bag from a drawer and handed it to Joan. "You can put your wet clothes in this."

She looked down at my borrowed pants and shirt. "What about these?"

"You can keep them." Joan seemed surprised by the gesture. She left the room quickly, as if she was afraid I'd change my mind.

I went into the front hall to wait for her when I noticed a blue glow from the direction of my car. Puzzled, I stepped outside. The wind had died down and a bank of fog hovered across the road. My shoulders tensed as the fog glided closer. A familiar scent hung in the air—cool and crisp—but I couldn't place it. I waited to see if the blue light reappeared.

Suddenly, the hairs on the back of my neck stood on end. Someone was nearby. My heart beat faster. The old rocking chair creaked back and forth as if someone had just gotten up. I leaned over the edge of the railing and peered around the corner. For the second time that night I saw a tall, thin man wearing a cap. He darted across the lawn and disappeared into the trees bordering my property so quickly that I wondered if it was my imagination. My eyes watered from staring so long at the spot where he'd disappeared.

I gave up and turned to go back inside when I noticed something written on the car's passenger window. My eyes widened in shock. The word "BEWARE" was carved into the mist clinging to the glass. It looked like icy fingers had scrawled a message on a steamy locker room mirror. The fog glided closer, enveloping my car. The mist was so thick only the outline of the blue SUV could be seen. I hurried back inside and locked the door.

When Joan came downstairs I told her to look out the front door window. She shrugged. "It doesn't look that bad."

"It does to me," I said more sharply than I'd intended.

Joan stepped back from the window and said, "Guess I'm

staying after all." She followed me upstairs to the guest room. It was papered in a small floral print. An antique double bed was centered against the front wall between two windows. A stuffed bear was nestled against the pillows. Opposite the bed was a matching bureau topped with a bevelled mirror. The tables on either side of the bed were made of the same wood as the other furniture, although of a different design. They were antique jewellery chests repurposed as night tables. White, lace curtains made the room feel light and airy.

"The guest room's always made up. I'm not sure why, because I don't often have visitors." I shrugged. "Maybe it makes me feel like I'm not living alone." As I scooped up the bear off the bed and placed him on top of the dresser, I noticed my reflection in the mirror. The face that stared back at me looked unfamiliar. My normally organized appearance was a chaotic mess. I'd given up on the ponytail. Now a wild tangle of curly, dark hair framed my round face. There were dark circles under my eyes and my usually ruddy, plump cheeks were pale and sunken. My full lips looked like they'd been sucked dry. I wasn't sure if I should tell Joan about the man. I'd already decided the message was due to some combination of light and fog.

"This's nice stuff. I like it when everything matches." Joan crossed the room and picked up the bear. She brushed her fingertips across his tummy. He had soft, caramel-coloured fur and a red ribbon around his neck. I'd gotten him from my boyfriend. He was still at the accounting firm where we'd both worked. She turned to me and smiled. "What's his name?"

Her question caught me off guard. "Name? Gerry."

"Gerry. That's an odd name for a bear."

"Sorry. You mean the bear? He doesn't have one." Joan's smile vanished. "Oh." She placed him gently back on the dresser.

I closed the door part way, then stopped. "Joan? I think the man from the lighthouse might have followed us." She frowned. "I'm sure everything is fine. I just…" She hardly paid any attention to me. She crawled into bed and closed her eyes.

I switched off the light and softly closed the door.

I lay in bed and thought about all I'd given up to move here—all the things that were no longer in my life—a partner, a secure job, and close friends. Gerry gave me the teddy bear on our last anniversary. I'd tucked it away out of sight in the guest room because I couldn't part with it. I only had three months left before I lost the house I'd given up everything for. Had I make the right choice?.

2 Chapter Two

*T*he misty, damp morning drained whatever energy I'd gotten from my night's sleep. I'd woken up a couple of times to check on Joan. I dragged myself downstairs and switched on the coffee maker. While I waited for it to warm up I poked my head outside and checked my car. There was no writing on the window.

I sucked in the heady smell of caffeine as I carried my mug over to the table. Just breathing in the smell of coffee kicked my brain into gear. I still found it hard to believe that she'd been by herself. I'd figure out some way to ask her about it again without sounding like I was prying when she came downstairs.

The local newspaper offered a welcome distraction from thinking about last night's bizarre events. The article on the front page was about lobster traps being vandalized off the coast near the lighthouse. Stealing lobsters was nothing new. It had been going on for generations. The ocean was too big for law enforcement to patrol and for centuries fishermen took care of any problems themselves. It was a tight knit community. They usually knew who was stealing from them, and if they didn't know their friends did. Men had lost their lives fighting over their fishing territory.

But now, with the price of lobsters higher than ever and fishermen stock piling their lobsters at the government wharf waiting for the prices to go even higher, there was enough money to attract a more sophisticated organization of robbers. The demand for lobsters in Asia and Europe had also made it worthwhile to highjack shipments of lobsters worth millions of dollars. Lobster was a big business. The government was stepping up their efforts, but it was still a huge job to patrol and enforce the law in the vast ocean waters surrounding the Maritimes.

I gave up waiting and made a fried egg and some toast. Joan came downstairs as I finished eating. She moved slowly and her face was pinched. The pajamas I'd lent her exposed a good two inches of leg above her ankles. It was a good thing the waist was elasticized or the bottoms wouldn't have stayed up.

"How are you feeling this morning?"

She walked over to the window and stared at the grey, cocooned morning. She shrugged. "Okay, I guess." She turned and gave me a small smile. "My arms are a bit sore and I've got a couple of bruises." She lifted her shirt and showed me large yellow spots around her ribcage. She seemed proud of them, like a boxer who'd gone nine rounds with the champion.

"Are you sure you don't want to see a doctor?"

She shook her head with a surprising amount of vigour. "No, I'm fine." She could see the doubt on my face. "Really." Joan sat hunched over her mug, her hair hung down covering her face. Her hand trembled as she took a sip, and she didn't look well enough to be on her own.

"You're welcome to stay here another night. It would make me feel better to know you're okay."

"No, thanks." She wrapped her arms around herself and stared down at her mug.

"Can I at least make you breakfast before you go?"

Joan glanced over at my empty plate smeared with egg yolk and dotted with toast crumbs. "No, just some toast." As I got out the bread she said, "I can make it myself."

"It's no problem." It was nice to have company. I cheerfully popped the bread into the toaster, took out a plate, and grabbed the jam and peanut butter.

Joan stretched her legs under the table and leaned back in her chair. "This kitchen looks kinda like something from one of those decorating magazines." She pointed at the wainscoting. "Those white boards part way up the walls make it look sorta old." She grinned. "But nice."

The yellow walls and white wainscoting made the kitchen bright and cheerful no matter what the weather. It faced east, so the meager amount of morning sun added to the warmth. The old pine floor added to the comfortable, relaxed feeling.

I waved my hand, dismissing the compliment. "Thanks. Most of my ideas are from decorating magazines. Ever since I can remember, my dream was to be an artist and live by the water, so I've had lots of time to plan my ideal home."

Refilling my coffee mug, I sat down in the same chair as the night before, like we'd already established a routine.

Joan nodded. "So, like, how come she left this place to you?"

That was a good question—something asked by more than one relative. The earthenware mug felt smooth against my thumb as I slid it up and down the curved handle. "I'd always wanted to be an artist, like my grandmother—my mom's mother. When we came down here to visit, Grandma always had bits of charcoal and scraps of paper around. She'd take me down to the beach and we'd sketch for hours. She even let me use her paints when I got older. She encouraged me." I smiled, remembering the way she pursed her lips at some of my less than stellar efforts. "She would make suggestions in such a way that I always thought I had a choice whether to follow them or not."

"She sounds nice. I just had my Grampy, but he never had time to do stuff like that. He was always working."

"Oh, what did he do?"

"He was a fisherman."

I took a sip of coffee. "My older brother likes fishing, but he does it as a hobby. It's a tough life."

"Yeah. Sometimes you got no choice." Her gaze drifted over to the window and she sat lost in thought for a moment. "So, where's your brother?"

"He's back in Ontario with his family. It's just me here." Anger surged through me as I recalled the conversation we'd had when he found out about Grandma's will. I had to wait a moment so that my voice wouldn't quaver before I answered. "My parents live in Ontario. They moved there after they retired so they could be closer to their grandchildren—my brother's kids."

"They must be happy you're living in the family home."

I laughed sharply. "Not at all. My mother left Pleasant Cove when she graduated high school and got a job in Halifax. She never looked back. When we came down for a visit, the car door was barely closed before she'd say that moving to the city was the best decision she ever made. When I wanted to go to art school, my parents weren't supportive." I shrugged. "Mom used to talk about how poor they were and how being an artist was a hard life. She was a good artist herself. My parents said they'd pay for my school, but only if it was something useful. So I became an accountant. The best jobs were in Toronto, so that's where I went." My mouth was dry, so I took a gulp of cold coffee and swallowed it quickly. "My older brother had already moved there, so it made sense." I smiled. "Then Grandma left me this place. I decided to chuck it all in and do something I've always wanted to do before it was too late." I shrugged. "So here I am."

Joan nodded. "So long as you sell a painting. Right?"

I grimaced. "My Grandma gave me two years to do it."

"When's your time up?"

"At the end of July."

Joan's eyes widened in surprise. "Wow! That's, like, only a couple of months away."

"Three, actually." I marched over to the sink and dumped the remainder of my coffee down the drain. "I probably have a few things that might fit you. I don't know why I moved them here. I can always use more closet space. Do you want to come upstairs and see? Then I can take you home."

As Joan followed me upstairs, it dawned on me that the tables had been turned. Instead of me being the one to ask questions and finding out about Joan, she'd found out all about me.

Joan sat on the edge of the bed while I pulled out clothes tucked away in the back of my closet and tossed them in a pile on the floor. Her eyes widened in amazement as the pile grew.

"Why were you at the beach last night?" she asked.

Bristling at her directness, my response was sharp. "I was there because of an assignment for my painting class. Well, it's more of a group than a class."

Joan looked puzzled.

"We use photographs as a guide for our paintings. My great idea was to photograph the lighthouse during the full moon." My defensiveness evaporated and was replaced with a smile, remembering the struggle to get down to the beach. "From the beach, of all places. I was just about to take the shot when I heard your cries."

"You didn't get your picture?"

I shook my head. "No. I took a couple of photographs before going down to the beach. I'll use one of them." Muttering under my breath I said, "It's not like I'm good enough that it'll matter."

Joan frowned but didn't say anything. She pointed to a garment bag that poked out of the jammed closet. "What's in there?"

I unzipped it and pulled out a vintage strapless dress. "This is for when I have my grand opening at a gallery, or at the very least sell a painting. My girlfriend convinced me to buy it when I decided to move here. Red is my lucky colour." I hoped it would still fit.

"I'm sure you'll get to wear it."

Bending down, I grabbed a T-shirt and shook out the wrinkles. It was one of those souvenir T-shirts—the kind with the logo of the resort tastefully embroidered over the left front pocket. I must've made a face because Joan said, "Teddy bear guy?"

I nodded and quickly added the shirt to the pile. "I don't regret moving to Toronto. When I got a chance for a buyout package at the same time as inheriting the house, well…it seemed like a sign. Plus, with my savings and the money I made when I sold my condo, I had enough money to live on, so here I am. I've always wanted to be an artist, but making a living at it is harder than I thought."

I sighed. Maybe my parents were right. I folded the clothes strewn on the floor and placed them in a pile on the bed. Joan shifted to make room for the colourful assortment of garments. She picked up a silk blouse and rubbed the sleeve between her finger and thumb.

I pointed at the blouse. "That stuff belongs to my old life. I'm not sure why I packed so many of my office clothes. There's a blazer here somewhere if you want it." I dug around and pulled out a black jacket with a design sewn in gold thread on the collar.

Her eyes widened. "Are you, like, sure?" Her expression softened and she looked more like a kid rather than a woman in her twenties.

"I've got a couple. That's more than enough."

"Cool!" Joan bent over to pick up a pair of jeans decorated with silver studs on the back pockets. She stiffened and grabbed her side. Slowly, she straightened. The jeans were clenched in her hand, and her face was drained of colour.

Taking the jeans from her, I said, "I'll leave these clothes in your room. Why don't you take a hot bath? I can wash your clothes from last night while you're in the tub.

I gave Joan some towels and pulled out a bag of Epsom salts from the back of the cupboard under the sink. Handing it to her, I said, "This should help relax your muscles."

Joan pointed to an old-fashioned bottle filled with lavender scented bubble bath on the vanity. It was there more for decoration than usefulness. Its shape reminded me of the

17

bottle on the beach. "What about that stuff?"

I shrugged. "Help yourself. It probably won't help as much as the Epsom salts, though."

Joan grinned. "I'll use both." She glanced at me. "If that's okay."

I couldn't remember how long the bottle had sat there untouched. There wasn't any good reason to save it. "Go ahead."

Joan started to undo the buttons on the pajama shirt before I had a chance to leave the room. I caught a glimpse of the tattoo as I quickly shut the door behind me. I could see a hint of other letters on either side of the word *Confuses*. I wondered what the rest of the tattoo said.

I checked the pockets before tossing Joan's clothes into the wash. She had a cell phone wrapped in a plastic bag. She must've forgotten all about it because of what happened last night. The rest of the pockets were empty.

The lavender bubble bath reminded me of the old bottle I'd found. It was still out in the car. After I put Joan's clothes in the wash I went to get the bottle.

I opened the car door and reached down to grab the bottle. My hand hovered above it as I remembered the jolt I'd felt when I touched it last night. I popped open the trunk and found a reusable grocery bag. Then I picked up the bottle with my fingertips and dropped it into the bag. I slipped back into the house and took the bottle into the kitchen.

I made sure not to touch the glass as I slid the bag down to reveal the bottle. It was the first chance I'd had to get a good look at it. The words *PRESCRIBED BY R.V. PIERSE, M.D. BUFFALO N.Y.* were embossed on the front. The body of the bottle tapered into soft curves like shapely shoulders narrowing into a long neck. The rim of the neck was chipped, but years in the water had smoothed away the sharp edges. Maybe it was a rare and valuable antique. I'd have to check the Internet and see if I could find out. In the meantime, it would be nice to display it somewhere in the house. I tentatively reached out and touched it. Nothing. I got braver and picked it up. Still nothing. The thick, clear glass made the bottle heavy for its size.

I wandered from room to room trying to decide where to put it. Then my eyes caught sight of the glass starfish. It was solid blue in the centre, with ribbons of colour stretching out its arms. The ribbons of blue were the width of a strand of hair. By the time the strands reached the ends of the arms they were so thin they disappeared, leaving the tips of the arms clear. Little air bubbles were trapped inside the glass, but the starfish was smooth to the touch on the outside. It would be a perfect partner for the bottle.

Placing the bottle beside it, I stood back to admire the result. At that moment, the sun broke through the cloud and the beams bounced through the glass of the bottle and the starfish, making a rainbow on the opposite wall. Even if it turned out to be valuable, there was something about it that made me loath to let it go. It belonged here.

* * *

I brought Joan's laundry upstairs. She was drying her hair. "Lunch is ready."

"I'll be down in a minute."

When Joan didn't come down a little while later, I went to check. I found her in the living room frozen in place. Her hands were clenched so tight her knuckles were white. She stared at the bottle.

"Joan?" I stepped into the room.

She jumped. "Oh, you scared me." She pointed at the bottle. "The bottle was glowing. It was some kinda blue light. I could see it from the hall, so I came into the room. Then the light disappeared." She snapped her fingers. "Just like that."

I waved my hand in dismissal. "It's the sunlight. It made a rainbow on the wall when I first put the bottle there."

"Hmm." She frowned. "I think the starfish was better all by itself."

I stepped closer to the window, admiring the way the shape

of the two objects balanced each other out. "It looks kind of interesting. And the starfish doesn't seem as lonely."

Joan shook head. "That old bottle gives me the creeps."

I laughed. "Your imagination is getting the better of you."

Joan glanced back over her shoulder as we left the room. "I hope you're right."

"By the way, I found your phone in your jacket pocket." I pointed at the phone sitting on the counter still wrapped in plastic.

"Thanks." She switched it on. "Where are my keys?"

I shook my head. "The only thing I found was your phone."

She glared at me. "I'm sure I put them in the pocket that zips up."

I shrugged. "The only pocket that was zipped up was the one with the phone. There was nothing in the other one. Maybe you forgot to zip it up."

Her eyes narrowed and her face darkened. Then she smiled. It was as if the clouds had parted and the sun came out. "No problem. Yeah, there's a spare set. I'll call and tell 'em, like, I need 'em."

Joan helped me clean up after lunch. She sloshed the soapy water around the bowls and placed them haphazardly in the drain rack. Once or twice I used the tea towel to wipe bits of food off the "clean" dishes. Something about her manner made me think that asking her to re-wash them wasn't a good idea.

When Joan left the room to make the phone call, I picked up the dishcloth she'd left in the sink. I wrung it out and hung it over the drain rack to dry. I tried not to eavesdrop, but Joan raised her voice. It was easy to tell things weren't going the way she'd hoped. When she came back into the room she tried to appear like things were all right.

"They can't come let me in, like, 'til tomorrow. They asked if I could stay here, if not, then I could hang at, like, a friend's place."

"No one else has a key?" She shook her head. "Of course,

you're welcome to stay here tonight." She didn't look happy about the way things had turned out. "Why don't we go into town? I hadn't planned on house guests and I could use a few things. Maybe we could get something special for dinner."

Joan went upstairs to get her jacket. Suddenly, there was a loud bang, followed by a piercing scream. I ran upstairs and pounded on her door.

"Joan! Joan! Are you all right?"

The door wouldn't open. I was about to try and kick it in when suddenly it flew open. A strong wind blew through the open windows. The curtains looked like large, white balloons. Strands of hair whipped around my face. Joan stood frozen in place, her eyes as wide as saucers. I rushed over and put my hands on her upper arms. "What happened? Are you hurt?" Her eyes were fixed on something behind me. I turned to see what she was staring at. On the mirror, written in the same icy handwriting as the message on my car window, were the words, "*I know what you did.*" The letters were unevenly formed and the "y" dripped down almost to the bottom of the mirror.

"I…" She licked her lips. "I went to get my jacket. When I turned around, there he was—in the mirror. I thought he was standing behind me. I turned around and that's when I noticed the window was open and there was no one there." She shuddered. "At first I thought I'd imagined it. But then…" She grabbed my forearms so tightly her nails dug into my skin. "When I turned back around, there was writing on the mirror."

"What did the man look like?"

"Tall and thin with dark hair. His clothes were like my Grampy's. The ones he wore fishing."

"What do you mean?"

"Pants with the straps over your shoulder. And an old jacket with…oh, I forget what it's called. You know, the red squares?"

"Plaid?"

Joan nodded.

I glanced over at the mirror. "What does it mean?"

Joan sunk down on the edge of the bed. "I don't know. A

blue light surrounded him. The same light that was around the bottle." She glared at me. "I told you that bottle was weird."

I sat down beside her. "You're right. I don't know if it's the bottle or not, but there's definitely something going on." I licked my lips. "Last night, it was so strange, you wouldn't have believed me. And this morning, well, it all seemed so unreal, I thought I'd made it up."

"What happened?"

"A blue light shone from inside my car. I went outside to check. No one was there. When I looked around the side of the house, I saw a man. He disappeared into the woods before I could get a good look at him." I stood and wiped my sweaty palms on my pants. "I think he was the same man I saw at the lighthouse."

"Do you know who he is?"

I shook my head. "No. I've never seen him before." I hesitated. "There's something else."

"What?"

I took a deep breath. "'*Beware*' was written on the passenger window."

Joan frowned. "Beware?"

I glanced at Joan. Over her shoulder I could see the mirror. I jumped up and grabbed Joan's arm. Joan followed my gaze and stiffened. The message was gone. Then she straightened her shoulders like she was ready to step into a boxing ring. She marched over to the mirror and leaned in to take a closer look.

I came and stood beside her. "Something else happened last night. A smell." I wrinkled my nose. "I've smelled it before, but I can't remember where."

Joan whirled around and headed for the door. "Alma, you need to get rid of that bottle."

I hated to admit it, but she was right. The bottle might be valuable but it wasn't worth the risk of keeping around. "I'll put it outside in the garbage can."

As soon as I stepped outside, the same smell as the night before hung heavy in the air. The cool, crisp scent was so familiar. It was comforting rather than upsetting. It bothered me that I couldn't place it. Quickly, I shoved the bottle into the garbage can and slammed the lid closed. The scent was fainter now. Closing my eyes, I breathed in deeply. A memory floated to the surface of my grandfather pushing me on a tire swing in this backyard. I looked over at the tree where it used to hang. The scent was Old Spice. My grandfather's cologne.

He'd always made me feel safe. Whenever I thought there were monsters under the bed or in the closet he would say, "They're more afraid of you than you are of them because you know the secret. Remember?"

I'd pretend that I hadn't. He'd put his forefinger on each side of his mouth, stretch his lips wide and stick out his tongue. I'd squeal with laughter.

"That's the secret!" he said. "Don't show them you're scared and they'll go away."

The memory was so clear that when I opened my eyes I half expected him to be standing there in front of me.

Before going back inside, I jogged over to the spot where I thought the man had disappeared last night. There were no signs anyone had been there. I saw the kitchen curtain drop back into place as I walked toward the house.

Joan was waiting for me when I got inside. "Did you find anything? Over by the trees?" Joan's voice had a sharp edge. Her arms were folded across her chest and her feet were spread apart in a defiant stance. I shook my head. She opened her mouth about to say something, then changed her mind. Slowly, she walked over to the window and leaned over the sink to get a better look at the backyard.

"The man... He was so angry." She gripped the edge of the sink until her knuckles turned white. It reminded me of last night when we'd met. She kept her eyes fixed on the view out the window. Her shoulders hunched up around her ears.

Tea wasn't strong enough and this didn't seem like the right occasion for a bottle of wine. I hunted through my meager selection of hard liquor for something stronger. The best I could come up with was a bottle of Grand Marnier. I'd purchased it ages ago for a dessert recipe.

I filled a glass and handed it to Joan. "Here, take this." Joan gulped the liquor down in one mouthful. Then I poured a glass for myself. The hot liquid burned as it ran down my throat. Joan sunk into a chair and reached across the table for the bottle. Her hand shook as she refilled her glass. She took a drink then carefully set the half-empty glass down. She dropped her head, resting her chin on her chest. Her hair hung like curtains on either side of her face, masking her expression. She whispered, "It was a ghost." She raised her head and her eyes flashed. More loudly she said, "It was a ghost. I'm sure of it."

My grandmother mentioned a few times that she'd seen her mother after she'd passed. She said it was comforting to know that she was watching over her. Growing up, I'd heard tales about haunted houses. I was often surprised by the nonchalant way people talked about finding their cutlery strewn around their kitchen when they woke up in the morning, as if having a ghost in residence was a normal thing. I had to admit there was definitely something strange going on, but leaping to the conclusion that the strange man I'd seen hanging around was a ghost? That was a little hard to believe.

3 Chapter Three

"Fine. Don't believe me. I don't care." She slumped in her seat and shoved the chair opposite her with her foot. The chair bounced back from the table and hit the wall. If she'd been standing, I'm sure she'd have stomped her foot.

I avoided the urge to go over and see if there was a mark on the wainscoting.

"Why would a ghost bother us?" To my ears, it sounded like I was talking to a child. I hoped Joan was too angry to notice.

Her head snapped up. "Not us, me."

"You? Why you?" I sat down across from her and licked my lips. They tasted of Grand Marnier.

She nodded toward the backyard. "It has something to do with that bottle. I know I'm right!"

I didn't want to admit it, but what happened in Joan's room scared me. I was glad Joan was staying another night. On our way out the door, I removed the grocery list pinned to the front of the fridge and stuffed it into my pocket.

The jingle of a local car dealership blasted from the radio as soon as I started the car. I reached over and turned the sound down as the news began. The deep voice of the news anchor washed over us.

"Last night's fog tops today's news. There was a three-car pile-up on the 103. One person was taken to hospital. There were no other serious injuries. The highway was closed for an investigation but is now reopened." I resisted the urge to give Joan a look that said I told you so.

"Police are asking for the public's help in solving a rash of lobster thefts in the county. Local fishermen have reported traps sabotaged and another government wharf was broken into last night. Officials aren't saying how much damage was done but do say the increase in thefts is due to the higher lobster prices this season. If you see anything suspicious, please call the RCMP. In other news, nobody won last night's radio bingo. Next week's jackpot will be two thousand dollars. Bingo cards can be bought at the following locations…"

Joan reached over and turned the radio down so low it was hard to hear. I glanced over at her, but she'd turned to look out the window. The news was over and music played faintly in the background. Although I wasn't happy with her touching the radio without asking, the quiet was fine with me. Without saying a word, we drove the short ten-minute ride into town.

We parked next to a white van with the logo of an alarm company plastered on the side door. We took a few steps toward the store when I stopped and walked back to the van. I pulled the grocery list out of my pocket and jotted down the phone number. Joan shuffled from one foot to the other, her hands shoved deep into her pockets.

She said sulkily, "An alarm's not going to do any good if he's a ghost."

I shoved the paper into my pocket. "Better safe than sorry." I quipped. Oh god, I sounded like my mother. "So what would you like for dinner?" I made my voice lighter to make up for my previous comment.

Joan watched as I unjammed a cart from the long line protruding from the covered shelter. "Steak. No broccoli." She practically skipped along beside me as we headed for the doors.

I grinned. "Why don't we go all out and see if we can get some lobster tails. We can have surf and turf."

Joan stopped dead in her tracks. "I don't like lobster." Her carefree mood evaporated. She stomped off down the aisle and disappeared from view. Keeping up with her changing moods was exhausting and I selfishly hoped she wouldn't find me until after I'd done most of the shopping.

I navigated my cart through the senior shoppers clogging the aisles until an older woman blocked my progress. I watched as she attempted to juggle her cane, the handle of her cart, and a tin of beans. She dropped her purse and it flew open. I helped her collect her belongings, even chasing down loose coins that had rolled under a display. When I stood, I noticed Joan scowling at me from the end of the aisle. I made sure the elderly lady had her can of beans safely stowed in her cart and all her belongings back in her purse. By the time I was done, Joan had disappeared again.

We finally connected in the meat section. Joan was bent over a refrigerated display of steaks nestled in Styrofoam trays and wrapped in plastic. I regretted my suggestion to buy steaks. Hamburger would have been more in line with the behavior she'd displayed toward the elderly lady. I pushed the cart over to the side and joined her.

"That old lady was stupid. It's her own fault she dropped her purse. She should've put it in the cart. It's, like, her problem, if she lost something." She grabbed one of the thicker steaks. She turned to put it in our cart and bumped into the elderly man beside her. Handing me the steak, she said, "Can't blame no one but herself."

The store wasn't the place to argue with her. We wandered up and down the remaining aisles. By the time we were ready to check out a long line had formed.

Joan scowled. "This is gonna, like, take forever."

"Why don't you go and wait in the car? There's no sense in both of us standing here."

I'd parked close enough to the front of the store that I could press the button on my key fob to unlock the doors from where we stood. Joan mumbled "thanks" over her shoulder as she walked out.

Buried at the bottom of the cart were a few items Joan must have added without me noticing. Nothing much. A couple of candy bars, some gum, a fashion magazine, and a tube of lipstick. I shoved the magazine back on the rack. I was about to wedge the lipstick between some candy bars when I changed my mind. I was being as childish as she was. Clearly, Joan didn't have much. I took the magazine back off the rack and placed it on the conveyor belt along with the lipstick and candy. Then I chose a decorating magazine and a couple of chocolate bars. I'd earned them.

The large glass windows gave a perfect view of the parking lot. While I waited in line, I saw Joan talking to a man. Although his back was to me, I could tell he was husky, with short-cropped hair. Joan was hunched over and her hair hid her face so I couldn't see her expression.

I scanned the parking lot looking for the man as I pushed the cart back to the car, but he'd disappeared. He didn't look like the man I'd seen before—Joan's ghost. But something about him made me uneasy.

Joan sat in the passenger seat, her head against the headrest, her eyes closed. She didn't move as I shoved the groceries into the trunk. I climbed into the car and slammed the door shut harder than necessary. My patience was wearing thin and I regretted purchasing the extra items for her. Sucker, I thought. Sharply, I said, "Who were you talking to?"

She opened her eyes slowly and gave me a blank look. "What?"

"In the parking lot. I saw you talking to a man with short hair."

Joan straightened up and reached for the seat belt. "Some guy. He wanted to know if they had any chicken left on sale."

"Chicken?"

"Yeah, there's some special and he wanted to know if there were any left. Said his wife sent him to the store just for that."

Joan's body language hadn't been consistent with a

conversation about chickens, but I wasn't going to argue with her. Instead I said, "Your candy and stuff are in a separate bag."

Joan flushed. "Thanks." She dug out the gum and stuffed a couple of pieces into her mouth. "I'll pay you back," she said as she chewed.

Embarrassed for snapping at her, I said, "Don't worry about it. I'm glad you're keeping me company."

"Hang on a minute." Joan reached over and pulled something out of my hair. She held it up for me to see. "A white feather. Your guardian angel is watching out for you." She gently placed it in the empty cup holder as we pulled out of the parking lot.

* * *

Dinner was a success. We accompanied the steaks with a nice bottle of red wine from the Nova Scotia valley. The combination of wine and last night's events left both of us ready for an early night.

Peeling off my jeans and T-shirt I pulled on some loose fitting pajamas. The anxiety around losing the house had added a few pounds. Feeling the soft flannel against my skin was as soothing as the wine flowing through my bloodstream.

I willed my muscles to relax, starting with my feet and moving up my body. By the time I reached my shoulders, the tension that had been building over the last few days was gone.

* * *

I woke up to the glow of a soft blue light coming from the mirror opposite my bed. At first I thought I was still dreaming. Then the scent of Old Spice filled the room. I gripped the edge of the sheets and pulled them up around me as if they would provide some sort of barrier. Suddenly, the window flew open. The pages of the book on my night table flipped so quickly they reminded me of an old-fashioned animated movie.

"Alma." It sounded like the wind was talking. "Alma, don't be afraid. I'm here to help you."

My eyes were drawn back to the mirror. The light was becoming brighter. Instead of my reflection, a thick bank of fog clouded the glass. Silently, the fog parted to reveal me on the beach. I bent down and picked something up and slipped it into my pocket before I could see what it was. Somehow I knew it was the bottle. Then I ran farther down the beach and disappeared into the fog. It was like watching a home movie.

A gust of wind blew through the room. The fog rolled off into the distance revealing my shocked face, reflected in the mirror.

A man's voice whispered, "Thank you for helping me. I've been waiting a long time."

The smell of Old Spice grew fainter. The blue light flickered like the flame from a candle whose wick was almost gone.

"Please, let me help you." He sighed.

Air brushed against my cheek. I imagined it was his breath as he whispered in my ear. A shiver went down my spine. Then, something inside of me snapped. This couldn't be real. Suddenly, the room was plunged into darkness. It grew colder and I wrapped the blankets tighter around me.

"Who are you?" I asked, ready to spring from the bed and run for the door.

His voice came out of the darkness. It was so close he could've been sitting next to me. "You are in danger. Please, let me…"

Something cold squeezed my hand. I screamed.

Footsteps thudded down the hall. The bedroom door flew open with such force it banged back against the wall. Joan rushed into the room.

"Alma? You okay?"

4 Chapter Four

*J*oan switched on the lamp beside my bed. "What happened?"

It took a moment for me to answer. "It was…" I sighed. "I don't know what it was." I glanced over at the closed window. "I must've been dreaming."

Joan raised her eyebrow. "More like a nightmare."

"Yes, I guess you're right. Thanks for coming to my rescue." Joan followed me toward the door.

"No problem."

I started to shut the door when the sound of a howling wolf vibrated down the hallway.

"Sorry," Joan called as she hurried the rest of the way back to the guest room. "My phone's ringing."

Joan's laughter floated down the hall as I shut the bedroom door.

The first thing I was going to do in the morning was throw the bottle back into the ocean. The garbage can wasn't a good enough solution. The bottle probably didn't have anything to do with the nightmare, but it was best to be on the safe side. I lay in the dark and listened to every creak and groan in the house. Dark shadows slipped out from the walls and slithered along the floor, arms outstretched toward me. Ghostly wraiths, wearing sailor's caps, circled the bed. I flipped the light back on.

The decorating magazine I'd bought when I was at the grocery store with Joan was on the night table. I flipped through the pages. Photographs of normal, sunny rooms eased my mind. Eventually, my eyelids grew heavy and I switched off the light. This time there were no visions of ghosts. Instead, my thoughts were filled with ideas on redecorating the living room with antique shelves, custom covered pillows, and artistically displaying expensive knick-knacks on a glass coffee table. In the centre of the display was an old-fashioned medicine bottle.

* * *

My blankets were twisted around my ankles. I yanked them free and pulled them under my chin. I snuggled into the warm cocoon. Then I remembered the events of the previous night. The sun went behind a cloud and there was a sudden chill in the room. My feet touched the cold floor as I got out of bed and I hurried to put on my slippers.

I wandered down the hall to the bathroom. I was so preoccupied with what I'd heard and seen last night that I didn't notice the message on the mirror when I first entered the room. When I did, I took a step back and almost fell into the toilet.

"*Don't trust anyone*" was written on the mirror above the sink.

The handwriting was the same as the message on the car window and the mirror in the guest room. My stomach clenched. *Was he watching me right now?* My gaze darted around the tiny room. I charged over to the tub and clutched the edge of the shower curtain. I pulled it back so sharply the rings snagged on the bar and tore the curtain. On the edge of the tub was the bottle of bubble bath Joan used. A film of hardened soap clung to its base. I flipped the toilet lid down. A loud bang reverberated through the room. I winced and hoped the noise wouldn't wake up Joan.

I sat down on the edge of the tub, the corner of the torn shower curtain dangling above my head. What was happening? Who shouldn't I trust? I remembered the voice warning me that I was in danger. Was he really here to help me? I grabbed one of the purple hand towels and rubbed out the message. I didn't want Joan to see it.

The message on the bathroom mirror made me more determined than ever to throw the bottle back in the ocean. I quickly scrawled a note for Joan to let her know I'd be back soon. The bottle was safely stowed in the trunk and I sat waiting for the car to warm up. Inch by inch the house came into view as the warm air blasted the inside of the windshield clear of the morning condensation. My grandmother wasn't afraid of ghosts, but something about this one, if it was a ghost, didn't give me the impression he was harmless.

I began to relax as my feet warmed. I rolled my window down an inch to let in some fresh air. I closed my eyes and sucked in the fresh morning air. I took another breath. The temperature in the car dropped much faster than was explained by the open window. I opened my eyes and watched as my breath hung in the air like a small cloud. The spicy, clean scent of Old Spice filled my nostrils. I grabbed the door handle. The door locks thudded closed. I leaned against the door and pushed but it didn't budge.

"Alma, don't be afraid. I'm here to help you." It was the same voice as last night." A man began to take shape in the passenger seat. He was tall and dark. A sailor's cap was perched on his head. He smiled and said, "My name is Nicholas Denyes."

"Who?" My voice squeaked. I slid as close to the driver's door as possible. "Why are you here?"

His eyes widened in surprise. "Why, the bottle of course."

"The bottle?" I licked my lips. "Joan was right?"

This was the first chance I'd had to get a close look at him. Dark, unkempt hair framed his weathered face. Tiny wrinkles creased the corners of his eyes. His clothes were worn. A patch covered one elbow of his plaid jacket. The collar of his white T-shirt was frayed.

His voice was soft, almost a sigh. "I've waited a long time for someone to come. I've come to save you."

"Save me?" Indignation quickly replaced any fear I had of Nicholas. "Save me from what?"

"That young lass you picked up on the beach. She's no good."

"Joan? How do you know?"

"I know the Nauglers, all right. They don't change. She's one of them, which means she's up to no good. Take my word for it. Don't trust her." His eyes flashed in anger.

"I don't understand. How do you know anything about Joan?"

He sighed. "Trust me, I know the Nauglers."

"Why should I believe you?"

He shrugged. "Believe me or not, it makes no difference to me." He frowned. "By the way, there's no point in driving to the ocean. He shifted in his seat and avoided my gaze. "We're connected."

I glanced back toward the trunk. "The bottle?"

He shook his head. "No, it's more than that." He began to fade away. "At least Joan Naugler won't be a problem for long."

By the time Joan came down for breakfast, I'd made a decision. Whatever was happening, I'd deal with it myself. I called the alarm company and set up an appointment to get an estimate. I doubted an alarm would keep out a ghost—the whole idea of a ghost was hard to wrap my head around—but doing something made me feel better. And Nicholas wasn't my only problem. This place wasn't exactly my house, at least not yet. I was hoping to convince my mother that a house alarm was a good investment and that I was concerned for my safety.

After the incident with Nicholas, I was sure I could sound convincing.

Joan walked into the room as I hung up.

"Who were you talking to?"

I shrugged. "Oh, no one special. Did you sleep okay?"

I think she nodded yes, but I couldn't tell because her head was stuck in the fridge. Moments later, she emerged with her hands full of yogurt, strawberries, and spinach. She shut the door with a nudge of her hip. "Do you have a blender?" I pointed to the cabinet beside the stove. My cooking, especially breakfast, never entailed a blender. "What about chia seeds?"

"What? Chai? I have some Chai tea."

Joan rolled her eyes. "No. It's not the same. Forget it. This'll be okay." She paused mid-stride, straightened her shoulders, and announced, "I'm going to make you breakfast. Just sit back and relax." She dumped the various containers on the counter then pulled out the blender. She peeled some bananas and dropped them into the blender along with the other ingredients. The whir of the blades drowned out any conversation. I watched, fascinated. She was confident and capable. From inside the pantry cupboard she pulled out a bottle of hardened honey I didn't even know was there. After a minute in the microwave, Joan added some to the foamy concoction in the blender. Moments later, she placed a frothy glass, filled to the brim, on the table in front of me.

Grinning she said, "I'd stick a straw in it, if you had one."

She peered at me anxiously. I took a sip. The creamy liquid was a perfect blend of banana and strawberry. You'd never know there was spinach in it.

I licked my lips and took a second sip. "It's delicious. Thank you."

Joan filled herself a glass and sat down. She was in good spirits. The trauma of being washed up on the beach and the incident with Nicholas seemed to have faded. "I love smoothies. I could eat 'em every meal." She laughed. "Well, maybe not everyone." She raised her glass in a toast. "Thanks for the steak." She drank half the glass in one gulp and licked her lips. "My foster family taught me how to make these."

"Foster family?"

Joan flushed. She slid her thumb and forefinger up and down the sides of the glass and stared down at the table. "Yeah, I stayed with them, like, for a bit. The McGregors. They, like, own the art gallery." She bit her lower lip. "Till my dad was…" She paused, searching for what to say. "Till my dad could look after me again." Quickly, she picked up her glass and took several swallows in a row without taking a breath. Setting the glass firmly down on the table, she locked her eyes on mine. "You've been great. But, like, I need to get back to my place." She swallowed and rushed on before I could say anything. "That stuff with the ghost." She tucked her hair behind her ear. "I'm not afraid. I don't want you to think I'm a chicken or anything. Like. It's just, like. Well, I need to get going." She met my eyes, daring me to challenge her.

"I understand. I'm glad I could help." I thought about the message in the bathroom.

I picked up my glass and put it in the sink along with the container from the blender. The glass was coated with the dried residue from the smoothies. I scrubbed until it sparkled. "So, when would you like to go?"

Joan handed me her glass. "Anytime you can take me."

"Whenever you're ready to go is fine with me."

Joan looked down at her jeans and shirt. "What about these? Like, how…?"

I smiled. "Keep the clothes. And if you don't want them, drop them into the donation bin at the mall."

The breakfast dishes were all cleaned up, but Joan still hadn't come back down. I dropped the tea towel in a sodden pile on the counter and went upstairs. The door was ajar and I peeked inside. Joan stood in front of the dresser. She'd pulled the sleeve of her shirt over one hand and was using it to wipe away tears. In the other hand, she clutched the bear—the one she'd noticed on her first night.

I crept downstairs and took the bag of clothes I'd given Joan and put them in the backseat. Then I grabbed the bottle out of the trunk. It was better to keep it away from Joan. I brought it inside and stuffed it into the back of a drawer full of tea towels. A few minutes later I yelled from the kitchen, "Are you ready to go?" I heard the guest room door close and then her footsteps on the stairs. Then, all of a sudden, there was a scream and a series of bangs. I rushed into the front hall. Joan was lying in a heap at the bottom of the stairs. The black button eyes of the teddy bear gazed up at me. His red bow askew.

"Oh my god. Joan, are you all right?" I knelt beside her. She struggled to get up. "Take it easy. Just lay still for a minute."

She turned her head. Her nose brushed up against the bear's soft belly. She stared at it at moment, puzzled. Then she struggled to sit up. She put her hand to the side of her head.

"Does anything hurt?"

She shook her head. Slowly she reached out and picked up the bear.

"How did this get here?"

She pushed herself up enough that she could sit on the bottom step. Joan carefully placed the bear down on the step beside her. She wiggled her toes and moved her head from side to side.

"Nothing seems to be broken." She stretched her arm up until she could grab hold of the bannister. Then she pulled herself up. She took a couple of deep breaths and took a couple of tentative steps toward the front door. "Let's get going." With each step, she stood straighter, and by the time she reached the door, her head was high and her shoulders were only slightly rounded. She didn't look back.

As we pulled out of the driveway I noticed a blue light coming from the guest room window. I hit the brakes and we both jerked forward.

"What?" asked Joan.

"Nothing. Sorry. My foot slipped." I carefully backed out of the driveway. Stopping before we turned onto the road, I said, "Where to?"

"Huh?" asked Joan.

"Where do you live?"

"Just a sec." Joan dug her phone out of her pocket and squinted at the screen. She brushed back her hair and glanced sideways over at me. The tiny jewel embedded in her nostril sparkled in the sunlight. It was a sharp contrast to her dark, withdrawn eyes. She stuffed her phone back into her pocket. "Drop me at the mall. Like, they're going to meet me there." Her jaw was set and she stared out the windshield. Her hands were shoved into her pockets. I pictured them clenched into tight fists. Joan stared straight ahead for a few minutes. Then, in a quiet voice, she said, "That bear. I used to have one like it when I was a kid."

I kept my voice neutral. "What happened to it? Did you lose it?"

Joan shook her head. "My older brother. He got a fishing knife one Christmas. He practiced using it." She shrugged. "The bear was old. My dad said it wasn't worth anything."

When we got to the main entrance of the mall, I asked, "Are you sure you're all right? Do you want me to come in with you?"

She gave an imperceptible shake of her head. "I'm good." I reached into the backseat and handed her the clothes. "Thanks," she said as she slammed the door closed. My last glimpse of Joan was her scurrying over to the main entrance. She stood aside to let a family of shoppers out before she grabbed the closing door. A man appeared beside her and grabbed her elbow when she stepped inside. The two vanished into the dark opening, but not before I noticed Joan try to pull her arm free.

It didn't feel right leaving her there like that. By the time I'd parked and returned to where I'd last seen Joan, there was no sign of her. Every time I pictured the man grabbing her elbow my imagination added more details. Were his fingers clenched around Joan's arm so tight that the fabric of her coat seeped between them? Had she winced in pain? I scanned the crowd and wandered through several stores. I even had a story ready in case I "accidentally" ran into her. But no luck. The pair had disappeared.

On the way home, I stopped at the monument dedicated to sailors lost at sea. The monument sat atop a small, grassy knoll with a perfect view of the ocean. The names of those lost at sea were engraved into black, granite pillars and grouped by year. Nicholas's name was third from the top for his year. There were only a handful of names that year compared to others when entire crews were lost. I traced his name; the rough, white letters stark against the smooth, black granite.

The anticipation of going home to work on my painting was overshadowed by concerns about Joan's safety. Maybe I was overreacting. The man hadn't grabbed her that hard. Maybe it was worry and not anger that made him grab her. Had she even tried to pull away? Was it her brother or a boyfriend? Joan hadn't told me much about herself. I didn't even know where she lived.

The jarring sound of music from the radio added to the unsettled feeling. I touched the button on the display screen and switched from the radio to Bluetooth. It connected to the playlist on my phone. The calming music of Pachelbel's "Canon in D" filled the car. I recalled Joan's story about the bear. She must have learned to take care of herself by now. There was nothing more I could do. Besides, maybe it was safer for her to be out of the house and away from Nicholas. She could have broken her neck falling down those stairs. He couldn't have put the bear there on purpose, could he? He said he was here to protect me, but what if he was lying? Now that she was gone, would he leave, too?

5 CHAPTER FIVE

*T*he red flag was up on the side of the mailbox at the end of my driveway. There was only one envelope inside the box. My heart skipped a beat as I noticed the simple, white envelope with the elegant monogrammed return address up in the left corner. The letter was from my grandmother's lawyer. I tossed it on the passenger seat and sped up the driveway. The car jerked to a stop just short of the porch stairs.

A van pulled up the driveway as I got out of the car. The logo on the side was the same one I'd seen at the supermarket.

"Afternoon, dear." The driver walked over to me with his hand extended in greeting. "Name's Ron. Ron Aldrich. Pleased to meet you."

He was dressed in the usual workman's garb. Work boots and pants hung low around his waist. His wrinkled face was dusted with black stubble from below his nostrils down his neck, and disappearing under the white edge of the undershirt that peeked through the unbuttoned collar of his plaid shirt.

"I thought you were coming tomorrow," I said more sharply than I'd intended. He didn't seem to notice. The smile on his friendly face didn't falter.

"The office told me about your call. I was driving right past your place so I thought I'd stop by. I can come back tomorrow if you want me to."

"No. Come on in. Would you like a cup of coffee or tea?" He followed behind me up the porch stairs and into the house without interrupting the flow of conversation.

"Tea'd be nice, dear. Thanks." He glanced around the kitchen saying, "So, what kind of alarm system were you thinking of?"

I dropped the lawyer's letter on the counter unopened and busied myself with making tea.

I shrugged. "I'm not sure. What do you recommend?"

Ron walked through the house, advising me on where to put motion sensors as well as alarms on the doors and lower windows. "We can add outdoor lights with motion sensors, too, dear." He looked up from his clipboard. "Do you want cameras?"

I shook my head. "No, that won't be necessary. I don't have the budget for that. I guess not too many places have that kind of equipment."

Ron pursed his lips. "You'd be surprised. I get all sorts of customers wanting different things. I always like to tell people what their options are."

"Do you have many people wanting cameras?"

He nodded. "We just finished a big job at the government wharf down the road a'ways. They didn't have none." He chuckled. "You know the government. Always trying to cut corners on the wrong things. I told 'em when I put in the system to get the cameras. It wasn't until the thefts last month they listened." He grinned. "Cost 'em extra to put 'em in after the system was installed."

"Did they catch the robbers?"

Ron shook his head. "Nope. They haven't touched the wharf since we put in them cameras. They're probably somewheres else. The price of lobsters is up, so's I can't imagine they'll stop until someone catches 'em."

"I guess it'll keep the police busy, or is it the coast guard?"

"I don't know about them, but folks 'round here take care of their selves. I remember one guy put razors in his lines. He knew who'd been stealing from his traps, but he couldn't prove it. Next time he was in town the feller he thought had done it had his hands all bandaged up." He chuckled. "Them lobster fisherman are cowboys out on the water." He grimaced. "You don't want to go messing with them, dear. No sir." He hitched up his pants, which was difficult as he was still holding his clipboard. "Okay, dear, that'll do it. The office'll get back to you and let you know how much the system'll cost." He followed me back to the front hall and handed me his business card.

"When would you be able to install it?"

He shrugged. "If we've got the parts, early next week."

Accompanying Ron to the front door, I noticed the large grey clouds that filled the sky, prematurely darkening the afternoon. The bright headlights from Ron's van were a sharp contrast to the gloom as they cut their way down the drive and onto the road.

The letter from the lawyer glared at me from the kitchen counter. I knew what it would say. I shoved the unopened letter into the junk drawer along with the duct tape, a hammer, and random screwdrivers. Then I tried to slam the drawer shut but it stuck inches from closing. I left it that way.

"Nicholas?" I whispered. Then a little louder, "Nicholas?" I felt a little silly calling his name. I waited a few moments. The house was quiet. Seeing his name carved into the stone monument made him seem more real, but at the same time raised more questions. I decided to see what I could find out on the Internet. A few variations of his name came up but nothing about him or his death. I wasn't surprised. A fisherman's death off the coast of a small town in Nova Scotia in 1950 wasn't big news. The stiffness between my shoulder blades grew the longer I clicked through websites without learning anything new. Sitting in front of a computer wasn't my idea of fun. My spirits rose as I turned off the screen and went to get my camera from the front hall. Finally, I could spend some time looking at the photographs from the lighthouse.

So much had happened since then, it seemed like a life time ago. I scanned through the pictures I'd taken the night I'd found Joan. Each of them had something I could work with. A full moon peeking between grey, angry clouds, waves cresting onto the beach, and finally, a beam of light cutting through the darkness. My canvas was primed and ready to go. Quickly, I sketched out a composite of the pieces I liked from each of the photographs. The lighthouse, just off center and positioned so that there was enough water and sky to create a path of light stretching off the canvas. I stood back to take a look at my work. The painting pulled you in.

My hands flew across the canvas in sure, confident strokes. The lighthouse stood atop the cliff, the path down to the beach barely discernable. The straight line of the horizon divided the water from the sky. Then I ran into trouble. The waves were too flat. Too lifeless.

The afternoon light was fading. I switched on the lamp near my easel. The glow from the lamp cast shadows around the room.

"Feel the wind on your face," a voice whispered.

I whirled around. The paint dripped from my brush onto the floor.

"Hear them crash onto the shore. Feel their energy. Don't be afraid to paint their anger."

"Nicholas? Is that you? Where are you?"

I went into the kitchen and unearthed the bottle from the pile of tea towels. A jolt of energy coursed through my body making me drop the bottle. It gave a loud thud as it hit the floor. I bent down to pick it up when the room got so cold I could see my breath coming out in puffs of smoke like bits of white candy floss. The bottle began to glow, a soft deep blue at first, then changed to a bright turquoise. The change in colour was mesmerizing. I sat back on my heels, captivated. Suddenly, I felt a presence behind me. I jumped. Nicholas stood partly in the shadows. His eyes were dark pools, devouring any light that came near them. His arms were hugged tightly across his chest. Waves of energy pulsed around him making the hairs on my arms stand on end.

"Why are you so angry?" I asked.

His voice sent a chill through me. "Because you let her leave."

"What?"

"The girl. You let her leave."

"What do you mean, I let her leave? She was my guest, not a hostage." My right wrist throbbed from the bolt of energy that shot through me when I touched the bottle, but I didn't care. "And her name is Joan. What does it matter to you? You said not to trust her. I'd have thought you were happy to see her go."

"Happy!" He almost spit he was so angry. "It is justice I'm after, not happiness, you foolish woman." He took a menacing step toward me and I shrank back.

I forced down the lump in my throat. I wasn't going to give him the satisfaction of seeing me cry. The whole room began to pulse with a blue glow so intense it looked almost white. It was so bright it hurt my eyes. The cupboard doors flew open and closed. Bang, bang, bang. A stack of papers on the counter blew around like leaves. I shivered as cold air wrapped itself around my legs and climbed up my body.

Nicholas raised his fists and shook them at me. "How can I get revenge if she's gone?"

Something snapped inside of me. "I don't know, and it isn't my problem. I didn't ask you here." I pointed an accusing finger at him. "What have you got against Joan, anyway?" I took a step toward him, shielding my eyes from the light with my left arm. "What do you want?"

"Revenge." His voice rolled like thunder.

He glanced over his shoulder at the seascape and then turned back to look at me. His next words were sharp but less angry. "I lived most of my life on the sea. Either you love it or you hate it." His eyes flashed. "You've got to love it, if you want to paint it proper."

The pulsing blue light vanished from sight like a bit of

debris in a stormy ocean.

I stood blinking at the spot where he'd stood a second ago, then collapsed onto a chair. The longer I sat there, the angrier I got. He told me he was here to help. I never should have believed him. *Trust no one.* That included Nicholas. The only one I could trust, the only one I could count on, was myself. I struggled with the painting for a while then gave up. I'd lost the flow. Maybe tomorrow's meeting would give me some suggestions.

* * *

Painting can be a lonely occupation and it was both stimulating and fun to get together with other artists on a regular basis. I always picked up new ideas, and the structure of having an assignment due forced me to be more disciplined. I'd taken courses for years back home, and, being new to the community, the group gave me a social outlet. And learning about great places to paint and where to get art supplies was worth connecting with other artists. The group had been together for a few years and it was only by chance that I learned about it.

One day when I was at the grocery store I'd noticed a woman posting a notice on the community bulletin board. It was actually her bright orange hair, big hoop earrings, and colourful silk scarf that drew my attention. She noticed me and came over and introduced herself. Faye's warm smile drew me in, and her enthusiasm about the group encouraged me to check them out. The first meeting was like being home. Throughout the fall session I got to know several of the other artists, but none as well as Faye Crouse. She was so positive and supportive. Each of my canvases drew words of praise and gentle hints that improved my paintings. Once the sessions were over, we continued to stay in touch. Now, I counted Faye as one of my best friends. And she knew about the deal with my house.

There were already a couple of other cars parked along

the side of the road. The studio was on a side street, neatly sandwiched between a hairdresser and a private home. The building had undergone a renovation, which transformed the studio space from two dark smaller rooms into one big room, complete with large windows and skylights. The white walls made the room feel open and airy. Bev Donaldson and Gwen Glasgow were already hard at work. Faye was getting her paints and easel set up to do a demonstration. Today she was wearing a subdued scarf—a simple black-and-white design.

"Your sky is amazing," I said to Gwen as I passed by on my way to the kitchenette with a tray of homemade cookies.

"Thanks. How is your lighthouse painting coming along?"

I shrugged. "Not so good. I can't seem to get the water right. The waves are too stiff."

Faye looked up, a tube of paint squished between her finger and thumb. "Have you been out on the water?"

"No. I don't know anyone who owns a boat."

"Seeing the light bounce off the waves, the different colours…" She put the cap back on a tube of paint. "The smell of the sea air and the boat moving up and down under your feet." She smiled, revealing teeth squished together because there was one too many. "There's nothing like it."

Bev interrupted. "You don't get seasick, do you?" She grimaced. "Then it's not so fun. I remember one time, we were out on my brother's boat. The weather was fine when we left, but my god, partway through the afternoon, storm clouds appeared on the horizon." She shuddered. "We headed for shore, but the storm was faster. I was never so glad to feel the earth beneath my feet. My stomach was upset for ages. I haven't been out since. That was enough for me, thank you very much." She'd been waving her paintbrush around while she spoke. Now she stopped and pointed it at me. "Check the weather before you go. And there's no need to go out very far."

Faye came and stood in front of my easel. "This is good, Alma. The lighthouse is exactly the right size and you've placed it just off center. Nicely done." She gave me one of her warmest smiles.

"I don't know, Faye. The waves aren't right."

"My cousin owns a boat. If you're interested, I could ask her if she'd take you out."

I sighed. Would that help? "I don't know. That seems like a bit of an imposition. She doesn't even know me."

Faye brushed aside my comments. "She and her husband go out all the time. I don't think she'd mind taking you along." She grabbed her purse. "I'll send her a text and see if she's going out one day this week." Before I could say anything she'd found her phone and was typing away.

During break time, while the others were busy gossiping about the goings on in the community, Faye came over and showed me the text she'd received from her cousin Theresa. They were going sailing one afternoon this week.

"Are you sure it's okay?" I asked Faye.

"It's fine. Don't worry." She handed me a piece of paper. "Here's Theresa's phone number. I'll let you guys sort out the details." Faye nibbled at one of my cookies. "These are great. They remind me of the ones my mother used to make."

"It's from the *Green Shutters* cookbook. I found a copy jammed in with a bunch of old books at that antique store up the road from my house."

Faye smiled. "I remember that cookbook. Almost every household in Nova Scotia had a copy. Have you made the chocolate squares yet?" I shook my head. "Oh, you've got to try them. They were my absolute favourite when I was a child." She neatly folded her napkin and dropped it into the compost bin. "I haven't had one in years."

At the end of the session, Faye came over and took a look at my canvas. I'd worked on shading the rocks and lighthouse. Maybe it was because of the relaxed atmosphere, but I was pleased with my efforts. The rocks almost jumped off the page and the shadows on the lighthouse walls blended so smoothly the building looked more like a photograph than a painting. I'd made much better progress in one afternoon than I had all the time I'd been working on it at home.

"You are very talented, Alma. Have confidence in yourself. I'm sure this painting will be amazing." She took off her glasses and wiped them on the edge of her scarf. "This painting is going to be the one. I can feel it in my bones." She slipped her glasses back on. "Have fun on the boat. The wind in your hair, the boat rolling beneath your feet, the whole ocean wide open before you. Then go home and capture that in your painting."

"You make it sound so simple."

She winked. "It is."

She started to walk toward her car when I called out, "Faye, just a second. You wouldn't happen to know about a fisherman who died by the lighthouse?" She frowned. "His name was Nicholas Denyes."

She shook her head. "No, the name doesn't ring a bell. When did he die?"

"In 1950." It dawned on me that I didn't know much else about him.

"Why are you asking about him?"

I hadn't thought this far ahead. I shrugged. "Just something I came across."

"You might want to ask Theresa's husband. I'm sure he'll be on the boat. I think someone in his family was a fisherman, or had something to do with fishing."

* * *

I spent the rest of the afternoon painting. Nicholas left me alone. The mirrors didn't have any messages, and there was no blue light. I thought about getting rid of the bottle, but Nicholas said we were connected. I didn't want to tempt fate or draw his attention, so I'd left it in the drawer. It was nice to have the house to myself again, for however long it might be. I decided to celebrate with a glass of Chianti. The wine rack was empty which meant I needed to give up on the idea or go out to the store. I chose to drive into town.

My favourite cashier was as the express checkout. While I

waited in line I scooped up a design magazine and added it to my pile. And, for good measure, I added a chocolate bar. Then I put it back. I thought about the frozen cookies waiting for me at home. I changed my mind again and put the chocolate bar back on the conveyer belt.

Margie smiled. "Hey, Alma. Back again so soon?" She laughed. "Quiet night at home?"

"Yeah. It's been a bit busy. Too tired to cook tonight. You'll probably see me here again tomorrow. I have no idea what food is even left in the fridge." I laughed. "I'll probably pull out of the parking lot and then remember something else I was supposed to buy." I gathered my purchases and helped Margie put them in my grocery bags. "How's your family? Has your son gotten over his cold?"

She rolled her eyes. "He's back to normal and then some. I wish I had half as much energy as he does."

I had a soft spot for Margie. She and her son were one of the first people I'd met when I moved here permanently. I'd bumped into her and her four-year-old son one day at the small café in town that doubled as a children's play centre. Michael was having a wonderful time disappearing in a large, screened-in area filled with small, colourful balls. It looked like a giant box of Smarties. His infectious laugh as his head surfaced was contagious. Instead of taking my coffee to the outside table like I'd planned, Margie invited me to join her at one of the tables inside. We talked mostly about her son. My niece and nephew were a bit older, but I'd babysat them often when they were younger. I'd entertained Margie with stories of some of their escapades. Sitting and talking with her made me feel like I belonged. That I wasn't a visitor.

As I walked out of the store, I felt someone staring at me. When I looked back over my shoulder, the manager was bustling over to Margie. He nodded in my direction. Margie glanced back at me and frowned. I debated walking back to ask if there was a problem, but I was tired and the bags were heavy. I waited for a moment, but neither of them paid any more attention to me.

The drive home was uneventful. I turned off the radio and enjoyed the peace and quiet for the short distance home. I never got tired of glimpsing the water through the trees as the road twisted and turned along the coast.

The phone rang as I unlocked the front door. By the time I dumped the grocery bags and walked over to the phone, the ringing stopped. I scrolled through the caller list but the name was unavailable. A few moments later, the screen showed one message waiting. I punched in the code and listened to the message.

"Ms. Sinclair. This is Officer Eisner. Could you please call me as soon as you get this message?"

The switchboard directed my call and a few moments later, Officer Eisner was on the line. He didn't waste any time with pleasantries. "Will you be home tomorrow morning? We'd like to come by."

"Why? What is it?"

"We'll discuss that when we see you." His voice was terse.

Maybe it was from watching too many police shows, because I said, "Do I need a lawyer?"

The officer sounded surprised. "No, ma'am."

I'd eaten the whole chocolate bar before my dinner was ready. *What did the police want with me?*

There'd still been no sign of Nicholas, and with Joan gone, the house felt emptier than usual. Even my new decorating magazine didn't distract me. I called one of my friends in Toronto but she didn't pick up. I sent her a text but she didn't respond. When I first moved out east, a couple of my friends came out for a visit. They'd never been to the Atlantic Provinces and they jumped at the opportunity to get shown around by a local. But now that they'd been here, there were so many other places on their list to visit they hadn't been back. Instead, I caught up with them when I was back in town visiting my family. But after two years of living out on the East Coast, living the life of an artist, I had so little in common with their big city jobs and lives. I flipped through the television channels looking for something to fill the empty evening.

There wasn't much to choose from. Eventually, I gave up and went to bed early.

* * *

I woke up before the alarm went off.

I showered, dressed, dried my hair, and did my makeup in record time. I'd chosen to wear one of my favourite dresses. The turquoise lining smoothed out the bulges, allowing the blue and silver gauzy outer fabric to flow around my body in soft curves. Silver inuksuit dangled from my ears. I checked my reflection in the mirror and smoothed out a couple of wrinkles in the fabric hugging my hips.

A visit from the police couldn't be good news. I mentally corrected myself. In Ontario the provincial police were the OPP. Here in Nova Scotia the provincial police were the Royal Canadian Mounted Police, or RCMP for short. Some of the larger towns and cities had their own police force in addition to the RCMP, but in many of the rural areas, 'The Force' was it.

I jumped at the sound of the doorbell. They were early.

Two officers stood on the front porch. One old and one young. The day wasn't that sunny, but both men wore aviators. They removed them at the same time, as if they'd rehearsed it.

The older policeman had thick, iron-grey hair and a crop of bristles which cast a shadow over his cheeks and down his neck. He probably had to shave twice a day. Deep lines were etched into the corners of his eyes, like he'd spent too much time staring at the sun or glaring at criminals. A small paunch hung over his belt.

The younger police officer's blond hair and athletic build was a sharp contrast to his partner's appearance. The hair on his face was so fair it gave him the appearance of a much younger man. It wasn't until he stepped closer and I saw the coldest blue eyes I'd ever seen that I realized he was much older than I'd first thought. The air around him bristled with energy.

They introduced themselves. Toby Eisner was the younger officer, Carl Brennan the older one. Neither of them returned my smile.

"Hello, please come in." They followed me into the kitchen. I'd planned on offering them some coffee but their manner was so cold and formal I didn't bother. Sweat rolled down my sides and droplets formed on my forehead at the hairline. They made me feel guilty of something. I just didn't know what. Officer Eisner did the talking while Officer Brennan scanned the room. I was certain he noticed every little detail. He asked me routine questions about how long I'd lived in the house and where I'd lived previously. He also verified my name and date of birth. Then his tone changed. He asked me if I was at the grocery store on Monday. His partner pretended he wasn't interested, but his eyes had stopped scanning the room and now rested on me.

"Yes, yes I was."

"We had a report of money stolen from a car in the store's parking lot at the time you were there. A passerby noticed a young blond woman hanging around the car where the purse was stolen. She left before we could arrive." He glared at me. "The witness got part of the licence plate. Your car matches the description."

I told them about finding Joan washed up on the beach. They were surprised when I said Joan had stayed with me for a couple of nights.

Officer Brennan stepped toward me and put his hands on his hips. "Do you usually invite strangers to stay overnight in your home?"

The scent of Old Spice wafted in the air. I stood up straighter, all signs of guilt about their visit disappeared. "I don't turn away people in need of help." I didn't have to explain about the fog and the car keys.

"Why didn't you report the incident?"

"Well, she assured me she was fine. That's why she stayed at my house. I wasn't comfortable letting her stay on her own."

"Are you a nurse?"

"Pardon?"

"I was wondering what qualifications you have to decide

if someone needs medical help." He took another step closer and glared down at me.

Officer Eisner chimed in. "What would you have done if something had happened to her during the night?"

I didn't correct them about Joan staying for two nights. I glared back at them, refusing to take a step backwards. "What do you think I'd have done? I'd have called an ambulance." I crossed my arms. "As it was, nothing happened. She was fine." Heat spread up my neck and into my cheeks.

"Where is the young lady now? Do you have her address?"

"No, I don't." They looked at me as if they didn't believe me. "I dropped her at the mall." I thought about telling them about the man she'd met, but I'd hardly seen him. They didn't appear to trust the information I'd given them so far. I doubted a vague description of some man would be of interest. They both flipped their notebooks closed at the same time.

At the front door, Officer Brennan paused. "It's odd that you invite strangers into your home, yet you're interested in a home alarm?" I must have had a blank look on my face because he added, "You have fridge magnet from the alarm company." He handed me a business card. "If you think of anything else, please give me a call."

I took the card and stuffed it into my pocket without looking at it. "I'm not in the habit of inviting strangers home. Joan was an exception. As it happens, I'm thinking of taking a holiday and I thought it might be a good idea to install an alarm." It took all my self-control not to slam the door behind them. The story about the holiday was a lie, but I certainly wasn't going to tell them about Nicholas. The scent of Old Spice followed him out the door.

I went back into the kitchen and started to make coffee, but I couldn't stop thinking about Joan. Did she steal the purse? So much for helping strangers. I should have taken her to the hospital like I'd first planned. I abandoned the coffee making and went to check my wallet. My cash and credit cards were all there. Maybe Nicholas was right about Joan after all. Then I remembered the smoothie she'd made that last morning. She seemed so happy. It was a sharp contrast to my last glimpse of her. Although I didn't get a good look at the man, it was more Joan's body language that bothered me. What had happened to her? Was she safe?

I went up to the guest room and started to go through the drawers. Maybe there was some clue to her whereabouts. A piece of paper was wedged in the back of the dresser drawer. It was an old photograph of my great-grandparents standing in front of their famous rose garden. I'd found the photograph when I was looking through some old albums. I'd set it aside, planning to frame it. The photograph reminded me of how much things had changed over the years. The picture showed the beautiful rose gardens in the foreground and the side of the house off in the distance. You could see a bit of the front porch. Today, the rose gardens were no more than a few bushes. I'd planned to take a picture of the house from the same spot and hang the pair of photographs side by side but somehow I'd never gotten around to it. I didn't even remember where I'd left the old photograph.

I flipped the picture over. On the back was written, Bert and Edith Bush, Rose Cottage, Pleasant Cove. 1924 was neatly printed in the bottom right corner. A thick, red line was drawn through their names. Above it was the word "THIEVES" in large uneven block letters. And the word "rose" was crossed out. In its place "Naugler" was written in large letters that took up most of the space. The pen strokes were so deep they left a mark on the other side of the picture. I sat on the edge of the bed. What could this mean? Was Joan pretending this was her home? After learning the few pieces about her childhood, I wouldn't blame her for wishing she'd had a different life.

Did Joan leave anything else behind? I pulled on the chain to turn on the light bulb screwed into the ceiling of the closet. Other than some dust bunnies floating around, the closet was empty. I turned to go when my hand brushed against something rough on the inside moldings around the door. I bent down and took a closer look. The initials "S.N." were carved into the wood. They looked like they'd been there for years except, someone had recently carved a heart around the initials. The rough edges of wood made by the heart stood out like a fresh scar. I took the photograph back to my bedroom and propped it up on the night table.

I was ready for that cup of coffee now. Actually, the situation called for something stiffer, but it was a little too early in the day. I went back downstairs and finished making the coffee. When I opened the cupboard to get a mug, the doorknob came off in my hand.

The visit from Officer Brennan and Officer Eisner had set the tone for the day. I decided I may as well read the letter from the lawyer. When I ripped open the envelope, a cream-coloured business card fell to the floor. I didn't bother to pick it up.

Dear Ms. Sinclair,

In anticipation of the sale of Mrs. Sarah Maitland's home, this is to notify you that arrangements have been made with a sales representative from Coastal View Real Estate to assess the value of the house. Please contact them to arrange a date for a viewing at your earliest convenience.

Sincerely,

Robert Morris, LLB

6 CHAPTER SIX

I stared at the business card for a few moments before picking it up. The name Erin Stokes was embossed in black calligraphy. Centered below her name, in smaller lettering was the slogan, *Finding the right place that means home to you.* Her business and cell phone numbers were in the lower right hand corner.

The nerve of the lawyer, assuming that I wouldn't be able to sell a painting. I still had almost three months to go. Why didn't anyone have any confidence in me? Without thinking, I tore the card into pieces. My hand shook as it hovered over the garbage can. Then I came to my senses. Sighing, I stuffed the pieces back into the drawer. I might need it.

I'd done the right thing all my life. I became an accountant because my parents told me that it would get me a good job, and they were right. But I'd always wanted to be an artist. Grandma's will had been like a sign. I'd always done what everyone else thought I should do. The idea to move out here wasn't an impulsive decision, although my parents—my mother especially—thought I was crazy. I sold the condo and made a tidy profit and jumped at the buyout package my firm offered me. Didn't I deserve the chance to live my dream? Instead, I had police at my door and the lawyer breathing down my neck.

I gulped down the rest of the coffee and went outside. The old photograph reminded me of how beautiful the yard once was. My grandmother was too ill to keep it up properly and my mother never spent time on the garden when she came to visit. I grabbed the rake out of the shed and attacked the sodden leaves trapped in the thorny branches of the few remaining rose bushes. The smell of damp, rotten vegetation rose up from the soil.

On the other side of the garden I noticed footprints visible in the mud. Someone had stood there watching the house. I thought about the day I put the bottle in the garbage can when I had the feeling that someone was watching me. I went as far as the grove of trees at the edge of the yard searching for more footprints. A chipmunk, startled by my approach, darted across the ground and ran up a tree. It was the only sign that anyone or anything else was out there. After a few minutes I went back to raking leaves, but every so often I turned around and peered into the woods. I couldn't shake the feeling that someone was watching me.

A couple of hours later, I stopped to survey the results of my hard work. My lower back ached and blisters were evident on my palms. I'd been in such a hurry I hadn't bothered to wear my gloves. The good news was that the gardening had changed my anger into a pleasant exhaustion. My shoulders ached and my palms protested as I half-heartedly dragged the rake along the grass.

Suddenly, a gust of wind came from nowhere. Damp leaves swirled around my ankles a few times then flew up into the sky. They should have been too heavy for the wind to blow. Soon the whole backyard was filled with twisting leaves. It was as if they were caught up in a hurricane. Round and round. Faster and faster. The wind whipped my hair. Tugged at my pant legs. Pulled at my jacket. Made my eyes water. Then, as quickly as it started, the wind stopped. The leaves fell to the ground in a neat pile at my feet. The air was heavy with the scent of Old Spice.

Someone was watching me. A blue light pulsed like a beating heart from my bedroom window. A figure stepped in front of the light, surrounding him like an aura. Nicholas.

He'd disappeared by the time I reached the bedroom. I walked over to the mirror and pressed my fingertips against it.

"Nicholas?" I whispered. "Did you do that with the leaves? If you did, then thank you."

"I'm sorry," he whispered but he didn't appear.

I picked up the old photograph of the house resting against the lamp on my night table. The rose garden was beautiful. Right then and there I made a decision. I'd return the gardens to their former glory. I'd make Rose Cottage worthy of the name again.

* * *

I pulled out a bottle of wine and filled my glass. I stood in front of my easel and raised my glass in a toast.

"To Rose Cottage!"

I drained the glass and went back into the kitchen for a refill. That's when I noticed I had a phone message. They must've called while I was outside. My mother's number came up. I put the phone on speaker and poured a second glass of wine.

"Alma, this is your mother. I hope you're all right. I wanted to give you a quick call. The lawyer—Grandma's lawyer…" as if I didn't know which lawyer she meant, "…said he sent you a note." She made it sound like a question. She knew perfectly well what was going on. She kept tabs on everything. I could hear her take a deep breath before she continued. "As executor, I thought it best to get in touch with the lawyer and suggested he call a real estate agent. You know how long it takes for properties to sell down there. I think it would be the best thing." She sounded defensive. Then her voice lightened and her words came out in a rush. "Not that this would stop you from your plans." Deep breath. "It would be a safe guard, a plan B so to speak. Anyway. No need to call back. I'm sure you're busy with your painting. Love you."

So that explained the letter and the business card from Erin Stokes—*Finding the right place that means home to you. —Real Estate agent.* A woman who prints that on her business card must be full of it. I poured a third glass of wine.

Most times I didn't mind being single. But right now, I wished there was someone who was going through this with me.

I pulled the card out of the drawer and slid the pieces back together. May as well get it over with. I hoped to get the agent's answering machine, but she picked up on the first ring. She's like a vulture circling, I thought.

"Erin? Erin Stokes?"

"Yes?"

"This is Alma Sinclair." I paced up and down the kitchen. "I got a letter about having you come do an appraisal?"

"Pardon?"

"My grandmother's lawyer, Robert Morris, sent me a letter asking me to contact you."

"Oh, Bob. Yes, you live in the cottage in Pleasant Cove. It was your grandmother's, I believe?"

I gripped the phone tight. "Well, sort of. She's left it to me."

There was a pause. "Oh, I thought it was for sale."

"No, it isn't. Not yet." I gripped the phone tighter. I didn't want to go into all the details. Especially since the story wouldn't be very flattering to me. At least not right at the moment. I rushed through the next bit. "It won't come on the market until the end of July, if at all."

"I guess I must have misunderstood Bob. He told me that there were some buyers interested and he needed to get the property evaluated as part of the estate."

"Buyers?"

"Ms. Sinclair?" She chose her words carefully. "Perhaps there has been some mix-up. I'll give Bob a call and we can get this straightened out. I'm sorry for the confusion."

I imagined the conversation between her and "Bob". The whole story about the will and my failure to sell a painting would come out. I'd have to deal with her eventually.

"Erin, hang on." My resolve of a few minutes earlier was evaporating quickly. It was hard to say the next few words out loud. "The house *may* come on the market. Perhaps Robert, I mean Bob, is simply being proactive. If you'd like to come by to do an assessment, that's fine with me."

"Are you sure? I'm happy to get in touch with Bob and confirm."

"No. That's all right. I'll give him a call myself and let him know you're coming by." I opened up the cupboard and checked the calendar taped inside the door. "When would you like to come?" The date for Erin Stokes's visit reminded me that Mother's Day, the second Sunday in May, wasn't far off.

I slid the pieces of the business card around. If only the pieces of my life fit together as perfectly as this. My life. My mess. I was almost forty years old. So much for trying to live the rest of my life the way I wanted. It had turned out poorly. Thanks to Grandma, this was my chance to live my dream. She was the only one who had ever believed in me. I guess she was wrong.

* * *

I passed by the living room on my way upstairs when the painting above the fireplace caught my eye. It was one of my grandmother's paintings. She called it her Jackson Pollock. She'd taken all the leftover paints she and my grandfather had used over the years from painting the various rooms and splashed them, dripped them and smeared them across a large canvas. The wire on the back was even set so the drips ran up the canvas rather than down, like they were defying gravity. The harmonious chaos reminded me of my grandmother. My eyes filled with tears.

The painting reminded me of a conversation I'd overheard between my mother and my grandmother. They were in this room and I was outside under the window. I remember noticing a tear in the screen. I'd never seen it there before and I'd stopped to see if I could fit my finger through the hole. My mother and grandmother thought I was out in the garden sketching some flowers, but it was so hot, I was going round the house to sit on the porch when I heard them. I was thirteen or fourteen at the time.

My grandmother's voice was soft and gentle. "Let her be."

My mother's voice was sharp and angry. "I'm not going to burden her with the disadvantages of living an artist's life. That job doesn't put food on the table."

"Ruth, you didn't have such a hard life."

My mother gave a bitter laugh. "Mom, you wouldn't know what kind of life I had. You and dad had your heads in the sand." She spoke in a deep voice, imitating my grandfather. "It's not how much we have, but how much we enjoy that makes us happy." She snorted. "You and Dad had your painting. It made *you* happy. We went without so much. New clothes, going to the movies, second-hand bikes. Always having to watch how much we spent. I don't want the same thing for either of my children." She sighed, and I could hear a chair creak as she sat down. "I love you, and Dad, too, may God rest his soul, but times have changed. You inherited this house. You didn't have a mortgage. Life was simple back then. It won't be the same for Alma. I wouldn't be a good parent if I encouraged her to be an artist."

My grandmother was about to say something when my mother interrupted her.

"Don't say it, Mom. I do know what I'm talking about. She can't live down here with you. There is so much out there for her to explore. And I want her to be able to take care of herself, no matter what comes along. Financial security gives you choices."

"Ruth, I don't want her to hide away down here. Far from it. I want her to have the chance to build up her confidence. She has talent. I know it's a hard life being an artist. If she gets the opportunity to have a few successes, then I know she can make a go of it."

My mother sounded tired. "Mom, what do you know about making a living in the art world today?"

"I know that it takes more than talent. Hard work always pays off. Maybe not right away, but eventually. And you feel good about yourself, happy."

"Are you saying Alma isn't happy?"

"No, of course not. I'm just saying that it would be good for her to have the chance to build up her confidence. It would be a shame to see her talent go to waste because she didn't believe in herself.

My mother's voice softened. "Alma is fine. I know you want what's best for her, and so do I. So does her father. The world has changed. Alma is a smart girl. She can always do her art as a hobby. She needs a plan that will give her a job so she can take care of herself." She laughed. "You can't count on rich husbands anymore."

My grandmother bristled. "Your father's family wasn't rich. He worked hard for what we had. Your grandfather bought this house during the Depression. It was a good investment. Her voice sounded resigned. "Well, at least let her spend the summers here. I'll teach her what I can." Then her voice regained some of its energy. "You never know. Things may work out so that she can pursue her art." She paused then said, "If she wants to."

My mother's voice grew louder. She was coming toward the window. "Mom, Alma needs to learn responsibility. She needs to get a summer job to help pay for university. Bob and I have told all the kids that they need to contribute to their education. They can't expect us to pay for everything. That's why her older brother isn't here. He's working up north planting trees. Next summer, Alma will have to find a job."

I scurried around the side of the house and up the front porch steps. When my mother came to tell me dinner was ready a few minutes later, she found me sitting in the old rocking chair, absorbed in my sketchbook, as if I'd been there all day.

7 Chapter Seven

*T*he morning sun shone on the uneven edges where I'd used too much paint. I thought about all the times I'd been to the beach. The crash of the waves as they hit the shore. The swooshing sound as they were sucked back into the ocean. The blue water turning into a white froth and changing back to blue or grey or green or black depending on the weather. I stared at the waves. How would Nicholas paint them?

I tried to imagine I was Nicholas, standing on the rolling deck staring out to the endless horizon, the sea air sharp in my nostrils.

I heard his voice before I saw him. "You need to love the sea if you're going to paint it."

Nicholas stepped out of the shadows and into the light. He smiled at me and the wrinkles around his grey eyes deepened. I forgot I was holding my brush and I dropped my hand to my side. Paint smeared against my pant leg. The scent of Old Spice mingled with paint filled the air. His calm demeanour was such a contrast to our last meeting. It slowed my racing heart. I carefully put my brush back in the jar of water.

"My apologies for being so angry the last time we met." He

extended his arm in a gesture of reconciliation.

Brushing my hair back from my face, I took a deep breath and shook his hand. His grip was firm. I could feel calluses rough against my palm. His hand was cold as ice. His eyes softened. He nodded at the painting.

"Remember. Let the sea into your soul. She'll guide your brush."

Then he disappeared and the temperature of the room rose.

I stared at my painting and thought about what Nicholas had told me. I closed my eyes and visualized the night I met Joan. I filled the tip of the brush with a blob of turquoise and added a bit of white. I ran the brush along the canvas. The white paint formed a thin line above the turquoise. I made small, uneven strokes and blurred the line between the two colours. Standing back, I closed one eye and squinted. Then I quickly stepped forward and filled my brush with more paint and quickly added more colour before I could lose the spot where colour was needed. The waves became larger, angrier, untamed. I added the smallest hint of dark blue to my brush and dragged it through the turquoise, making a smooth, even horizon.

I stood back again, assessing the result. The waves crashing into the shore needed more white. I filled my brush and made sharp, quick strokes near the bottom of the canvas, leaving enough room for a sandy beach. Bits of grey added dimension to the waves. I worked until my mouth was so dry I couldn't swallow. I traded my brush for a glass of water.

I looked at my work with a critical eye. The waves were better. I could sense their power. But what about the moonlight? I dug out my camera and scrolled through the pictures I'd taken. I held the screen up to my painting and compared them. The moonlight in the photograph lit a path along the water. My painting had no hint of light. I'd have to think about it. I stretched and ran my fingers through my hair. I was so absorbed in my painting I didn't realize it was almost dusk until the fading sunlight made it difficult to see. I closed the cover on my pallet, protecting the paint from the air. It would keep the exact colours I'd mixed fresh and ready to use again.

* * *

"Nicholas?" I said. I sat up and pulled the quilt tight around me.

The bottle glowed. Nicholas appeared. I shivered. This time I think more in anticipation than fear.

He sat beside me on the edge of the bed. The mattress sunk a little lower and the sheets that were tight up around my neck loosened.

"I'm sorry I couldn't protect you."

"Protect me?" What did he mean?

He vanished before I could ask him to explain.

8 Chapter Eight

I stood a few feet back from the painting and took in every detail. It looked good, very good. My heart sang as I snapped open the pallet and saw the rainbow of colours as fresh as when I mixed them.

I scrolled back through the photographs until I found the one that showed a path of warm, yellow moonlight fluttering on the surface of the water. The path of moonlight looked like a subdued version of the yellow brick road. I put a dab of yellow on my pallet and added a hint of white. Then I set to work. The yellow wasn't right so I chose a softer shade. A few brushstrokes later, I stood back to check the colour. It still wasn't right. After the fourth attempt I gave up and snapped the lid closed on the paint pallet. If I kept painting I'd ruin what I'd already done. Maybe worrying about the upcoming visit from the real estate agent was stifling my creative energy, or maybe it was the fact that it was Mother's Day and I needed to call my mother.

Maybe Faye could help. Our regular painting session wasn't

for another week, but even talking to her for a bit would give me some ideas.

She picked up on the first ring. "Hi, Alma."

"That was fast. Were you waiting for me to call?"

Faye laughed. "No, but I was thinking about you. How's your painting coming along?"

"Not so good. Maybe I should give up on the lighthouse and try something else."

I went upstairs to my bedroom.

"Maybe once you get a chance to go out on Theresa's boat, that'll help."

"Maybe. I have another idea. I have this old photograph of the house. I was going to frame it alongside a new photograph of the place. You know, make a nice contrast." I picked up the photograph resting on the night table and stared at it wondering how best to turn it into a painting.

"Sounds interesting."

"Well, I was thinking maybe I'd paint it. My family's lived here since the Depression."

"I know. It was the Nauglers' place before that."

I almost dropped the phone. "Your grandmother referred to my home as the Nauglers' house?"

"Yup. She always referred to your place that way, not Rose Cottage. My grandmother used to live near your place. She worried about moving away when she got married." Faye laughed. "Even though moving away meant only a few miles, back then it was like moving clear across the country. Some families have lived here for generations." She sighed. "People around here are slow to change."

"Thanks for helping me make up my mind. I'm going to take a break from the lighthouse and try painting Rose Cottage."

"If you want any help, give me a call."

"No, I'm okay. Thanks for the offer. I'll give you a call if I change my mind."

I went into the guest bedroom and opened the closet door. I ran my hand over the rough edges of the heart. Joan must have carved it. I bent down and looked at the initials. They were barely visible. How did Joan know they were there? Did she know Rose Cottage was her family home? If she did, why hadn't she said anything?

The photograph was tucked in the night table drawer. I'd shoved it there after the ugly scene with Nicholas. I thought he might have been responsible for the writing on the back. Now I wasn't so sure. I decided to get a black and white photocopy made. The contrast between light and dark would show up better and make it easier to paint.

* * *

It was almost the long weekend—the weekend that heralded the beginning of summer. I thought about how different it was to live in another province. I missed the familiar Victoria Day long weekend rituals.

When I lived in Ontario, the weekend was called "two-four". It referred to the date and the fact that beer was bought in cases of twenty-four, since large amounts of beer were consumed over the long weekend. And there were fireworks. The displays ranged from backyard shows ending in the "burning schoolhouse" to spectacular fireworks sponsored by cities and popular venues like Canada's Wonderland. Some of the displays were even choreographed to music. But here in Nova Scotia, fireworks were not as common on the May holiday weekend. The big displays were saved for the first weekend in August. In my youth, my family didn't go down to the East Coast until July, so I wasn't aware of the provincial differences in celebrating the holidays until I'd moved permanently to Nova Scotia. When I'd asked about where to see the fireworks display on Victoria Day, the locals looked at me blankly.

Margie, my favourite cashier at the grocery store had said, "Some people do something in their backyard, but the town doesn't do anything special."

The customer in line behind me had chimed in. "The

campgrounds open. That's the big thing around here."

There may not be fireworks but the garden centers were open. I decided to celebrate the imminent arrival of the summer season with a trip to the garden center. On the drive into town, Taylor Swift's "Shake It Off" came on. I turned up the volume.

The hourly news report came on next. I turned it down.

"Police announce another break-in at another government wharf. This time in Shell's Harbour. An unknown quantity of lobsters were stolen. A state of the art alarm system was recently installed, and authorities are puzzled as to how the thieves managed to bypass the new system. Local fishermen believe it was someone familiar with the facility. There is a reward offered for any information on the apprehension and arrest of anyone involved in the case. Fishermen only have a matter of days left before the lobster season ends.

In other news, a Lunenburg county resident was charged yesterday for possession of illegal firearms. Police are not releasing any names at the moment.

The visitation for Albert Maitland will be held today and tomorrow between two and four at the Millway Funeral home.

Now for the weather. This unseasonably warm spell will last a couple more days before a low pressure system returns to the area, bringing with it colder temperatures and rain for the holiday weekend."

I grimaced. At least the rain would be good for the plants. I thought about the gardens the cottage was named for. Was it too early to plant rose bushes? The real estate agent was coming by this week. I'd stick the plants in the shed and wait until after she left to plant them. I didn't want to her to be too impressed with the place.

The grocery store had a section of its parking lot fenced off for a temporary garden centre. The large circus tent was filled with shelves displaying a variety of annuals, herbs, and vegetables. Flowers cascaded over the edges of pots hung from metal bars, which supported the tent. It was Mother's Day, so there were plenty of baskets to choose from. The roses were in the corner, nestled together to keep warm, as frost was still a real possibility.

The smell of earth and the colourful display of fresh flowers raised my spirits. Humming the Taylor Swift song, I cruised the aisles. I thought everyone would already have their Mother's Day flowers but I guess a garden centre was the best place to get that summer feeling earlier than Mother Nature intended.

When I walked back toward the cash register, I noticed a young woman with bright orange hair watering the hanging baskets. Something about the way she carried herself reminded me of Joan. Her back was to me so I couldn't tell for certain. My gaze was glued to her as I walked nearer. I wondered why she didn't sense someone staring. The orange hair made it difficult for me to be certain. Then I noticed the jeans. The rhinestones decorating the back pocket. My old jeans. The girl turned and faced me. A flash of recognition crossed her face. She dropped the hose and began to walk away.

I quickened my pace. The aisle was full of shoppers. I caught up to her.

"Joan?" She pretended not to hear. "Joan." I called louder. I was close enough now to grab her by the arm. She spun around and I let go of her arm.

She quickly regained her composure. "Sorry, ma'am. My name's not Joan." She chomped down hard on a piece of gum.

"Joan. I know it's you." My voice was loud and shrill. A couple of ladies nearby glanced over at us.

"Like I said. My name's not Joan."

I glanced at her name tag. Beth. No last name, just Beth. "I don't know what's going on, but I know it's you." Anger surged through me. "The police were at my house."

Her face hardened. "Like, I wouldn't know about that." The whole tent had gone quiet. No one was even pretending to shop. A man who'd been busy unloading a skid of flowers looked over at us. He stood up and brushed the dirt from his hands. He, too, looked familiar. I must have seen him stocking shelves in the store or something.

My voice shrill, I repeated. "What's going on?" I grabbed her arm. She pulled away. The opening of her shirt widened and more of her tattoo was revealed. *Lust* was clearly visible as well as *Confuses*. I'd been so absorbed, I hadn't noticed a man had crossed the distance in record time. He stepped up to me, almost knocking over the shelf of plants. Joan moved out of the way. There was something about her manner that made me think this was the older brother she'd mentioned and not a boyfriend. He spat out the words. "Lady. She said she doesn't know you." I could feel his hot breath on my face. I was shocked when I realized he was the same man I'd seen grab Joan's arm at the mall.

I was familiar with older, bossy brothers, but this guy was way beyond the norm. I looked down at his hands. They were clenched into tight fists and his arms were stiff at his sides. I got the sense that he was trying hard not to grab me like he'd done to Joan. Well, he wasn't going to intimidate me. Just as I was about to say something to him, an older, balding man stepped between us. "I'm the manager. Is there a problem here?"

We had an audience now. I glanced around at the curious faces. Warmth crept up my neck. Embarrassment and anger vied for control.

I glanced at the girl. Fear. I glanced at the man. Anger. I stepped back. I shook my head. "I thought I knew this girl. I must be mistaken."

Her shoulders eased. The manager smiled. I could feel eyes burning into my back as I walked away.

What just happened? I was certain the girl was Joan and the man was her older brother. He was quite the piece of work.

9 Chapter Nine

My phone rang as I opened the car door.

"Hi, Mom."

"Hello, Alma. I got your message. Thank you for calling. We were all at brunch. The children were so well behaved. How is your painting coming along?"

Talking to my mother was never relaxing. It was getting warmer outside. Beads of sweat dotted my brow, so I pushed the button to roll the window down a few inches.

"I'm working on something right now. I still have a couple months." I pictured her sitting at the kitchen table flipping through a fashion magazine, sipping a glass of Perrier.

"Actually…" She paused for a moment. I could hear the hesitation in her voice as she struggled to find the right words. This was unusual for my mother. She decided on an upbeat and positive tone and said, "The lawyer called to tell me someone was interested in buying Grandma's house." I started to protest, but she cut me off. "Don't worry, the lawyer made it clear that we can't consider any offers until the end of July." She took a sip of her drink and continued. "He said the buyer…" She immediately corrected herself. "The potential buyer used to live in the house or have family around, or something. I'm not sure of the details. Anyway, I thought it was interesting."

I was so stunned it took a moment for me to reply. Someone who used to live in the house. It must be Joan. Who else could it be? "Mom, was it the Nauglers?"

"Naugler?" I heard the glass thump as she set it down on the table. "Alma, I honestly can't remember. I'm not sure what difference it makes."

"Did Grandma ever mention them? Or your grandparents?"

"No, not that I remember. Why?"

"Someone told me our house used to be the Nauglers' home before it was Rose Cottage."

"Well, that's news to me. As far as I know, it's always been Rose Cottage. Besides, what does it matter who owned it before my grandparents? If the Nauss's want to buy it then all the better." I didn't bother to tell her that wasn't the right name. "I think it's nice to know that the estate wouldn't have to carry the cost of an empty house."

I couldn't restrain myself any longer. There was no way Joan was going to live in my house. I said angrily, "What do you mean? I thought I could stay until it was sold. *If* it even has to be sold. I still have a few months left."

"You've probably used up most of your savings by now. Making a living as an artist is difficult. Your father and I, well, we're worried about you."

I gazed up at the roof of the car. Nice touch, including Dad. He probably didn't even know about the phone call. "Mom, I'm fine." I could feel a headache starting.

She gave a small laugh. "I know you're fine. You're good at taking care of yourself. I, we, just don't want you to get hurt, to get your hopes up. A lot of people have tried to make a living being an artist. It isn't a reflection of your abilities if you don't succeed." I heard her take another sip. Then she changed the topic—her usual approach to any conflict. "I bumped into that friend of yours, Susan? She seems like a nice girl." I cringed at the word "girl". Susan was almost forty. "Your father and I saw her at that new restaurant in the Distillery District. She asked how you were doing."

"I called Susan the other day." I turned on the car and pressed the buttons to open the windows all the way. "Mom…" I sighed. I tried to remind myself she wanted the best for me, but this latest turn of events made it hard to believe. I slumped back down in the car seat. The leather was hot against my back. "If you hear anything more about the Nauglers or anyone else buying the house you'll give me a call?"

I was about to hang up when I heard her say, "Alma, are you still there?"

"Yup. What, Mom?"

She laughed. "I forgot to mention. Your brother was thinking of coming out to see you." She took another sip of her drink. "Is there a good time for him to come?"

I paused for a moment thinking about what just happened. Brothers! "Why isn't he calling me himself?" I said aggressively.

In response to my tone, my mother sounded defensive. "Oh, he was going to, but I told him I planned to call you so he asked me to check dates with you."

I'm sure Mom offered to make the call. My brother let her take care of things if it meant he didn't have to. His visit was to check up on his—inheritance. He wanted to make sure I hadn't done anything to de-value the house. His wife probably already had plans on how to spend the money.

"There's no need for him to come. I can't work if I'm busy entertaining him."

My mother came to his defense. "You know you don't need to entertain him. He's perfectly capable of taking care of himself."

I was so upset I could hardly get the words out. "If you really want to help, then leave me alone to paint. I don't need him or anyone else checking up on me."

I heard the chair legs scrape on the ceramic tile as she stood up. "No one is checking up on you. We're worried about you."

"I came back for a visit at Christmas."

She sighed. "It's just that…"

"I know the East Coast isn't where you or anyone else in the family want to live, but I do." My eyes filled with tears. "Why can't you support me?"

"We do." She sounded surprised by my question.

I brushed away the tears that spilled down my cheeks. "This is important to me." A realization came to me. "And you know what? Even if I don't sell a painting, at least I've tried and I'm proud of that."

She didn't say anything for a moment. "Honey, we've always been proud of you." She cleared her throat. "I'll tell your brother to wait. Let me know if you change your mind."

I rolled my head from side to side to get out the knots that were taking up permanent residence in my neck. "I have to go."

"Okay, dear. Good luck with the real estate agent." Then she quickly said, "And the painting. Love you."

"Thanks, Mom. Love you, too." I disconnected and rubbed the back of my neck. I'd hoped to convince her that a house alarm would be a good investment, but today wasn't the right time. With the potential sale of house looming on the horizon, I didn't know if an opportunity would ever present itself.

Something cold to drink on the drive home would make me feel better. The air conditioning in the store was so refreshing I decided to get a carton of milk and a few other groceries as well as the cold drink.

As I walked past the meat section, I caught sight of Joan through the window in the door that led to the employee-only area. I glanced around for the man I guessed to be her brother before pushing open the double doors. They swooshed closed behind me.

We stared at each other for a moment. Then she stepped forward and said, "Alma. I'm sorry."

"It is you." I tried to keep my voice even. "What's going on?" She gave me a blank look. My voice rose. "The RCMP came to see me."

A man in a white apron streaked with blood entered through the door that led out to the loading bays. He glanced in our direction, but the side of beef balanced on his shoulder looked heavy and he was clearly on a mission to get to his destination as quickly as possible. He disappeared behind the glass wall where a long counter and an assortment of knives were visible.

She shrugged. "I don't know anything about it."

A man's voice bellowed. "Joan?" It came from outside, by the loading docks at the back of the store."

Before I could ask whether she'd tried to buy my house Joan grabbed my hand and dragged me toward the swinging doors that led into the store. "My brother Lonny's coming. Get out of here." I barely had time to feel a sense of satisfaction that I'd guessed right about the man being her brother before she pushed me so hard I stumbled out the door. The door swung back so quickly it hit the back of my leg.

I ran over to the milk display and grabbed a carton. I expected Lonny to come barrelling out and toward me. The carton slipped from my hands. Luckily, it fell into my basket and not on the floor.

It wasn't until I reached my car that I realized I hadn't bought a cold drink—my reason for going into the store in the first place.

* * *

I kept checking my rearview mirror the whole drive home. The incident with Joan's brother, Lonny, scared me. It wasn't his appearance. It was the way he stared at me. I didn't think he'd have any qualms about hitting me, or worse. I recalled how he'd squeezed Joan's arm at the mall. My own brother could be annoying, but he'd never hurt me. Then I remembered the story Joan told me about the teddy bear. What kind of person would take delight in doing something like that? I couldn't imagine living with Lonny. It was easy to understand why Joan was afraid of him.

Was he the reason why the Nauglers were trying to buy my house? Joan wouldn't be able to come up with the money by herself. Why would Lonny want to buy my house after all this time? His family hadn't lived there for ages.

Maybe Nicholas knew something.

I didn't bother to admire the scenery the whole way home. The bottle was still hidden under the tea towels. I wasn't sure how to contact Nicholas, but this seemed the best way. I waited for a jolt of electricity to hit me as I picked up the bottle, but nothing happened. He'd always just appeared. The only thing I could think of was to rub the bottle like it was a lamp and I was summoning a genie. Not even a flicker of blue light appeared. I called his name several times, but that didn't work. There was only one other way I could think of to reach him. I wrote a message on the bathroom mirror. *Please help me.* I stood back and stared at it for a moment. Then I grabbed a towel and erased the message and wrote. *I need your help.* Then, after a moment, added, *please.*

The tension from the last few days had left my neck and shoulders stiff. I glanced over at the bottle of bubble bath. Instead of leaving the room, I bent down and turned on the taps. Soon soap bubbles rose from the surface of the water and the air was filled with the scent of lavender. The soothing touch of the hot water was welcome relief. I adjusted the bath pillow and closed my eyes.

The sound of the phone ringing startled me. Water sloshed over the side of the tub and bubbles clung to my arm as I leaned over the side of the tub to pick up my phone. "Hello?"

A tentative voice. "Hello, is this Alma?"

"Yes." The air was cold against my skin. Goosebumps appeared on my arm. I swirled warm water around me while trying to keep the phone dry.

"Oh, hi. This is Theresa, Faye's cousin. I hear you'd like to go out on a boat. Faye mentioned that you're an artist and it would help with your work. I know this is short notice, but are you free on Tuesday? The weather is supposed to be good."

10 CHAPTER TEN

*P*uffy clouds skittered across the brilliant, blue sky. Boats bobbed on the water, disappearing and reappearing with each bend in the road. The water sparkled like a sea of tiny diamonds. The radio blared with Sinatra singing "My Way" as I navigated the twists and turns on the road to the yacht club. I belted out the lyrics louder than Frank. The line about paying the price struck home. Today it felt like giving up financial security and friends to live my dream was worth it.

Theresa waited for me on the dock, next to the *Hale Terry*. Her bright red hair and lithe figure reminded me of Faye. There was one big difference. No dangling earrings. Maybe they were too dangerous on a sailboat. She waved and smiled as I approached.

"I hope you don't mind. My brother-in-law's joining us. He doesn't get a chance to sail often. He's an RCMP officer and his schedule is kind of crazy. He called last night and asked Harry if he could join us."

"It's your boat. I'm just along for the ride." I laughed. I handed her a bottle of wine. "I hope you like white. I know you said not to bring anything, but I wanted to thank you for taking me out."

Theresa brushed the hair back from her eyes. She pulled her sunglasses off the top of her head and slipped them on. "Thanks. You may want to wait to thank us until after we come back. The wind is a bit strong." She turned to climb aboard the boat and stopped. Over her shoulder she said, "You don't get seasick, do you?"

My boating experience consisted of an old rowboat belonging to my grandparents. I shook my head. "Not that I know of."

"Good. Take my hand. I'll help you step aboard. Harry's up at the clubhouse. He'll be back soon."

"Wow, this is quite a boat. I pictured something a bit smaller."

"The *Hale Terry*," she gave a tiny smile when she said the name, "is forty-five feet. We've gradually moved up in size over the years. She can sleep six. Not that we ever have that many people stay aboard overnight."

The cockpit was shaded by a green canvas bimony. A bright yellow dingy, tied to the back of the boat, bobbed gently in the water. Seating ran along three sides of the cockpit, and cushions were stacked in one corner.

The boat rocked gently as I stepped aboard. Theresa pointed under the bench and told me that was where the life jackets were stored. Then she disappeared below to put the wine away. I pulled a cushion off the pile and put it on the bench on the port side, giving me a good view of the dock. It seemed to be the best spot to stay out of the way. I looked over my shoulder at the water. The water around us was full of boats. Sailboats, motorboats, large and small. The taller sails looked like white wings skimming across the surface of the water. I shielded my eyes with my hand. The sun reflecting off the water made it hard to see. Too bad I'd left my sunglasses in the car. I debated whether to go back and get them when I felt the movement of the boat. Someone else had stepped aboard.

I looked up to see Carl Brennan. A Boston Red Sox baseball cap was pulled so low on his forehead that his aviator sunglasses seemed overkill or maybe I was jealous of the protection they provided. My eyes watered from the bright sunlight.

Theresa climbed up the companionway hatch. She was unaware of the tension. She gave him a quick hug. "Carl. This is Alma Sinclair."

He nodded. Would he admit to knowing me? "Hello again." He didn't extend his hand.

"Hello." I stood and looked him in the eye. At least I think I did.

Theresa looked from him to me. "Do you know each other?"

There was an awkward pause. Brennan answered, "Yes. We've met." He didn't elaborate.

Theresa's husband, Harry, bellowed from halfway down the dock. He waved and called out a cheerful greeting. He had the same colouring as Carl, but he was shorter and wider. Harry's belt vanished under his stomach. There was a case of beer under his arm and a big grin on his face.

Carl took the case of beer from his brother and confidently navigated the ladder down to the galley. Clearly, he'd done it many times. Harry stepped onboard. I stood to greet him, but the boat dipped so dramatically that I sat quickly before I lost my balance.

He grinned. "You must be Faye's artist friend, Alma. Welcome aboard."

He and Theresa busied themselves with releasing the lines, then navigated out of their slip. Carl emerged from below deck and helped. I stayed out of the way. The open water lay before us. I relaxed, soaking up the sunshine and fresh air. I could almost forget Carl Brennan was three feet away. Theresa went below and brought up a beer for each of us. She disappeared below deck once more and returned with a heaping bowl of tortilla chips and salsa. Carl stood and unfolded the table attached to the same pole as the wheel. Harry sat up on the back of the bench, put one foot on the wheel and the other on the cockpit floor. He took a long swallow of beer. I'm sure he drained half the bottle.

"So, Alma. What kind of painting do you do?"

"Landscapes, flowers, that sort of stuff." I glanced over at Carl. Our eyes met and I looked away. "I'm trying my hand at a seascape. Faye thought it would be helpful for me to have some experience out on the water. To help me make the painting more realistic." I wasn't much of a beer drinker. I took a big mouthful and swallowed the bitter liquid quickly.

"Nothing like being out on the water on a day like today. Right, Carl?" Harry glanced from me to Carl. I think he sensed the tension between us. Carl gave a slight nod but remained silent.

Carl stood and pointed. "Isn't that Martin's boat?"

"Yup. The old fella's gotta be eighty if he's a day. He's out here every chance he gets. He'd curl up and die if he stayed on land for more'n a few days. Nobody knows the water better'n Martin."

Martin's weathered face, fisherman's sweater, and colourful fishing boat were like a picture out of a calendar. I didn't bring my camera because I was afraid of it falling overboard, so I grabbed my phone and snapped a photograph. It might make a good subject for a painting. I'd have to check with Martin to see if he was okay with it. The boat drew closer, and the men called out a greeting. We were heading in opposite directions so there wasn't much chance for a lengthy conversation.

Carl stared thoughtfully at the boat as she grew smaller in the distance. Sound carried easily over water. We could hear Martin singing the Kenny Chesney song "Summertime". Both Carl and Harry joined in and the tension evaporated.

Theresa winked at me and laughed. "So, where are you from, Alma?"

"From here, sort of." She waited for me to continue. "My family's lived here on the South Shore for a few generations. My mom got a job in Halifax when she finished school. She met my dad there and they stayed. My mother is more of a city person. When my brother and I finished school, we moved to Ontario to find jobs. My parents moved out there a few years ago to be closer to my brother's children."

Everyone nodded at the familiar story. I took a sip of my beer. Condensation made the bottle wet and slippery.

"My Grandma lived here all her life. She died a couple of years ago. I was the only one in the family interested in living out here, so she left the family home to me."

"Lucky girl," said Harry.

I picked at the edges of the beer label, wondering how much to tell them. Sometimes it was easier to confide in total strangers. "Yes, I am."

"Were you an artist in Ontario?" asked Theresa.

I laughed. "No, far from it. I was an accountant." I set the bottle back in the drink holder and wiped my damp palms on my pants. "I liked my job, but I'd always dreamed of being an artist and living here.

Carl asked, "What do you miss most living in Ontario?"

I thought about it for a moment. "The scenery. The pace of life. The space."

He chuckled. "Not the food?"

"Well, I'm not big on fish. I don't mind the occasional lobster. They're a lot of work for not much meat."

Harry perked up at the mention of lobsters. "I remember my mother saying that when she went to school the poor kids had lobster sandwiches and the rich kids had the baloney. Times have certainly changed. Now you pay a fortune for a lobster roll. The price of lobster keeps going up, which is great for the fishermen but not so good for the rest of us.

Carl was a little intense. "It's about time. It is dangerous work and the fishermen deserve every penny.

"What's going on with those lobster thefts? Any leads?"

"Nope, nothing so far." Carl picked up our empty bottles and disappeared below deck. Moments later he re-appeared with a second round for everyone. It was difficult to finish the first beer; I knew I couldn't do a second one justice.

I shook my head. "None for me. Thanks."

Harry said, "Keep it up here. It won't go to waste."

Carl handed him the bottle and sat down beside me. "Do

you know any of the islands around here?" I shook my head. He pointed over to our left. "That's called Hawk's Point." A sandy beach curved along part of the shoreline. A house stood part way up the cliff that rose high above the water. "My family's house is around the other side. Our place has a better view and the beach is sheltered. Our dad grew up there but moved to the mainland. He hung onto the house, though." He took a sip of his beer. "It was a good life. We'd go out fishing with my grandfather. I don't know how he did it. He just used a watch and a compass, but he could navigate these waters in the thickest fog. Nowadays they have so much equipment you could almost let the ship steer herself."

Grass covered the land around the house. Trees covered the rest of the island as far as I could see. We sailed around to the other side. I squinted up at land above us. A roof peeked out from among the trees.

Carl pointed to the spot with a sense of pride. "That's home. Well, at least that's the way I think of it. Once I retire I plan to live there full-time—at least that's the idea. I have a place in town, but I try and get out here as much as I can. I bought out Harry years ago." He waved his hand around, indicating the boat, and said, "They wanted this instead."

Harry grinned. "The *Hale Terry* is our place to get away."

Carl pointed to the shore saying, "That's a great beach for sea glass." He looked ten years younger as he talked about the island. "Good spots for painting, too."

Theresa overheard the comment. "Would you like to go ashore?"

"No, I don't want to trouble you," I said.

Harry laughed. "No trouble at all. We'll drop anchor. Carl can take you in the dinghy. Theresa and I can stay here and relax." He nodded at the bottle of beer beside him.

After I navigated the ladder back up from the closet-like washroom, Carl took my hand and guided me into the dinghy. We quickly covered the distance to the sandy beach.

"I'll take you up the path so you can get a better view." He shaded his eyes with his hand. "The house on the other side is probably empty this early in the season. You might like to use it. It would give you a chance to spend some time here to paint. There's lots of nice spots and great views of the ocean." He pulled the dinghy above the tide line.

We walked up the steep path that led up to Carl's house. A dense forest surrounded it, giving the house a certain amount of privacy. A wide deck spread across the front and faced the ocean. We climbed the few steps up to it.

"Do you want to come inside?" Carl asked.

I got the sense that he was asking out of politeness rather than wanting to show the place off. "No, that's okay. The view out here on the deck is lovely." The *Hale Terry* looked like a toy boat floating in an enormous bathtub.

Carl pointed toward some large rocks towering out of the water farther down the shore. "There's a hole between those rocks. You can see it at low tide. The locals call it the Devil's Hole." He smiled. "We used to swim there when we were younger. I'll see if Harry can get us close to it when we're on the boat." I could feel his excitement. "If you're up for it, there's another place I'd like to show you."

I wanted to sit on the deck and enjoy the view, but he seemed so keen to show me the island. "Sure."

He quickly covered the distance between the house and the edge of the woods. My heart rate increased and sweat beaded around my hairline trying to keep up with him as we climbed higher up the cliff. My poor physical fitness level wasn't responsible. It was my short legs that put me at a huge disadvantage, I told myself. Carl walked like he had a destination in mind. I prayed it wasn't too far away.

He glanced back at me. "You okay?" I didn't answer. My panting would give me away. I nodded. He disappeared into the trees. The path was so overgrown you'd have to know it was there.

It felt like hours later before we stopped. He waited for me to catch my breath. "We're almost there." His excitement was contagious. I was curious about our destination. "I hope it's still there. You know how your memory can be deceptive. I haven't been there for ages. Not since I was…" He stopped and frowned. "Hum, I don't remember how long it's been."

A few minutes later, he stopped short. I bumped into him. He took my hand before I could lose my balance. "It isn't much farther."

Together, we stepped into the clearing. "My brother and I used to come up here all the time. We'd pretend there was no one else in the world except us."

Mother Nature was the only one in evidence as far as the eye could see. The ocean stretched to the horizon, making it feel like we were at the edge of the world. I turned around to look back the way we'd come. The entrance to the path melted into the woods.

"I thought you might like it." He took off his cap and wiped his brow. At least I wasn't the only one sweating.

"This is lovely." I walked around the clearing, seeing it from different angles. The two rocks he'd pointed out earlier were beige dots surrounded by many shades of blue. That always fascinated me about the ocean; how many different shades of blue there are. I never got tired of seeing it. Since I didn't have my camera, I took out my phone and took a few photographs from several different angles. Carl busied himself with checking out the path and the clearing. I'm not sure what he was looking for. He was concentrating so hard the tip of his tongue stuck out from between his lips. I snapped a picture of him. He heard the click, glanced over at me, and smiled.

"Thank you for taking me here, Carl. It's beautiful." My hand brushed his arm as we turned to go. We both pretended not to notice. The tingling in my hand lasted for several steps.

The walk back went faster. Down on the beach, Carl stopped and picked something up. He turned it round and round, rubbing the sand from it. He handed it to me. "Sea glass. That piece could be as much as fifty years old. The salt makes it cloudy."

I gazed down at the frosted stone, admiring the various shades of blue it contained, like the ocean it came from. Then I held it up to the sun. The light reflected through, showing colours I hadn't noticed in the palm of my hand.

He waved his arm. "This beach is a good place to look for it." The frosted glass was different from what I was used to seeing in Ontario. He must have read my mind. "You're probably used to clear glass. Beach glass. Fresh water acts differently. It's not as cloudy as sea glass." I handed the glass back to him. He shook his head. "No, keep it. Some folks like to make jewelry out of it."

I rubbed the smooth surface. Imagine, fifty years of being tossed around by waves. "Thanks." I tucked it in my pocket.

Back on the sailboat, Harry took us past the Devil's Hole. The waves crashed against the rock wall. The narrow gap between the two stones seemed impossibly small. I was mesmerized by the relentless beating of the waves against the stone. I pictured myself navigating through the passage, the waves either carrying me gently through the narrow gap or throwing me up against the rocks.

Carl stood beside me. "Amazing, the things we did when we were younger."

Harry called out. "Up for a swim, Carl?"

Carl laughed. "Sure. You first, Harry. I'll be right behind you."

The choppy water reminded me of what had happened to Nicholas. I caught Theresa's eye and said, "Do you know anything about a sailor who drowned near the lighthouse? His name was Nicholas Denyes." Before she could ask I said, "I don't know much about the accident. I don't even know how long ago he died."

Theresa asked Harry, "Was that the fellow who died a couple of years ago during the big storm that washed out the old bridge?"

Harry shook his head. "No that was Abe Nickerson." He frowned. "Nicholas Denyes, eh? Too bad you don't know more about him. The name doesn't sound familiar, but if it was a long time ago, you'd best ask someone like Martin." Carl and Theresa nodded in agreement. "He remembers everything and everyone. If someone drowned out by the lighthouse, Martin would know about it."

Harry spied a white buoy floating a few metres away and that was the end of the discussion about Nicholas. He sailed the boat closer and said, "Someone's lobster pot, eh?"

Carl glanced up toward the spot where the other house on the island stood. He didn't say anything for a minute, then he spoke so quietly it was like he was talking more to himself than to us. "Maybe someone's staying there after all."

Harry came and stood beside him. "You never know who's around. Some of these places are so isolated people could be there and you'd never know."

Carl looked thoughtful. He turned to me and asked, "Have you got that alarm installed yet?" I shook my head. "You might want to get it done soon."

He didn't know about Nicholas. I already had an alarm system better than any kind a company could install. I said, "They gave me an estimate. I'll give them a call and set something up."

"Any more visits from Joan Naugler?" he added.

"The Nauglers?" asked Theresa.

Carl frowned. "Alma had Joan staying with her for a bit."

"Really?" Theresa leaned over and put her hand on my arm. "Watch yourself. The Nauglers are a nasty piece of work. I taught at Joan's elementary school. She was never my student, but all the teachers knew her. She was the smart one in the family, and a real manipulator, too. She talked about being scared but she never distanced herself from the family. I think she said it because that's what people expected her to say." She shrugged, "Trouble was always around her, but she was never the one who got caught. Someone else always got blamed."

Harry said, "I heard Lonny talking some foolishness about his sister staying at the family house. He was shooting his mouth off at the pub, same as usual. Said something about soon enough they'd be living there, the way they used to." He frowned. "She was staying with you, eh?"

Theresa glanced at the horizon. "The sun's getting a little low in the sky. I think we should head back."

Harry nodded and began to hum the Willie Nelson song "On the Road Again".

"That's not much of a sailor's song," I teased.

Theresa grinned. "Don't encourage him. One of my husband's many talents, at least he thinks, is singing."

Harry joked. "We may be too old to swim through the Devil's Hole but we aren't too old to entertain the ladies, eh, Carl?"

Harry slapped his hand on his knee. Carl's leg bounced in time. For all Theresa's supposed disdain, she joined right in. A thumping rendition of "Whiskey in the Jar" carried across the water to any boaters within a kilometre of us. We spent the trip back singing, sipping cold drinks, and, most of all, laughing.

We sailed back to the yacht club faster than I'd wanted to.

Carl helped me out onto the dock. "It's still early. Would you like to grab some supper?" Theresa and Harry were busy with tidying up the boat and pretending not to listen. "Nothing special. There's a good fish and chips place not far from here." He paused, "And they serve good burgers, too."

The restaurant didn't look like much from the outside. The paint was peeling and the décor hadn't changed since it opened. My guess was it had been around since the sixties. The menus were grease stained laminated pages. The new prices were written on tape that covered up the old ones.

Carl was so easy to talk to it was hard not to tell him about Nicholas. He didn't discuss work. Instead, he talked about his plans for fixing up the family home once he retired, which wasn't too far in the future. He didn't ask me any questions about my past. I guess he'd already heard enough on the boat. He listened while I talked about my painting and my efforts to sell something in a gallery.

"So you have until the end of July and then the house gets sold?" He whistled. "That's tough. Can't you get a little more time?"

I laughed. "My mother is anxious to sell. She has an agent already lined up so that she can put it on the market August first." I shoved the remaining french fries around on my plate.

They were cold, but I thought about eating them anyway. "She thinks it will get me to come to my senses." He raised an eyebrow. "My parents think being an artist is not the wisest career move."

He laughed. "It isn't, but if it makes you happy…" He raised his glass in a toast. "Here's to doing what makes you happy."

* * *

When I got home, I was almost too tired to change into my pajamas. The day had turned out better than I'd hoped. My jeans were glued to my legs and when I yanked them off, the sea glass Carl gave me fell out and rolled under the bed. I considered leaving it there I was so tired. I changed into my pajamas then crawled under the bed to retrieve it. Even in the small bit of sunlight left in the day, the sea glass reflected the colours trapped inside.

The boat trip made me think of Nicholas. He'd made himself scarce the last few days. I wondered what happened to him. Was he tracking down Joan and her family? "Nicholas?" I said softly. "What are you up to?"

Just as I pulled the covers up around me, the window flew open. The wind made the curtains dance. Nicholas appeared beside my bed. Blue light glowed softly around him.

"Nicholas, where have you been?"

"Did you have a nice time out on the water?" He stepped closer. "I can smell the sea." He took a deep breath. "Do you think it will help with your painting?"

I swung my feet out from under the blankets and sat on the edge of the bed. "Oh, I don't know. I've set that painting aside. I'm working on one of this house." I couldn't touch the ground and I swung my foot back and forth. "Did you know this place used to belong to the Nauglers?" I watched his expression closely.

He nodded. Then his eyes widened in surprise. "Didn't you?"

"No, I didn't. My family never mentioned it. I'd always assumed we'd lived here for ages. I guess I should have figured out that my great-grandparents bought it from someone." I sighed. "It just seemed like such a long time ago, but I'm not sure if it feels the same for the Nauglers." I walked over to the dresser and picked up the piece of sea glass. I rubbed it between my finger and thumb. "I get the impression that it still matters to them—a lot." I turned and held it up to Nicholas. "Did you know it might have taken as much as fifty years for the sea to smooth all the rough edges off this piece of glass?"

He shook his head.

"And that the frosted look is because of the salt?"

He didn't say anything.

"It's beautiful." I set it back down on the dresser. "I was on Cape Head Island today. "Have you been there?" Before he could answer I laughed. "Of course, you have. You probably know it like the back of your hand."

He smiled. "Yes, I know it. There's a nice sandy beach. The other side of the island is much rougher. There's a spot called the Devil's Hole." He grinned. "I spent many an afternoon swimming through it in my younger days."

I shook my head. Some things never change. "Yes, I understand that's a popular activity with local boys." I emphasized the word boys. "The fellow I was with, it was his family's place. He was one of the RCMP officers who was here about Joan."

Nicholas smiled. "I'm not surprised your paths crossed again. I think he was smitten by you."

Warmth spread up my neck. "He's investigating those lobster thefts." I glanced over at him, "You wouldn't know anything about them, would you?"

He frowned. "Perhaps." I could tell he was debating about how much to say.

"Does it have something to do with Joan and her family?" I asked.

He snapped at me. "Alma, Joan's family has been stealing lobsters for decades. They haven't changed."

"Funny, someone else said the exact same thing to me. So if everyone knows they're guilty, how come they've never been caught?"

"Fear." His face darkened and he clenched his hands. "And they're guilty of a lot more than stealing lobsters." He rubbed his hand across his face. "I tried to protect you from them."

Nicholas turned on his heel and walked over to the mirror. The reflection of the bedroom disappeared. In its place, the sea waves charged toward me. They seemed so real, as if they could surge out of the mirror and into the bedroom. Not far from shore, a boat bobbed up and down. A man leaned over the side of the boat. He held a long stick with a hook on the end of it. He caught the rope in the hook and guided the object over to the side of the boat. It was a lobster pot. Another figure, smaller than the first one, moved from the other side of the boat. He looked like a younger version of Martin, the fellow we'd met when we were sailing on the *Hale Terry*. Together, they bent down toward the pot. Minutes later, the pot was dropped back over the side. The boat moved on. Nicholas turned and faced me and the scene vanished. The mirror was just a mirror again.

"The Nauglers." He spat out their name. "They're to blame for this." He looked down at his outstretched hands, his fingers spread wide. He spun back toward the mirror and shook his fist. "I'll get you, Stephen Naugler. If it's the last thing I do. May your soul rot in hell."

"Nicholas. I don't understand. What does Joan have to do with this?"

He raised his fists. "She's one of them." His eyes were sunk deep into their sockets. If I didn't already know that he wouldn't harm me, I'd be frightened. He was gaunt and pale. "Her grandfather murdered me."

"What?" I shoved the sheets aside and scrambled out of bed. "Her grandfather killed you? How?

"I was a lobster fisherman, same as Stephen." He grimaced. "Well, not quite the same. I fished legally. He didn't." He sighed. "My buddies told me not to mess with him.

Everyone was afraid of the Nauglers. They told me to let it go." He shook his fists at the mirror. "But I couldn't. It wasn't right. Stealing from hard-working folks. It made me angry." He paced back and forth. "He was a mean son of a bitch." He glanced over at me. "'Scuse my language. I knew he was the one stealing lobsters from my traps. I couldn't prove it, so I rigged the line with razor blades." He stopped and caught my eye. "If he hadn't touched them, he wouldn't have gotten hurt." He rubbed his hand across his face and resumed pacing. "When I saw him in town, with his hands all bandaged up, I knew it was him. I never said nothing. I didn't need to. I figured that was the end of it."

"What happened?"

He gave a bitter laugh. "Stephen got even with me."

"How?"

"It was foggy. He came out a nowhere and rammed me. Got me right on the starboard side. I saw his face as the boat hit, before I fell into the water." His face filled with rage, his fists clenched. "He was smiling."

"But what does this have to do with Joan? She didn't do anything to you."

His face hardened. "I swore that I'd get revenge. I cursed Stephen and all his offspring. I won't rest as long as any of the Nauglers live." I was so stunned I didn't know what to say. "Keep away from them, Alma. For your own safety, keep as far away from them as you can."

A shiver went up my spine. The teddy bear on the stairs hadn't been an accident. "Nicholas…" Before I could finish, the bedroom door flew open and he stormed out of the room. By the time I reached the hall, he'd vanished. I'd missed the chance to ask him when all this happened.

11 CHAPTER ELEVEN

I sat on the front porch and waited for Erin Stokes. She'd sounded eager about the potential listing when I spoke with her, so I wasn't surprised when she was right on time. She slammed the car door shut on her shiny red SUV and marched up the front steps, clipboard in one hand, the other stretched out, ready to shake my hand. Her grip was strong and confident. Her smile stretched wide to reveal impossibly white teeth. They couldn't be natural.

"Hi, Alma. Pleased to meet you. Thanks for letting me drop by. This shouldn't take too long." The whole thing came out in a rush.

"Hello, Erin. So, where would you like to start? Inside or outside?"

She shrugged. "Whatever's easiest for you?" She tucked a strand of brown highlighted hair behind her ear. "You don't need to come along. I'm used to doing this on my own."

I crossed my arms. "It's no problem. I'm happy to help hold your tape measure or something."

Her smile stretched even wider. "Sure." She glanced around the yard. "Let's start outside. Do you know where your well is? How old is your septic system?"

It was my turn to shrug. "I don't know. I can find out."

She took a pen and tape measure out of her purse. "No worries. I can find that out." We wandered around the house to the backyard. "You have a lovely piece of property. Not too far away from the ocean." She glanced over at the grove of trees lining the edge. "And very private." She nodded toward the rose gardens. "You could put a pool where those gardens are. There'd be lots of sunshine."

I gazed around at the property I'd known all my life, seeing it through fresh eyes. A pool had never occurred to me. "I suppose. Lots of work, though, when the ocean is a few minutes away." I bit my lip. The thought of trading a rose garden for a pool was ludicrous. I shuddered to think what would happen if she got her hands on the property. "You mentioned something about there being a buyer interested?"

She looked flustered. "Oh, I misspoke." She clicked her ballpoint pen a couple of times. "My visit is simply to get all the paperwork ready in case the property goes on the market." She wouldn't look me in the eye.

"But if someone was interested in buying the house, I'd be informed, right?"

She walked toward the backdoor. "The lawyer would inform the executor or executors. Let's take a look inside. I can't wait to see what you've done to the place." She gave me one of her impossibly white smiles.

She wasn't going to give me any more information. Lots of things could happen in the next couple of months. There was no need to panic yet.

Erin and I spent the next hour measuring the different rooms, her paying me hollow compliments, me smiling and biting my lip. I was surprised it wasn't bleeding by the end of her visit.

She stood out on the front porch, tape measure safely stowed in her purse, clipboard clutched under her arm. She extended her hand for a final handshake when a gust of wind came out of nowhere. The rocking chair tipped forward then back. Erin loosened her grip on the clipboard to wrap her coat around her when the wind grabbed at the pages, tearing the top page free. It fluttered down the steps and onto to the lawn. Each time Erin almost reached it, the wind blew it just out of reach again. A blue glow emanated from the living room window. It pulsed brighter with each gust of wind. I almost laughed out loud. After a few minutes, I felt guilty standing on the porch watching her struggle. I stepped out on the lawn. The paper swirled through the air and landed at my feet. Grudgingly, I handed it back to her. If only losing a piece of paper could stop the sale of the house.

Her pages safely tucked away in her car, Erin gave me a cheery wave good-bye and carefully backed down the driveway. I wasn't surprised to smell the familiar scent of Old Spice as I turned back to the front porch. The chair had stopped rocking. Nicholas sat there, feet planted on the worn floorboards, hands clasped in his lap.

"Well now, that was one cheerful lady. She made you want to put a pin in her and watch all the hot air explode."

I laughed. "I couldn't agree more. Thanks for entertaining me." The grass was green and the air had that sweet smell special to spring. It was a smell full of promises. "If only losing that sheet of paper could stop things, but life isn't that easy, is it?"

"I know, but it was good for a laugh. Don't worry. Your painting will have art galleries fighting to show it."

I pulled my hand away. "If only I were as confident as you."

Instead of going inside, I wandered around to the back of the house. The rose bushes were beginning to turn green. A pool. I huffed. I closed my eyes and pictured the garden in full bloom.

"Grandma," I whispered, "I promise I'll plant a new rose bush every year I live in this house." I opened my eyes and looked up at the sky. Loudly I said, "Starting with this year!" I waited to hear if she'd heard me. The branches of the trees bent in the breeze. That was good enough for me.

* * *

Our art group meeting was this afternoon. The painting of Rose Cottage was almost finished. I couldn't wait to show it to Faye.

The parking lot was full and I had to squeeze my car into the spot farthest from the door. By the time I dragged all my stuff into the studio I was out of breath. Thank goodness I didn't have a tray of cookies with me this time. Faye noticed me arrive and hurried over to grab one of my bags.

"Wait 'til you see my painting." I set up my easel. I was so excited it took me a couple of tries to get it set up properly. The legs kept collapsing. I positioned it so the sunlight would shine on my canvas. Faye stood a few steps back. We always joked about the ten-foot rule. Things always looked better farther away. "What do you think?" I said eagerly.

She remained silent. Turning her head this way and that. "Hmmm. I like the angle of the front porch. The door half hidden makes the painting a little mysterious. That's a different idea, painting the house from the side view rather than the front. And the Adirondack chairs are a nice touch. She stepped closer and peered at the painting. "Who's that in the upper window? A mysterious stranger?"

"What?" I moved to stand beside her. She pointed at the face staring back at us. "That's, that's…" I muttered. "How did he get in there?" She was right. Instead of the glass reflecting the light the way I'd painted it, the window now framed a perfect likeness of Nicholas.

Faye laughed. "You're too close to your work." She pointed at the garden. "I'd add some shading here to show more depth. Don't be afraid of the contrast between light and dark. Be courageous with your colours." She smiled. "It's really coming along, Alma. You must be proud of it."

I was too distracted to pay her compliments much attention. How did Nicholas get into the picture? I debated about whether or not to paint over his face. His expression was thoughtful, his gaze drifted over the rose garden and out to somewhere beyond the painting. I didn't have to decide right away. I could paint over him later. Right now, I needed to make the changes Faye had suggested before I forgot what she'd told me.

The next hour and half flew by. Before I knew it, Faye announced it was break time. Bev and Gwen had a couple of cookies balanced on the edge of their saucers.

"Have either of you painted in the clearing overlooking Devil's Hole?" I took a small bite of my cookie.

They looked at each other. Bev said, "Clearing? What clearing?"

Gwen shook her head. "We always stayed down on the beach. We didn't even go up to the house much. We never went to any clearing."

Gwen turned to Faye. "Have you ever painted in the clearing at Carl's place?"

"Not for ages." She looked thoughtful. "Something happened up there. I'm not sure what. Then, all of a sudden, we couldn't go there anymore."

Bev and Gwen held their cookies suspended in mid-air, mouths hanging open. "You never found out why?"

Faye shook her head. "I got married the next summer and soon after that, Susan, my oldest was born. The last thing I was worried about was painting. I never gave the clearing another thought until you mentioned it now."

Surprised, I said, "Really? It never came up in conversation with Theresa?"

Faye's eyes flashed. "Theresa and I had other things to talk about over the years. Besides, she doesn't paint. Both of us were busy raising kids and working. Theresa taught school, and I taught painting classes." She turned on her heel and went into the kitchenette before anyone could respond.

The three of us stared at each other. No one said a word.

"Well, break time is over." I carried my teacup over to my easel and set it down beside my palette of paints rather than brave going into the kitchenette. Maybe there'd be another opportunity to ask Faye about the clearing without anyone else listening.

The opportunity came sooner than I expected. Faye came up to me as I packed up my things. "I'm sorry I was so abrupt earlier." She glanced at the door. "I just didn't want to say anything in front of those two."

"It's no problem. You don't need to explain." Secretly, I was hoping she would.

"Do you want another cup of tea?" She walked toward the kitchenette. "It was so long ago. I'd forgotten all about it." She looked at me in earnest. "Really, I did. Besides, it didn't have anything to do with me. Not personally." She plugged in the kettle and leaned back against the counter, arms folded across her chest. "Even Theresa never mentioned it and she married into that family."

"Carl's family?"

Faye nodded. "Those Nauglers." She pursed her lips. "They bring trouble wherever they go." Why was she talking about the Nauglers? I was about to ask when the kettle began to whistle. She turned around to make the tea so I couldn't read her expression. "Not that Carl's family is blameless. I often wondered if he became a policeman because of his dad."

"His father?"

Faye handed me a teacup filled to the brim. "Yup. His dad hung around with Stephen Naugler. The rumour was they had a good business going in illegal lobsters. The Nauglers would steal them, and Carl's dad would store them at his place on the island. She sighed. "I guess there was a fight one day up in the clearing. No one really knows for sure what it was about." Her eyes locked on mine. "Folks say Carl had something to do with it. He'd just started in the RCMP." She shrugged. "It was years ago. All I know is Stephen Naugler disappeared and Joan was put into foster care. Her older brother Lonny, skulked around town. He went out west for a while—at least that was the rumour—but he's back." She took a gulp of her tea. "Folks say they spotted him near Devil's Hole." She rinsed her cup and put it in the drain rack. "Anyway, it was so long ago, I didn't want to stir up any rumours. The story would be all over town by nightfall, if those two in there got wind of it."

"And you never wondered what happened?" I finished my tea and handed the cup to Faye.

"Nobody ever said anything directly. It was just understood that the place was off limits." She smiled. "Besides, there's enough other places around here you can set up an easel." She laughed. "And you don't need a boat to get there."

"That does make it more complicated." I recalled the amazing view of the ocean from the clearing. Faye was right, there were lots of places, but few were as spectacular. "You didn't need to tell me about the clearing, but thanks. It helps me understand things better."

Faye chuckled. "You mean understand Carl better."

I flushed. "Life is complicated, isn't it?"

"Carl's got a bee in his bonnet over those lobster thefts. And anything connected to the Nauglers brings out the worst in him."

"So I've heard. I've met both Joan and Lonny." The picture of him grabbing Joan's arm flashed through my head.

"What? Joan Naugler?" She sounded puzzled. "How would you cross paths with her or her brother?"

I laughed. "Actually, in a way it's your fault."

"My fault?"

"Yeah, I was out taking pictures for your moonlight assignment." I told her about finding Joan washed up on the beach.

She put her hand on my arm. "You be careful, you hear?"

I laughed. "Oh, I'm sticking close to home. Nothing's going to happen to me there." *Not as long as Nicholas is around.*

Together, we walked over to Faye's car. Rather than continuing on to my car, I set my bags down. "Can I ask you something?"

"Sure. You're doing a great job on your painting."

I smiled. "Thanks, but that's not it." I bit my lip. "Do you believe in ghosts?"

"Ghosts? Why are you asking that?"

"Nothing really." I could tell she didn't believe me. "It's just living in that old house. Sometimes I think someone is there." I glanced down at the canvas leaning against my leg. "Like a face in the window."

"There's lots of things in this life we can't explain. I think ghosts are one of them." She nodded at the canvas. "Maybe you have a story to tell me sometime." She smiled. "You take care." She gave me a cheerful wave as she drove off.

I picked up my bags and hurried over to my car. I got the strangest feeling that someone was watching me. I glanced back over my shoulder, but, of course, no one was there. I quickly stowed my things in the trunk and drove out of the lot without looking back.

Carl phoned as I got in the door. His voice was low and strong without being aggressive. A pleasant tingle travelled up from my legs and through my torso as I listened to him. He wanted to show me one of the hidden gems on the South Shore, a beach that would rival the Caribbean. I offered to pack us a picnic lunch.

When I hung up I felt as giddy as a teenager going on a first date. Even though I'd felt an attraction to Carl from the beginning, I'd resisted it. Police officers had a dangerous job, crazy hours and worst of all, they saw the dregs of humanity. That had to take a toll on them. But the time we'd spent together was so positive it had made me reconsider.

Then it occurred to me. Maybe I was getting ahead of myself. *What if the feelings aren't mutual? He probably just wants to show someone "from away" around, that's all.*

12 CHAPTER TWELVE

*I*t was a good thing I got up early. I changed three times before I decided that I'd dress for comfort rather than trying to impress.

There was so much food, I could barely close the lid on the cooler. We could feed everyone on the beach. There were three different kinds of sandwiches, a couple of salads and, of course, dessert. Plus a couple of apples and oranges thrown in for good measure. Grandma's wicker picnic basket was dusted off and sitting by the door. I threw my second cup of coffee down the drain rather than finishing it. I was jittery enough already.

Carl was right. The beach was amazing. And best of all, there wasn't another soul in sight. The only way anyone would know about it is if they were a local. There was a tiny sign nailed high up on a tree with an arrow pointing in the right direction, but that was it. We pulled into the hidden parking lot, carved into the trees lining the shore. It was big enough for about three cars. The only indication that it was even a public spot was the heavy duty garbage can with a plywood cover next to the path that led down to the water.

Carl's arm brushed against mine as we walked along the sandy beach. Each time we touched, a rush went through me. He led me around a bend and I gasped at the view. It was like we'd turned a corner and arrived in the Caribbean. The lagoon was beautiful. The shallow water stretched out in front of us in stripes of blues and greens. All around us, the beach was littered with sand dollars. I kicked off my shoes and rolled up my pant legs. The water was surprisingly warm for the Atlantic. We were protected from the wind, but Carl anchored the blanket down with his shoes, the basket, and the cooler. The afternoon flew by. It was one of the best afternoons I'd spent on the South Shore. We stayed late enough to watch the sun start to set over the ocean. I agreed to let him take me to a fish and chips shack for dinner on the way home. He promised it was the best fish and chips I'd ever tasted and he was right.

I invited him in for a coffee, but he said he had something he needed to do. He wouldn't say anything more. He was working over the weekend so we made plans to get together sometime the following week. Before he drove off, he asked me again about the alarm system. I told him I had an appointment to get it installed. I don't know why I lied.

* * *

Spring was leaving and summer was finally on its way. Everything was fresh and green. Even the air smelled new. A breeze blew strands of hair across my face, tickling me. I brushed the hair aside and bent forward to take a closer look at the bushes. Brown spots covered some of the tiny green buds. I reached out to take a closer look when one of the brown spots moved. I jerked my hand back. The spots were tiny bugs. I'd have to go and get something. A cloud moved across the sun and blotted out the light.

On my way back up to the house, I noticed the footprints. This time, there weren't any dead leaves to obscure them. They looked like the same ones I'd seen before. I stared over at woods even though it was unlikely the person was still there. Maybe I should try and convince my mother an alarm system would increase the value of the house.

The quote for the alarm system was more than I'd anticipated. I couldn't decide what to do, so I went back outside and cut the lawn for the first time since winter. Faye arrived as I finished. She wore a bright orange pashmina thrown loosely around her shoulders. Her earrings were like something out of a Bollywood movie. I stood up and met her at the foot of the steps.

"Good afternoon, Alma. I was at a flea market and I found something for you. Thought I'd take a chance you were home and stop by." She unwound the pashmina, the bright gold thread of the weave getting caught on her hoop earrings. She untangled it, then took a picture frame out of the trunk and followed me inside.

I took a couple of wineglasses out of the cupboard and filled a plate with a block of cheddar cheese and some crackers. I handed Faye a glass of red wine.

She took a sip. "Nice. Thanks." She went out into the hall and came back with the old picture frame. "I saw this at one of the tables and thought it would be perfect for the painting of your house."

Faye followed me into the sunroom. She walked up to the painting then took a few steps back. Then she stepped forward again and studied it closely. After a few minutes she said, "There's a couple of little things you could do, but it's almost finished." She pointed out a couple of spots that needed a little more shading, an angle that wasn't quite right. Small things, but they would make a difference. She took the canvas off the easel and fit it into the frame. We stood back and admired the effect. The painting was transformed from good to amazing. Once I made the small changes she suggested, it would be stunning.

"You'll be wearing that red dress of yours soon, my dear. Let me know when it's finished and I'll make a few calls to some of the gallery owners I know."

It was a few months after we met that I told Faye the story

about buying the dress to wear at my grand opening at an art gallery. Back when I was certain of my success. I confided in her about the inheritance. She was sympathetic about how difficult it was for an unknown artist to get their work shown in a gallery.

I gave her a big hug. "Thank you Faye." This was a big deal. Faye used her contacts sparingly.

"Glad I could help." Faye wandered back into the kitchen and sat down. "Any more run-ins with Joan or her brother?

"I've thought about the story you told me." Faye raised her eyebrow. "There's no way Joan would be out there alone. She was protecting her brother. The two of them were up to no good."

"Those Nauglers." She shook her head. Her hoop earrings swung back and forth with the motion. "Nothing good's ever connected to that family."

"How well do you know them?"

"I knew her father, Stephen Naugler. He was around my dad's age." She paused. "My dad always referred to him as a bad apple. They say the apple doesn't fall far from the tree, but he was more rotten than his father and that was saying something. Old Man Naugler, Stephen's father, was a piece of work." She shook her head. "It was like there was some competition between father and son about who could be a meaner son of a…" She let the word hang. "Stephen's father lived a hard life right up until the day he died, but I think in the end, his son won. Stephen was a bit of a legend around town. He spent more Saturday nights in jail than anyone else." She sighed. "I wasn't surprised to hear that Stephen Naugler lost his kid to the system."

"Joan told me she'd been in foster care."

"Yup. Joan's brother Lonny was too old." Her earrings tinkled as she adjusted her pashmina. "In my opinion, they should have taken Joan when she was born. It was too late by the time they did something."

"She told me about her brother cutting open her teddy bear."

Faye's mouth tightened.

"What happened to her father? She seemed reluctant to say much about him."

"I'm not sure. My family wasn't part of that crowd. The rumour was that Stephen was hiding out somewhere. He must've been close to seventy-five by then. I can't imagine why it took the police that long to figure out he should have been in jail years ago. He had a few friends that'd help him." She chuckled. "But I guess none of them wanted Joan around. Let me think." She took a sip of wine. "She was just starting high school, which is a tough age for any kid, never mind one going into foster care."

"Sounds like she had a rough time."

"Yup. Stephen Naugler attracted trouble like a magnet." She snorted. "I think he liked it that way. Joan's mother was almost young enough to be his granddaughter. Not sure if he ever married her or not. She took off soon after Joan was born. Too bad for the kids, but nobody blamed her. Maybe it was the only way she could survive." She tilted her head in the direction of the painting of Rose Cottage. "Well, that's enough about the Nauglers. Are you going to tell me the story behind that face in the window?"

"That's the other part of the story about the night I found Joan on the beach. I found this old bottle washed up on the shore. It seems that when I took it home, the ghost came along with it. Apparently, we're now connected."

"Like a genie and the lamp? Do you get three wishes?" She laughed.

"I wish." I thought about how simple it would make selling a painting. "He says he's here to protect me."

"Really? What's your ghost's name?"

"Nicholas Denyes."

"I don't remember any family named Denyes living 'round here. What's his story?"

"According to him, Stephen Naugler is the one who killed him." I hesitated for a moment. "Would you like to see the bottle?" I dug it out of the kitchen drawer and set it on the table in front of her. She leaned forward, watching intently as I slid the plastic down from around the bottle. I think she was hoping Nicholas would appear. Faye stretched out her hand to touch it.

"No!" I held my hands up in warning. "Don't touch it."

She frowned.

"It…it…" I rubbed my palms on my thighs. "Sometimes it can give you a nasty shock like you've stuck your finger in a light socket."

Faye sat back in her chair. I think she was trying to put as much distance as possible between her and the bottle.

She leaned back in her seat, a thoughtful expression on her face. "Nicholas says he knew Carl's father." I cut a piece of cheese off the block and popped it into my mouth. "I asked Theresa and Harry but they didn't know anything. They said to ask Martin." Then I remembered the photograph. I jumped up, saying, "We met him when we were out sailing." I found my phone and scrolled through the pictures. "This is him."

Faye squinted down at the picture. She nodded and handed back the phone saying, "That's a good photograph. Looks like something from a calendar. It'd be good to paint."

"Do you know him?"

She laughed. "Everyone knows Martin."

"Do you know how I can get in touch with him?"

"Let me see what I can do." She glanced at her watch. "Well, I have to be going." She picked up her bag. "I'll be in touch." She gave me a light peck on the cheek before she left. I was a bit surprised. She'd never done that before.

* * *

I finished painting *Rose Cottage* around lunchtime. I stood back and evaluated my work. The rose bushes were lush and colourful. You could almost smell their sweet perfume. The red Adirondack chairs were inviting. I'd positioned them so they faced the viewer, enticing them to take a seat and relax among the roses. The sky had a hint of purple. I hoped one day real life would imitate art. With a flourish, and a steadier hand than I believed possible, I signed my name. Now I just needed a gallery to sell it for me.

I'd turned off the phone so I wouldn't be interrupted. When I went to call Faye to let her know I was ready for the gallery, I noticed there was a message. My grandmother's lawyer wanted me to drop by the office. He said it would only take a few minutes of my time. What could he possibly want? I thought about what my mother had told me about the Nauglers. Would she have told me if there was another buyer? I doubted it. Certainly, the lawyer couldn't even consider an offer until August first. The idea of someone buying my home played over and over in my head as I drove into town. By the time I got to the lawyer's office, I was furious.

* * *

I barely got into his office before I said, "The house is going to be sold?" My voice shook, I was so angry.

"No, no, my dear." He held up his hands as if to say, *Don't shoot.* He didn't even bother to ask me to sit down. He reached across his desk and handed me a mauve envelope. My name was written in my Grandma's handwriting on the front.

"Her will instructed me to give this to you."

"I don't understand. Why are you giving this to me now?"

"Your grandmother was very specific about the timing. She wanted you to have this shortly before the house was to be sold."

"So the house is going to be sold."

"No, no." Beads of sweat appeared on his forehead. He pulled out a handkerchief and dabbed at his brow. "That was a poor choice of words. She simply asked that if things were still not settled, then you were to get this note."

He pointed at the sturdy vinyl-covered chair in front of his desk, indicating I should sit. He sunk into his large leather chair, placing his elbows on his desk, fingertips together. The position of his hands reminded me of the finger game I used to play as a kid, *"This is the church and this is the steeple…"*

"I don't understand," I repeated.

"Your grandmother instructed me to pass this along to you in the event that you hadn't inherited the house yet." He repeated.

So even my grandmother had planned for my failure. I stood and stuffed the envelope into my bag. "Thank you. Is there anything else?"

The lawyer shook his head. He placed his palms firmly on the desk and pushed his chair out from under him. He walked me to the door of his office. "Don't worry. Nothing's been decided about the house yet." My expression must have conveyed my doubts. "Ms. Stokes's visit was simply a precautionary measure in case the house needs to go on the market." He cleared his throat and stuck out his chest. "It is my responsibility to ensure the heirs receive the most money possible for the estate." He held the door open wider. "I wouldn't want to be negligent in my duties."

Stiffly, I responded. "Yes, I see."

I imagined his hand on the small of my back, pushing me out the door. My purse felt heavy, like it was full of bricks. The strap dug into my shoulder. I walked blindly back to my car. I hadn't bothered to park in the shade and now the sun had heated the inside of the car. I opened the door and the warm air rolled out around me. I flung the purse off my shoulder and tossed it onto the passenger seat. All the way home I kept glancing over at it, dreading the moment when I'd have to open my grandmother's letter. For once, there was no pleasure in the view on my drive home. The sparkling water and sailboats moored in the bay brought me no joy.

I avoided touching the envelope for a good half hour. I made a cup of tea, straightened the cushions in the sunroom, and stared at the painting of Rose Cottage. There had to be an art gallery out there that would sell my painting. I crossed my fingers and prayed. Then I opened my grandmother's letter.

My dearest granddaughter,

You must be wondering why I'm writing to you now. I can only imagine how worried you must be about selling a painting in the time that is left. Don't despair! The house may still be yours. Selling a painting can happen in an instant. Alma, you are a very talented artist. Believe in yourself and keep working hard. You are already doing what makes you happy. Enjoy every precious moment. I will always be with you, cheering from the sidelines.

With all my love,
Grandma

I let the tears run unhindered down my cheeks while I slowly put the letter back in the envelope. "Thank you, Grandma," I whispered. "I promise I won't let you down." I brushed my fingertips over her handwriting on the envelope. "I love you, too."

The frame Faye had brought lay over on a side table. I picked it up and placed the painting inside it. *Rose Cottage* would be good enough for an art gallery. It had to be.

13 CHAPTER THIRTEEN

I called Faye to let her know the painting was done.

"Alma, that's great news. I'll get in touch with a few of the galleries. Actually, I was going to call you about another matter. Can you come by this evening? There's someone I'd like you to meet."

It had been one of those days that made you think summer had come and gone and winter was on its way. When I arrived, Faye had a pot of coffee brewing and a fire going in the living room. The smell of coffee and the warmth from the fire were comforting. Faye's studio was in a corner of the room. A handful of canvases leaned up against her easel. Everything was as neat as pin.

An older gentleman stood up as I entered. Martin Keaton extended his hand in greeting.

"So we meet again, young lady." He wrapped his calloused, weather-worn hands around mine. Harry had told me the day we met him out on the water that Martin was in his eighties, but he had the grip of a young man. He pointed in the direction of the little studio and said, "You're an artist too, eh?"

I sat on the edge of an overstuffed easy chair and set my mug down on a spotlessly clean glass-topped side table. "Actually, I have a wonderful picture of you I'd like to paint someday." He glanced quickly at the photo on my phone.

"Who's that handsome son of a gun anyway, eh?" He smiled, "You go right ahead, my dear. Maybe I'll be famous one day, hanging in some museum or something."

Faye picked up a paisley pashmina from the back of her chair and wrapped it around her. She nodded encouragingly. "Remember you told me about your ghost?"

I took a sip of coffee, then set my mug back down. I reached for my bag and set it on the coffee table. I didn't say anything for a minute. I pulled the sides of the bag down to reveal the bottle and said, "This is where the story begins."

They listened to the whole story without interruption, their coffee cold and untouched. After I finished, the room was quiet for a moment. The only sound was the crackling of the fire. Faye crouched down and stared at the bottle. The edges of her pashmina brushed the floor. She held out a tentative finger, almost but not touching it. The flames shone through the dull blue glass. We held our breath and waited to see if Nicholas would appear.

I sighed, "I've asked Nicholas how it works, how he appears and reappears, but he didn't seem to know, either. He said he gets a sense of when he's needed or when it's the right time." I shrugged. "He didn't explain it very well. I don't think he really knows." I took a sip of lukewarm coffee. "It's a little frustrating, but there's nothing we can do about it."

Martin chuckled. "If it is Nicholas Denyes, then I'm not surprised. He was a stubborn man. He wouldn't listen to anyone or do anything different if it wasn't something he agreed with." He shook his head. "I think that's what got him killed."

Before I could ask he said, "I don't know for sure, my dear. I'm only guessing, but anything that involved the Nauglers was hard to prove. I told Nicholas to leave it alone, but he wouldn't listen."

Faye said, "He crossed Stephen Naugler? No wonder he didn't live to tell about it. Was it about lobster traps?"

Martin nodded.

"There's always been trouble about traps and territory for as long as I can remember. It doesn't usually come to…come to…" Faye wrapped the pashmina around her tighter. "Usually it means losing some traps or having the lobsters taken from your pots before you can get them yourself."

Martin frowned. "Now, Faye, Stephen Naugler wasn't all bad." Faye was about to argue when he said, "I admit, you didn't want to cross the man, but he did help out some when guys were hurtin'." Faye rolled her eyes. "When I was younger, he was a bit of a legend. It was something to be able to hang around with him. The bigness kinda brushed off on you. Then you got to see some of the other stuff, and you learned not to cross him." He chuckled. "The best thing was to mind your own business." He winked at me. "That's the best advice I can give you for a long life."

I leaned forward. This is the question I'd been waiting to ask since I'd first heard Nicholas's story. "Martin, do you know what happened to his family? I have this idea that if I can find out, then maybe it will help Nicholas to rest in peace. If he knows his family is okay, he won't have to exact revenge on Joan and Lonny after all."

Martin rubbed his chin. "It was such a long time ago. I was just a young lad." He got up and poked at the fire. "His missus moved to Kilbride, if I remember correctly." The flames grew taller and the fire crackled and snapped. "I'm not sure what happened to her after that." He sat back in his seat and rested his gnarled hands on the arms of the chair. The flames cast shadows across his face. "I'd hate to see something happen to Joan. I admit I've got a bit of a soft spot for the girl. It's not her fault who her daddy was."

I stood and got ready to leave. Martin and Faye followed me to the door. I thought Martin might follow me out to the car, but he shook my hand and went back into the living room.

Faye walked me out to my car. "You know, Alma. There's a way you might be able to contact Nicholas."

"What do you mean?"

Faye laughed. "Well, I'm not an expert on ghosts, but I think I know who you might ask." She shivered and hugged her arms around her chest. "Bev."

"Bev?" I gave her a blank look.

She laughed. "Bev Donaldson, from our art group."

"Really?"

"Her family's rumoured to have the gift."

"The gift?"

"The ability to speak with relatives who've gone beyond." She gazed up at the sky for a minute. The clouds had finally parted and a multitude of stars twinkled above us. "She can speak to the dead. Or so folks say. I've never asked her myself, so I don't know for sure."

The idea of confiding in Bev Donaldson was not appealing. She was such a gossip. Nicholas's story would be all around town within hours. "Surely there must be another way. Don't you know someone else?" I couldn't help the disappointment from creeping into my voice.

"Not anyone else that I know about." She shrugged. "It's just a thought, but it's up to you. I won't say anything to her."

I sighed. "Let me think about it."

* * *

Waiting around for Faye to give me a list of galleries wasn't an option. It was nice of her to offer, but I needed a Plan B. Besides, there was a certain satisfaction in being able to do it myself. I searched for art galleries up and down the South Shore. Most were artists who operated their own places. A few came up that represented different artists. I pulled out a map and planned my route along the old highway that skirted the shoreline. Kilbride was a little farther along the coast. I promised myself I'd go there tomorrow and see what I could find out about Nicholas's family. I could have sat in front of a computer, but somehow making the trip to Kilbride and experiencing the place for myself felt much more satisfying. And it gave me a good excuse to get out of the house. Maybe I'd be fortunate enough to find someone who knew his family.

The stores in town were unusually busy, even for a Sunday afternoon. In the bathroom at the gas station, I dragged a brush through my hair and put on some lipstick. It wasn't until I heard people in line while I waited to buy a coffee that I realized it was the May long weekend.

This weekend was the official opening of tourist season. Most of the galleries opened up now, but they wouldn't be too full of tourists yet. I pulled out of the parking lot, ready to face the day. I put on my sunglasses, even though the sun wasn't bright enough to need them, chose a playlist on my phone full of sixties and seventies tunes, and opened up the sunroof.

There was something about the South Shore that attracted artists from all over the place. The area was home to a variety of galleries. Some in old houses, others in shacks by the ocean. I stopped for a coffee refill and noticed the tiny general store displayed a collection of artwork on the wall opposite a glass case filled with cheese and cold meats. When I noticed the sign for a local winery, I broke from my planned route and followed the twists and turns inland away from the water.

The jammed parking lot indicated the place was doing a brisk business. Even the winery had a room off their main entrance filled with work from local artisans: wooden carvings of birds, brightly coloured hooked rugs depicting rolling hills rising from the shore, beautifully stitched quilts, and, of course, paintings in oil, acrylic, and watercolour.

Surely one of these places would be interested in my painting.

I got up the courage to ask the young lady at the counter as I paid for my bottles of wine.

"I'm not sure, miss." She turned to an older woman, who was busy helping customers taste the various wines.

The woman smiled at me pleasantly. "Maybe you could

drop by next week and bring along a few of your paintings." She nodded to a small wrought iron holder containing a stack of business cards. "Take one and give us a call. It's still early in the season, so you might have a chance to display some of your work."

I thanked her and took a card. The paper bag containing the wine bottles crunched under my arm as I stuffed the card into my pocket. Back inside the car, I breathed a sigh of relief. That wasn't so bad.

Then it dawned on me. All the artists had several paintings for sale. I only had *Rose Cottage*. Would the idea of one painting be easier to negotiate? I worried about it all the way home. Could I generate a couple of more pieces by the end of the week? I knew I was being ridiculous. Faye might be able to do it, but not me. It'd taken me ages to paint *Rose Cottage*.

It had been hours since I'd eaten. I pulled into a small café before five o'clock. Almost closing time. There wasn't much left—a couple of scones and the dregs of their daily soup. There was enough left to fill a bowl. I bought it, along with the last of the scones.

I sat at a small table by the window. The old wooden tables and chairs were painted in a variety of colours. Nothing matched, but somehow they all worked together to give the place a comfortable, homey feel. I was so hungry I practically inhaled the first scone. The soup was too hot so while I waited for it to cool I glanced around the room. Framed paintings of different sizes, different mediums, and, most importantly, by a host of artists, decorated the small space. I got up to take a closer look. Many were single works by an artist. I finished off the best bowl of hamburger soup I'd ever tasted in record time and left five dollars in the tip jar on my way out.

There were no lights on to greet me as I pulled up my driveway. Living alone didn't usually bother me, except sometimes at dusk. When it was no longer day but not evening. The stress of work was left behind and it wasn't late enough to fill your evening with television. I sat in the car for a moment, hoping for the flash of a blue light, the tiniest flicker, the hint of Old Spice drifting on the evening air. I stopped in front of the rocking chair for a moment, willing it to move.

I turned on the lights as I made my way through the house. I changed into pajamas and went back downstairs and opened the white wine I'd bought. I tossed a couple of ice cubes in the glass to make it colder. I didn't care if it wasn't the proper etiquette. I took a sip and splashed a little more wine in the glass until it reached the rim. Carefully, I carried it into the living room and switched on the television.

I forced myself to stay up late enough to watch the evening news. I almost made it. The announcer, reporting the headlines, woke me up. I wiped the dribble of spit from the corner of my mouth and rubbed the back of my neck. I'd fallen asleep in a most uncomfortable position.

The big story was about the lobster industry. The season was almost over. A warmer than usual winter created the environment for large hauls. Plus, there was a high price for lobster. These combined factors made it a record-breaking year for fishermen. I had a nagging feeling I'd missed something important. I watched for the next few minutes, but there wasn't anything else. I drained the lukewarm glass of wine and dragged myself up to bed. It was almost the end of May. There was two months left to sell my painting. I didn't sleep well at all.

14 CHAPTER FOURTEEN

*I*t was a good thing Nicholas seemed to have disappeared for the time being. I didn't want him to find out why I was travelling down to Kilbride and get his hopes up.

The bridge across the river was busy. On one side, the river narrowed through the town, and on the other, the river widened out into the ocean. Historic homes built by wealthy seamen lined both sides. Kilbride was a vibrant seaport in its day.

I followed the signs to the lighthouse and parked the car. It was too late in the day to take advantage of the lighthouse tour, so I wandered along the boardwalk. The view of the water from the boardwalk was exactly what I needed. I sat on a bench and watched the waves rush up against the rocks. Across the water, I spotted another lighthouse. I shouldn't have been surprised. After all, this was the lighthouse route.

Now that I was here, I didn't know where to go next. Martin hadn't given me enough information to give me an idea of where to start.

I decided the best place was the visitor information centre attached to the lighthouse. Perhaps someone there might give me an idea of where to begin my search. The worn steps led up to a newly painted white screen door. Flyers announcing local events were thumbtacked to a cork bulletin board inside the main entrance. An older woman stood behind an antique display case. She looked up when the door slammed closed behind me. I glanced back apologetically.

"Don't worry. I'm used to it." She grinned. "Welcome to the museum." She introduced herself as Elizabeth Nickerson, the museum's volunteer guide. She listened as I explained my problem. When I finished, she shook her head.

"The name doesn't sound familiar. You're welcome to check out our collection. We have some old journals and newspaper clippings. If you don't find anything here, there's always the Internet." She chuckled. "Not that I use it much. I get my grandchildren to help me if I need it." She winked. "And I try not to need it."

The museum's collection was fascinating. A dory complete with oars and fishing paraphernalia sat in the centre of the room. Full scale dioramas depicting the early nineteen hundreds ran around the perimeter. Elizabeth was a wonderful source of information. She was one of the most enthusiastic guides I'd ever encountered. She told me her family had lived in the town for more than three generations. And they had no desire to live anywhere else. She pointed out different artifacts, many from her own home or that of her parents—including her father's long underwear.

"It's important for folks to know what they used to wear back then." She shook her head. "Fishing's tough work." She ran her hand over the worn mitts. "Still is. My husband's retired now. I used to worry about him every time he went out."

When I asked her which local beach was the best one to visit, she said, "I wish I could get ahold of my husband. He'd know which one was the best because of which way the wind was blowing." She pulled a map from the pile sitting on the counter beside her and unfolded it. "If you're interested in sea glass, this beach—" she pointed to a spot on the map, "—is the best." She drew a red circle around the dot and handed me the map.

When I mentioned the lighthouse, she launched into another explanation, her enthusiasm as strong as ever.

"If you want a tour of the lighthouse over on the island, give me a call later in June and I can let you know when we have our tour. The men take visitors over in their boats. You've got to watch yourself when you step ashore, but it's a great day. If you have any children, we have ice cream and games, too." She smiled broadly.

A couple came in as she was telling me about the tour of the lighthouse. They waited politely for her to finish. Elizabeth wasn't in any rush. Her warmth and enthusiasm was a pleasure to be around. I could have stayed and talked to her all day. I moved away from the counter and let the new visitors take my spot. Elizabeth gave me a cheerful wave as I left. I was careful not to let the door slam behind me.

Although talking with Elizabeth was interesting, it hadn't provided me with any information about Nicholas. I didn't expect finding out about him would be that easy, but I couldn't help being little disappointed.

I wandered over to the bench farther away from the entrance to the museum. Elizabeth's joy at living here was contagious. I sat and relaxed. Looking out over the water, the sun shining, the leaves turning green, and the promise of summer heavy in the air. I bent my head back and raised my face to catch the sun's rays. The heat was wonderful. I took off my sweater and draped it over the back of the bench. Then I unfolded the map Elizabeth had given me and checked out the route to the beach she'd recommended. Maybe I could find some more sea glass to add to the one Carl had given me. Maybe I'd even find enough to make a bracelet or a necklace. The idea energized me. When I picked up my sweater, I noticed a plaque fastened to the back of the bench.

In memory of my father
Nicholas Denyes
Died at sea 1950
May he rest in peace

I could barely contain my excitement. I never would've found this sitting in front of a computer.

***

I rushed back to the visitor centre. There was no sign of Elizabeth. Then her head poked up from behind the counter. She must've been rearranging a display. She looked surprised to see me.

"Back so soon? Did you forget something?"

I pointed in the direction of the boardwalk. "I've found him!"

"I thought the gentleman you were searching for was dead."

"He is. I found a plaque with his name on it." I moved back toward the screen door and motioned for Elizabeth to follow. "That bench down the boardwalk. The one that faces out toward the lighthouse on the island." Elizabeth peered around me trying to see the bench. "You can't see it from here. The plaque on the bench is dedicated to Nicholas Denyes." The look on her face was more one of puzzlement than delight. "It's from his son."

"That's nice. People love to sit on those benches. Not so much in the winter. The wind can be mighty fierce."

"So this means his son lives in town."

Elizabeth shook her head. "Some folks moved away but when they heard about the boardwalk they sent money for the benches. The historical committee, well, mostly Naomi Atkinson, got the television station to do a news story about it." Elizabeth chuckled. "That Naomi was a pistol. When she put her mind to it, things got done. Anyway, it must've been a slow news day, or she knew someone, because a fellow came down and interviewed a couple of people—Naomi being one of them—about the project. A few people who'd moved away heard about it and sent money. The benches were a big hit. If you check out the gazebo you'll see a few more plaques. Bill Fogler over at the hardware store made a good profit engraving all those plaques."

My heart dropped. "So Nicholas's son might not live here?"

"Oh no! So many folks have moved away. Out west mostly." She walked back behind the counter and slid the glass door closed on the case she'd opened.

"Well, there must be records of the donations. Can you tell me where to find Naomi?"

"Unless you can talk to the dead, she isn't going to help you much."

"What about the historical society?"

"That'd be me, Henry Richardson, and Ethel Smith."

I smiled. "Then I've come to the right place."

Elizabeth shook her head. "Those plaques were so long ago. We didn't keep the receipts." She waved her arms around the room. "We don't have a lot of storage space. Most of the papers were over at Naomi's." She gazed out the window in what I'm assuming was the direction of Naomi's house, or maybe the cemetery. "When she died, her family cleaned the place out. There was so much stuff. I don't think Naomi ever threw so much as a grocery receipt out. There were so many papers." She sighed. "They asked us, I mean the Historical Society, if we wanted any of her papers, but there was so much junk. We had our hands full with setting this place up. We checked with the accountant and he said anything older than seven years we could get rid of." She smiled proudly. "So we did. You don't know how hard it is to get a bunch of old people to let things go. So much clutter and most've its worthless."

"So none of the information was entered into some sort of data base?" My hopes of tracking Nicholas's family were quickly disappearing.

She sighed. "My children told me we should put all those

records on the computer so people like you can get at them. I told them to go right ahead. Young people are full of talk but ask them to do something..." She shook her head. "I don't have time to do it and even if I did, I wouldn't want to. I prefer talking to all the people that come in. You can't have a conversation with a computer."

I thought about my own choice to drive to Kilbride rather than sifting through websites. "Computers don't replace the need for human contact," I agreed.

Elizabeth smiled. "But look on the bright side. Clearly his family loved and remembered him enough to get that plaque. That's got to mean something." She looked at me, her eyebrows raised, and said, "Doesn't it?"

Elizabeth so wanted to be helpful. I couldn't let her see how disappointed I was. "Yes, that's a good way of looking at it." I pushed open the door. "Thanks. You've been very helpful." I glanced back over at the visitor's book. "If you think of anything else, my name and phone number are written down in the book."

She shrugged. "I don't want to give you false hope, but you never know."

I couldn't believe it, so close and yet no nearer to solving the problem. I half-heartedly took a few photographs of the lighthouses before going home. The trip wouldn't be a complete waste of time.

I was in such a funk the whole way home. It wasn't until I pulled in the driveway that I accepted Elizabeth's point of view had merit. At least the plaque was proof that his family had survived well enough to have the means to dedicate the bench. It also showed that they clearly had a soft place in their hearts for his memory, too. Maybe they were also unhappy about not knowing what happened to him. I slowly climbed the steps to the front porch. If only there was a way Nicholas could be reunited with his family, or at least know they'd overcome the hardships caused by his death.

15 Chapter Fifteen

*F*aye hadn't called yet about the galleries, so I phoned the winery back. The owner could see me this afternoon.

The brown-paper-wrapped canvas lay in the backseat. I drove like there was an infant in the car, navigating the turns in the road with extreme caution. Tried not to use my brakes. Didn't pass any slow moving vehicles. At the sound of the package shifting in the backseat I'd squeeze the steering wheel, slow down, and quickly glance over my shoulder to make sure everything was all right. It took twice as long to get to the winery as it had the first time.

The only car in the parking lot was a brand new black BMW coupe. I guessed the owner was inside. A woman about my age but looking ten years younger stood behind the desk. She glanced up when I entered, a brilliant white smile stretched across soft pink glossy lips.

"You must be Alma." She came from behind the counter, hand outstretched.

The canvas was awkwardly tucked under one arm, my purse dangling from the opposite shoulder. I reached out to take her hand. My purse slid off my shoulder and stuck in the crook of my elbow, swinging back and forth. I set the canvas on the floor, leaning it against my leg while I hiked my purse back up onto my shoulder.

"Thanks for meeting with me, Susan."

She nodded at the package. "I'm guessing this is the painting." She led the way into the gallery. She cleared some brochures off a table in the centre of the room. My hands trembled as I untied the string and pulled away the brown paper. I felt lightheaded. I stood back and let the gallery owner fold back the paper. Her face broke into a smile. Relieved, I took a deep breath. She picked up the painting and searched the room for a place to hang it. "How about over here?" She walked over to a small space in the corner opposite the large window. She dragged a chair from the table and propped the painting up on the seat. Then stood back. I joined her.

"Artists always talk about the ten foot rule."

She laughed. "It is good to appreciate art from a distance. Your painting is lovely."

I waited, heart pounding, to hear the words.

"We don't normally display single works by artists. You don't have any more paintings, do you?"

Those weren't the words I was waiting for. I shook my head. "No, not at the moment. I have some almost ready."

"Hmmm…" She walked back up to the painting. "We get a lot of tourists. They like seascapes." She glanced back over her shoulder. "Especially ones with lighthouses." She picked up my painting and moved over to the window. "You don't have any paintings of lighthouses, do you?"

"Well, I'm working on one now. It should be ready soon."

She smiled. "Great. Why don't we wait until you have a few more ready for us to show? I'd be happy to display them." She placed my painting back down on the table and adjusted it until it was centred on the brown wrapping paper. "And do you have any postcards or brochures? Tourists like to know a little about the artist." She cocked her head to the side. "You are local, aren't you?"

"Oh, yes. I live in Pleasant Cove."

She smiled. "Good." She reached out to shake my hand. "Don't take too long to get the rest of the paintings to us. At least three or four would be perfect."

"Thank you." I smiled trying to hold back the tears. I wanted wrap up my painting and leave. "You must be busy. I can see myself out."

"Don't wait too long. I can't hold the space for you. If this weather stays nice, it'll bring the tourists."

"Yes, that would be great." I smiled like I couldn't wait for throngs of tourists to clog the old highway, restaurants, and, of course, this gallery/winery.

The wrapping wasn't nearly as neat when I left as it had been. The string dangled almost to the ground. The wrapping came undone as I put the painting in the backseat. Why hadn't I finished the seascape? I should've known it would be more in demand. Tourists were looking for paintings that reminded them of their trip to the Atlantic. And then another thought came to me. What if the seascape wasn't good enough for a gallery? I made myself focus on the positive. At least *Rose Cottage* was good enough for them to ask for more. It was a step in the right direction.

I replayed the conversation over and over as I drove along the old highway. How many paintings would be enough for a collection? Could I manage to get them done quickly? Maybe a series of smaller paintings that I could finish quickly would be the way to go. I needed to sit and think about what my next steps should be. When the sign for the café came into view, I pulled over.

The same girl was behind the counter as on my last visit. I don't know if she remembered me or not, but she smiled and said hello like she did. Since it was earlier in the day, the selection of baked goods was more plentiful. I bought a cinnamon bun to go with my coffee. I sat at the same table as last time, only I didn't look at the paintings. I stared out the window, unwinding bits of sugary dough and stuffing them into my mouth. The waitress came over and offered to refill my cup.

"Are you a tourist?" she asked.

"No." I shook my head. "I live here." I sighed. "At least, I'm trying to." She waited for me to explain. "I'm an artist." I chuckled. "A starving artist."

She laughed. "Lots of those around. You're in good company." She nodded to the paintings around us. "Some of these folks aren't starving anymore. The owner helped get lots of the people started. They still show one or two pieces here, even though they have bigger showings in Halifax." She nodded to a small oil painting. "Terence always gives the owner one of his paintings every year. And he never takes a penny of the sale. Says it's his way of giving back." She set her pot of coffee on the table. "It's hard to make a living as an artist, but it's also hard to make a living as a café owner, especially if you're only open during tourist season." She picked up her pot of coffee. "Beatrice, that's the owner, uses the money to help other artists and to keep this place going." She smiled. "This is my third year. It's nice to know you've got steady work."

"I've never heard about her, or this place."

The waitress smiled. "She doesn't talk about it. Just likes folks to enjoy the place and the coffee."

I pushed the half-eaten cinnamon bun out of the way and said, "You don't think she'd hang one of my paintings, do you?"

The waitress shrugged. "Don't know. The walls are pretty full right now. It's the beginning of the season. Beatrice always has more artists than space. Maybe later on in the summer? When she's sold some?"

My shoulders slumped. The cinnamon bun sat like a rock in my stomach. I smiled. "That makes sense." I sighed. "It's just, I have this timeline. And it ends at the end of July."

The waitress frowned. "That's only a couple of months away."

"I know."

The waitress glanced out the window. "Beatrice lives across

the way. In that old farmhouse. Her truck's in the driveway. You could pop over and talk to her."

I stared out the window at the farmhouse. An old dog wandered across the weed choked lawn.

The waitress said, "Don't mind Rufus. He'll bark like the dickens but he's harmless."

We watched a grey-haired woman come from around the back of the house. She was dressed in jeans faded from age rather than by design. She headed for the truck. Rufus jumped up and down, tail wagging.

"I guess I'd better get over there before she leaves." I left the last curl of cinnamon bun on my plate and quickly paid the bill.

As I hesitated at the door the waitress smiled and said, "Good luck."

The screen door swung back so quickly I had to quicken my step. Beatrice was already in the truck by the time I walked up her driveway. She rolled down her window and waited for me to approach.

Rufus noticed me at the same time. He was riding shotgun. He barked so loud I couldn't make out what she was saying. She gave up and waited until I was next to driver's door.

"Beatrice?" I asked.

She nodded. "Good afternoon." Her words were drowned out by Rufus. She turned to the dog and gave him a stern look. His tail drooped, his head dropped, and he stopped barking.

"My name's Alma Sinclair. I was having a coffee over at your café." I bit my bottom lip. "The waitress mentioned you help artists. Struggling ones?"

"Sometimes," she replied cautiously.

"Well, I have a bit of a unique situation." I realized how lame that sounded. Every artist probably thinks their situation is unique. How could I best explain the situation? "My family. Well, my grandmother, actually. She…she left me her house." That sounded like I was bragging. "Well, that's not the problem." I stared back over at the café. "You see, I only inherit the house if I sell a painting in an art gallery."

127

Beatrice smiled. "Honey, I may like to think my place is an art gallery, but it's just a café. With art."

"I know. But you help artists and…" I felt a lump growing in my throat. "I was wondering if you might sell one of my paintings."

She shook her head. "I'd love to help you out, but my walls are full up. Maybe later in the season."

The lump was the size of a cannon ball now. "I understand." I turned to go.

She called out, "Do you have a card or something?"

"No. But I do have something else. Just a minute. I'll be right back."

Rose Cottage lay on the backseat, the pinks and reds catching the sunlight. I grabbed my purse and on the way back, stopped, and took the painting out of the car.

Beatrice had gotten out of the truck while I was gone and stood beside it. I held out the framed painting.

She shook her head. "No, hold it up for me." I held the frame, my hands cradling it like an easel. Beatrice took a few steps back. She stared at the painting, then she came up to me and took the painting from me. She turned it this way and that. "It's good. Your brush strokes are even. The colours are lovely." She handed it back to me. "And it's a nice change from seascapes. Give me your name and number." She gave me the same stern look she'd given Rufus. "No promises, mind you."

I scribbled my name and number on a scrap of paper. Beatrice traded me the painting for the paper. She climbed back into the truck, and I stood back to let her pull out of the driveway. Rufus grinned and wagged his tail as they passed by me.

I walked back to my car and carefully wrapped the painting. I don't know if she was watching or not, but I gave the waitress a cheerful wave good-bye.

How many days would be polite to wait before I called Beatrice? I circled a date one week away. Maybe it would be better to drop by the café rather than call. I decided that would be a better plan. What could I do with myself before then?

16 Chapter Sixteen

I pulled out the half-finished painting of the lighthouse. The trip on the *Hale Terry* had helped me get a feel for the waves. I wondered if they would take me out again. I went upstairs to change. When I came back downstairs, Nicholas was studying the painting. I wished I could figure out what was it that made him appear. Did we have some sort of emotional connection? I read somewhere that twins could sense when the other one needed them, except that I wasn't in any trouble.

He turned as I approached. "You should finish this."

What an original idea. "Yes, one of the art galleries asked for seascapes. Apparently, they're a big hit with tourists," I said.

"Tourists. Humph. Why don't you paint what you want to paint and damn the tourists?"

"Because I don't have a choice," I snapped.

"What about the painting of *Rose Cottage*?"

"I've got it under control."

He nodded. "That's good news, isn't it?"

"I got some ideas about my painting." I picked up the canvas. "Maybe I need to spend a bit more time out on the water. Then maybe I could finish this."

"You just need to get on with it. You're good enough." He took the canvas from me. "I understand there is a ten foot rule." He motioned me to step back a few paces. "See, you're doing a fine job. Just keep at it."

I took the painting from him and set it back on the easel. "Thanks, Nicholas. Now if a gallery would say that, I'd be in luck."

"They will." Nicholas followed me back into the kitchen.

"Have you ever been to Kilbride?"

"Once. My wife had family there. We went for a wedding." He gazed up at the ceiling. "A cousin, I think." He shook his head. "It was a long time ago."

"That's where I was today." He didn't appear to be interested. "Would you like to hear about it?"

He shrugged. "If you wish."

"There are some beautiful homes there." I rinsed my plate and stuck it in the dishwasher. "At least there used to be. The economy has changed a lot. I guess it was quite the seaport."

"It was too busy a place for me. That's why we only went the once."

I kept my head bent down so he wouldn't see my expression.

"Did your wife like Kilbride?"

Nicholas laughed. "What woman doesn't like to shop?" He frowned. "Why all the questions?"

The sound of the phone ringing interrupted our conversation. Nicholas disappeared as I went to answer it. It was Carl. We talked about nothing in particular for a few minutes. Then I told him about my visit to the art galleries.

"I'm almost finished with my seascape. I might even have a buyer."

"Hey, that's great." He sounded genuinely pleased. Then he said, "I'm going to go out in a friend's boat. Lobster season is over at the end of the month and this might be our last chance to catch the guys responsible for the thefts."

Before I thought about it I said, "Can I come?"

There was a long pause. "I don't think it would be a good idea. Toby and I are doing this on our own time. We probably won't find anything but still…"

"So, really, you guys are just going to look around. That doesn't sound too dangerous. Besides, if you see something, you'll have to report it and wait for back-up, or whatever the right word is." I tried to keep my voice even. "I need to finish this seascape. Going out in the boat would help. Please? I promise not to get in the way."

Carl phoned back a little later to let me know the boat trip was set for the end of the month and I was welcome to join them. I guessed Toby didn't think anything would come of it either, or he wouldn't have let me go.

17 Chapter Seventeen

*W*aiting for a whole week to call Beatrice nearly killed me, but I did it.

"Alma?" I could tell she didn't remember me. I reminded her about our meeting.

"Right. The picture of the cottage, not a seascape." I glanced over at the unfinished seascape and my stomach tightened.

"Well, you're in luck. I just sold a painting yesterday. There's a spot open, if you want it."

I didn't hesitate. "I'll be right over."

Beatrice laughed. "Don't worry, honey. There's no need to rush. I've promised you the spot. I won't give it to someone else."

"No, I have time now. I'll be right over."

I didn't bother wrapping the painting up in paper this time. The drive to the café gave me time to get my head in a better place than I'd been in days.

The same waitress glanced up when I entered. "Is Beatrice

here?" I asked.

The woman nodded. "She's in the back. I'll get her." It didn't take long for Beatrice to hang my painting on the nail that already protruded from the wall. All three of us stood back and admired it. The waitress was all smiles. "I'm sure it'll sell. How much are you asking?"

I shrugged and looked at Beatrice for direction. "What do you think?"

"It's up to you. Take a look at how much the others are selling for and then decide." She handed me a piece of paper the size of a business card. "Once you've decided, put your name and the medium on this and tack it up next to your painting." She shook my hand and returned to the kitchen without a backward glance. The waitress was already behind the counter putting cinnamon buns on a cake plate.

I decided on an amount in the middle range of the others on display. I tacked the piece of paper up and at the last moment, took a picture. I sent it to my mother with the caption, "South Shore's up-and-coming artist." I waited a moment for a response. Then, feeling awkward standing in the middle of the café, I slipped out the door. Nobody said good-bye.

On the way back to the car, my mother sent a text. "I thought you were painting a seascape? What happened?" I deleted the text and tossed the phone onto the passenger seat. I don't know why I expected anything different from her. At least tomorrow I had the boat trip with Carl and Toby to look forward to.

* * *

Carl got out of the car and opened the back door for me. "Good morning," I said cheerfully." I glanced at Toby as I climbed in. "Thanks for letting me come along." He didn't meet my eye. Instead, he seemed absorbed by something in the upstairs window. He put his hand on the door handle as if he was getting out of the car. He couldn't see Nicholas, could he?

I said, "Let's get going. You don't want to miss this sunshine. I hear it's going to cloud over this afternoon."

Toby glanced back over his shoulder at me. He seemed about to say something when Carl answered. "Let's get this show on the road, Toby." Toby glanced once more up at the window before he put the car in gear.

The silence was uncomfortable. "I went to Kilbride last week," I said brightly. "There's a great beach there where you can find sea glass." My words jumbled together I was talking so fast. Neither man answered. "So, where are we going?"

Carl turned so that he could see me better. "We don't have a plan. We're just going to cruise around a bit. Check out a couple of places. You never know what you'll see or hear." He shrugged. "It's a long shot that we'll find anything."

"Well, I'm happy to tag along. I want to finish up the seascape I'm working on. I might have a chance to sell it." I paused for a moment for dramatic effect. "And guess what? I have a painting of my house up in a gallery."

Carl grinned and held up his hand for a high-five and said, "Good for you." I felt a little foolish slapping his palm.

Toby surprised me by saying, "You probably have a good chance with tourist season and all." I wondered what he knew about selling art.

Carl jabbed his partner in the shoulder. "Toby, here's a bit of an art collector." My face must've shown my surprise. Carl said, "You can't judge a book by its cover."

Toby grunted but didn't comment.

We drove in silence for a few minutes. Then Carl turned around and glanced down at my feet. "Good. You wore the rubbers like I told you. No fancy sailboat this time, eh Toby?"

Toby caught my eye in the rearview mirror and grinned. "Nope."

"Any clues about the latest lobster thefts?" I asked. Both men shook their heads but didn't say anything.

We turned down a dirt road riddled with potholes. It was so well hidden between the trees lining the road, anyone who didn't know it was there would've missed it. We bumped our way along until the road opened onto a wharf.

By way of explanation Carl said, "We came in the back way. Just in case."

"In case, what?" I asked.

The men ignored me. Toby slowed down then turned the SUV so it was parked up against a line of trees, hidden from the wharf. They got out and walked toward the only fishing boat tied up alongside the wooden structure. I'd seen these boats all over Nova Scotia but I'd never been on one. This was turning out to be an adventure. I picked up my pace.

"Hope you don't mind the rough amenities." Carl climbed aboard and held out his hand. My legs were just long enough to climb over the side without falling. Except for a box in the middle, the wide flat deck extended from one side to the other. The stern of the boat was wide open to the water. It provided no barrier to the wide-open sea. One could easily fall off the back of this thing.

Carl walked into the small cabin. He nodded over to the left. "There's a bathroom in there." He pointed back behind us. "Normally, that's full of traps, but it's the end of the season now. That's why my friend lent me his boat." He pointed to a stool off to the side in the narrow cabin for me to sit on. I shifted around on it, trying to get comfortable. And trying to stay out of Carl's way.

Toby waited on the wharf until Carl signaled that it was okay to untie the boat. Toby deftly undid the heavy ropes and tossed them onto the boat. Then he hopped aboard as we pulled away. Instead of joining Carl and I in the tiny cabin, he stood, legs planted apart, and stared at the receding shoreline.

We chugged around the bay, Carl pointing out small islands. Rock rose out of the water in the most unexpected places. Birds perched atop, watching us chug by. The air was cold this early in the season. I turned up my collar and wished I'd thought to bring a hat. At least I'd remembered my sunglasses this time.

When I stepped outside, Toby nodded. I stood beside him and clutched the side of the boat to keep my balance. His hands were shoved into his pockets. He didn't say a word. The sound of the engine and the wind made it hard to have a conversation. I settled for standing in silence and watching distant shoreline. After a while, the trees, rocks and beaches began to all look the same. I wondered if we were going around in circles. I wandered back into the cabin and asked Carl.

He nodded at the screen mounted above the throttle and pointed to the blinking dot. "This is us." I stared at the spot he'd pointed to and noticed the protection of land was about to be left behind.

Toby's voice startled me. I thought he was still out on deck. "Not much between here and England. You know, they've found buoys from some of our boats way over there. The buoys are marked so you know where they've come from. Sometimes the current grabs hold and doesn't let go until it reaches the other side."

We all stared at the stretch of open water before us. Carl gave the wheel a slight twist and the boat stopped heading out to sea and turned closer to the shoreline. As we got closer to shore, clumps of forest turned into individual trees and you could distinguish openings between the walls of boulders.

"There must be a thousand places for the thieves to hide," I said.

Carl grimaced. "It's like finding a needle in a haystack." The likelihood of us finding anything was next to impossible. The odds were overwhelmingly in favour of the bad guys.

"What were you looking for?" I asked.

"Anything that seems out of place." Carl smiled. "Mostly, this is a fishing expedition." He gave a wry laugh at the pun. "I just need to do something." He winked. "Besides, when you asked about going out on a boat, I didn't want to disappoint you." His tone became serious. "So, what do you think?"

"It's beautiful out on the water today, but I wouldn't want to have to be out here to make a living. I think it would ruin the enjoyment."

Carl shook his head. "That's where you're wrong. If the

sea's in your blood, you can't stay away. It's like breathing."

His face softened as he gazed out at the water. I wondered if he regretted his decision to choose a job that restricted him to working on land.

The trip proved to be a disappointment for Toby and Carl but a bonus for me. The experience of spending the day out on the water would help my painting be more realistic.

"Would you like to come in for a coffee?" I asked when we pulled up in my driveway.

Carl looked over at Toby. "No, we need to get going." He got out of the car and opened my door.

"Sorry today didn't work out the way you hoped."

"Police work is like that most of the time," said Toby.

Carl followed me up to the front door. "We got a tip Lonny Naugler was hiding out in one of the islands." He shrugged. "The lead didn't pan out."

"What would you have done if you found him?" I asked.

"Nothing. That's why we were in the fishing boat. We didn't want to scare him off. We thought we might get a location. Then we'd follow up with the proper support." He glanced back at the car. "Toby didn't want you to come along in case things worked out."

"Thanks for taking me."

Carl rubbed his face. "The price is good right now. The highest it's been in ages. I'd hoped Lonny would be greedy enough to stick around for a little longer. I guess he finally got smart and left town while he was ahead." He shoved his hands in his pockets. "Sometimes they get away." He smiled. "But we'll get him—eventually. Remember the tortoise and the hare? Well, I don't mind being the tortoise, as long as we win." He gave me a quick kiss then walked back to the car. I stood on the porch until the car disappeared from sight. When I turned around, Nicholas was sitting in the rocking chair.

18 CHAPTER EIGHTEEN

"How was the fishing trip?" Nicholas asked.

"How long have you been sitting there?"

When he stood, the chair didn't rock back and forth nearly enough for a man of his size. "Not long." He stared in the direction of Toby's car. I thought he was going to say something else, but he turned and vanished through the front door. When I entered the house the conventional way, Nicholas was nowhere in sight.

I went into the sunroom and stood in front of my painting. Water, sky, lighthouse, and moon. I moved over to the right and then to the left to study the seascape from different directions. I closed my eyes and pictured the water, the smell of the ocean air, the sound of the seagulls squawking. The horizon, a straight line that divided two shades of blue. Colour and movement. I needed my painting to feel alive. I wanted the viewer to imagine they were standing on the rocky cliff gazing out to sea, not looking at a painting of one.

The painting still needed work. I wanted to paint while the memory of being on the water was still fresh in my mind. I worked until the light faded but still, the water wasn't right. Frustrated, I snapped the cover down on the paint pallet. My shoulders ached. I turned my neck from side to side, hearing the cracks with each turn. My hands were stiff and cramped. I massaged my palms, rubbing my thumb deep into the meaty tissue.

Nicholas suddenly appeared and walked over to the painting. He stared at it for a few minutes then nodded. "It's coming along. You've been at this a while. It's time to stop and come back to it when you've had a chance to rest." He waved his arm in the direction of the kitchen. "Madam, I believe your table is ready." I followed him back into the kitchen. The table was set and the candles lit. A plate of steaming pasta sat in front of my place at the table. He pulled out my chair for me.

"You have hidden talents," I said.

Nicholas winked. "More than you know." The candle flames danced as he moved to sit across from me. While I ate, he entertained me with fishing stories. The one that got away. The storms. The endless days spent out on the sea. The places he loved best. His face was animated, his gestures wide, and his laugh infectious. I couldn't remember the last time I'd laughed so much. Not once did we mention the house, the painting, or the Nauglers. I saw a different side of him. The man he must have been.

"I know I've asked you before, but I don't understand it. Where do you go when you aren't here?"

Nicholas's expression darkened. "I don't know if I can describe it. It's like sleeping without dreaming. You exist, but not really."

"So you aren't aware of time? Or what's happening around you?"

He shrugged. "I don't know if I'm explaining it correctly. It's like waiting, except you don't even breathe."

"Can you control it?" I twisted the last of the pasta around my fork. I was full, but it gave me something to do. "So all of this…" I waved my arms around the kitchen. "Can you move things, or do you snap your fingers and things magically happen?"

Nicholas grinned. "I told you I had hidden talents. I can manipulate my environment, if the conditions are right. The temperature, things around me. It takes energy from me. Afterward, I…" He searched for the right word. "I sleep."

"What do you mean when the conditions are right?"

He shrugged. "It isn't something I can control. Something more powerful than me decides when and where I'm needed. I don't know any better way to explain it."

It suddenly occurred to me. "You don't spy on me, do you?"

His eyes opened in shock. "No. Why would I do that?" He frowned. "Somehow I just know when you need me around."

"But there's been times when I needed you and you didn't come."

Nicholas nodded in the direction of the seascape. "I don't know about that. You seemed to have managed things on your own pretty well. You are much stronger than you give yourself credit for." I felt his presence wrap around me like a hug. "Don't worry, I will be here if you truly need me." His gaze softened. "You've had a long day, and so have I." The flames from the candles flickered and went out. The room was plunged into darkness. When I switched on the overhead light all evidence of the dinner was gone. A single white rose was in the empty wine bottle, its sweet perfume mingling with the spicy scent of Old Spice.

* * *

Nicholas's kindness made me more determined than ever to find out what happened to his family. The seascape stared at me from the easel. I wasn't sure I was ready to finish it. Besides, now that Rose Cottage was up in a gallery, I could take a break and go back to Kilbride.

My route led right passed Beatrice's café. Even though the painting had barely been up for a couple of days, I couldn't resist the urge to stop. I popped in under the pretext of buying a coffee. Nonchalantly, I glanced over at the wall where my

141

picture hung. It was still there.

The waitress noticed and said, "People like your painting." I think she said it to be kind. "Don't worry. It'll sell. I've seen paintings here for ages and then one day—" she snapped her fingers, "—poof, they're sold." She smiled. "Just like that."

I didn't have the luxury of waiting "ages" for someone to buy it. I thanked her and hurried out of the café so she wouldn't see the tears. The coffee cup was full and the contents stone cold by the time I reached Kilbride. I decided to sit on the bench—Nicholas's bench, before going to the museum. I watched the waves. As soon as one would disappear, another would take its place. It was as if they were tugging at me, reminding me that I promised to paint them. I realized that depending only on *Rose Cottage* wasn't a good plan.

A voice from behind me said, "I thought it was you."

I turned to see Elizabeth's smiling face. She sat beside me and put a brown paper bag down on the bench between us. She pulled out a sandwich wrapped in wax paper. "Would you like half?" She held it toward me. "It's egg salad. With a touch of curry. Are you okay with curry?" Seagulls circled around us hoping for a few crumbs.

The smell of the egg salad made my mouth water. "Are you sure?" She handed me the sandwich and a napkin.

"I asked around about the donors for these benches," said Elizabeth casually, as if the comment was as unimportant as commenting on the seagulls. I crossed my fingers behind my back. "Henry and Ethel, the other members of the historical society...well, they said the same thing as I told you. The receipts were destroyed."

She kept talking, unaware of my disappointment at hearing the news. "But," she said brightly, "I did manage to find out a bit about your Nicholas's donors." It was agonizing to watch her finish the last bite of her sandwich. Then she said, "Henry." Was I supposed to know who he was? She must've seen the blank look on my face because she explained. "He used to be our mayor." She laughed. "He's a natural born politician. Henry knows everything that goes on in this town.

Who's getting married, who bought a new car, whose son or daughter moved out west to work." She waved her arms. "You know, the stuff that helps you connect with the voters. Henry was mayor for almost thirty years. He did a good job, and people liked him." I wasn't sure how this information was going to help find Nicholas's relatives. "Can I interest you in either of these?" She held homemade cookies wrapped in wax paper in one hand and an apple in the other. It was a Granny Smith, my favourite, but I couldn't take her only apple.

"I'll have a cookie." She unwrapped the paper and handed me two. Hearing the crunch of the apple as Elizabeth bit into it made my mouth water.

"I know it isn't apple season, but I'm grateful for the modern world. Nowadays, we can enjoy apples anytime of the year." She glanced at her watch. "I only get a half hour for lunch," she said apologetically. "I usually take a walk along the boardwalk, especially on nice days like today." I had to admit, although it was only June, the hot sun made it feel more like mid-July. "Global warming." She nodded sagely. "That's what I think." She stood up and brushed nonexistent crumbs from her lap.

"What about Henry?" I shifted the conversation back to the mayor as politely as I could.

"Well, he remembers the family." She sighed. "There were women who had to raise their families alone because of the war, but during the sixties there weren't as many." She shook her head. "It's tough enough raising kids, never mind doing it on your own. The youngest was a little one." She stopped for a moment to undo the top button of her blouse. "Mind you, she had family here, but still…" Elizabeth stopped and waved to an elderly couple walking nearby. "She volunteered on Henry's first campaign for mayor; that's why he remembered her in particular." She glanced at her watch again then picked up her pace.

I still hadn't figured out the connection to Nicholas. I was afraid she wouldn't finish her story before she had to get back to work. "Nicholas?" I prompted.

"Well, that was the name of her dead husband. The boys, I'm not sure which one, maybe it was all three, donated the money for the bench. Their mother was dead by then. The boys were all grown up and moved away." We'd reached the door to the visitors centre. "Henry said he thought it was the fellow that went into the RCMP. He might've been the one who came down for the memorial ceremony. Said he couldn't be sure, but he thought his name was Nick Eisner."

"Eisner?" I frowned. "I thought you said he was Nicholas's son.

"Didn't I tell you she'd remarried? I don't know the whole story, but Henry's sure that's the family. I was going to find out a little more before I called you." She chuckled. "Henry's memory isn't always to be counted on. But if you ever get a chance to meet him, you don't go telling him that. No sense in causing upset if it isn't needed."

We walked along the boardwalk like we had all the time in the world rather than the half hour limit Elizabeth's break imposed on us. Several other people were taking advantage of the beautiful afternoon. Young and old alike strolled along as if they didn't have a care in the world. The mood was contagious. The knot between my shoulder blades began to ease. My face muscles stretched my mouth into a smile, an action they hadn't been called on to do for some time. It felt good. My spirits rose as I filled my lungs with ocean air and let my skin be warmed by the sun's rays. I thanked her and wandered back over to Nicholas's bench. How much could you count on the memory of an old mayor?

My phone buzzed on my way back to the parking lot. It was a text from Faye. "Congratulations. Saw your painting at the café. Beatrice only supports the best artists. Well done!"

The drive home gave me a chance to think over the conversation with Elizabeth. Could there be a connection to Toby? His last name was Eisner. Unfortunately, it was almost as common a last name in some parts of the county as the last name Smith. I decided to give Carl a call when I got home. He'd know if Toby's father was in the RCMP. I hoped there weren't too many Eisners in the force. I spent the rest of the drive home trying to figure out the story I'd tell Carl to explain why I was asking about Toby's family.

19 Chapter Ninteen

A few days later I was working on the seascape when the phone rang. My heart skipped a beat when I saw the name on the caller display.

"Alma? This is Beatrice. I have great news. Your painting sold this afternoon. I thought you'd like to know right away."

"Thank you!" I stood so quickly the chair rocked and it hit me in the back of the knees. "That must be a record."

Beatrice laughed. "It happens that way quite often. People see something they like and buy it right then. Often the tourists are on their way somewhere else the next day so they don't have the luxury of thinking about it for very long." Her voice became muffled as she turned away from the phone to speak to somebody else. "Sorry about that. The café is busy today. Would you like a cheque or cash?"

I thought about it for a split second. "A cheque please." I wanted proof I'd sold a painting." My luck had finally changed. Grandma was right, my hard work paid off. And she was right about how fast a painting could sell, too.

The first person I called was my grandmother's lawyer, Robert Morris. It was the weekend, so I didn't expect him to answer, but I thought he might check his messages. There was still a few weeks left before the deadline to sell a painting, but I wanted him to know right away. I left a message for him to call as soon as possible. I scrolled down my contact list ready to call my mother. Then I thought how surprised she'd be when Mr. Morris called to tell her the house was mine. Let her hear the news from him.

I couldn't contain my excitement. I needed to share my news with someone.

"Faye," I shouted into the phone. "Guess what? Beatrice sold my painting of *Rose Cottage*."

"Congratulations! That's wonderful news. Your grandmother would be very proud of you."

I remembered the text she'd sent me. My enthusiasm lessened. "You didn't buy it, did you?"

Faye sounded hurt. "Alma, you don't need me to do that. You're a good artist. The painting sold itself."

"Sorry. It's just that I can't believe my luck. I've been trying for so long." I looked around me and my eyes filled with tears. "I can't believe the house is finally mine."

"You deserve it. You should celebrate." She laughed. "I see you wearing that red dress."

I'd forgotten about the dress. A celebration worthy of the dress would take some planning, but I felt like doing something tonight. "How would you like to go out for a lobster dinner tonight? My treat."

"That sounds lovely, thank you."

Next I called Carl and invited him to join Faye and me for a celebratory lobster dinner. I told him I'd explain over dinner.

Carl was picking me up, but I was ready a little early, so I went outside to the rose garden. My rose garden now. My luck had finally changed. All the risks had been worth it. This feeling was something I'd never experienced before. It was better than falling in love. I looked up at the sky and whispered, "Thank you, Grandma." Then, I couldn't hold my excitement in any longer. I raised my hands in a cheer and shouted, "I did it!"

* * *

It was a good thing I'd called and made reservations. There was a line out the door and down the steps when we arrived. We stood against the wall near the reservation desk waiting for our table. The restaurant was built in the late 1940s as a dance hall. Looking at the wooden floor and wide-open space it was easy to picture couples kicking up their heels to the music of a live band. Above us, large fishnets were draped from the ceiling. The stage at the front of the large room overlooked the long lines of tables. Waitresses carrying trays full of lobsters were navigating the aisles with practiced ease. Bright checkered tablecloths and big rolls of paper towel decorated the tables. The energy was high and the place buzzed with happy conversation and lots of laughter. The restaurant was where all the locals took their visitors "from away", and it was exactly what tourists imagined an East Coast restaurant to be. Although none of us were tourists, it was the best place to go for a great lobster dinner.

The waitress filled our wineglasses and moved on to another table. Faye raised her glass in a toast.

"To your new home."

Carl was puzzled. Faye looked at me, silently asking permission to explain. I nodded.

"Alma's grandmother left her this house on the condition that Alma sell a painting."

Carl smiled. "Congratulations to the best new artist on the South Shore." He clinked his glass against mine with such enthusiasm I was afraid it might break.

On my way to the washroom, one of the waitresses looked familiar. This time the young woman had black hair almost down to her shoulders, but she had the same heart-shaped face and slight figure as Joan. When the waitress turned slightly I caught the glimmer of a diamond stud in the side of her nostril.

This time I wanted to avoid her. I didn't want any interaction with Joan to spoil the evening. I'd decided anything to do with Joan or her brother would only bring bad luck.

When I came back to the table, Joan must've noticed me. She sauntered over to the table.

"Hi, everyone."

We all nodded a greeting.

Joan smiled. "What's brings you all out here to tourist country?"

Before I could stop her, Faye piped up, "Alma sold a painting. We're celebrating." She grinned and raised her glass in another toast."

Joan rested her empty tray against her hip. Her cold eyes conflicted with the smile on her lips. "Cool. I know, like, how big a deal it is. What gallery sold your painting?"

"Beatrice's place. I'm not sure you know it," I answered.

Joan frowned. "It isn't, like, that café place along the highway, is it? I didn't, like, know she had a gallery there, too." She congratulated me again and disappeared into the back kitchen.

I said to Faye and Carl. "I saw her at the garden centre. I didn't know she worked here, too."

"Joan has probably worked here for a few years. They make great money in tips. She can't be making much money at the garden centre, so I'm sure every little bit helps," Faye said.

Carl nodded. "You're right. So many people often have a couple of part-time jobs rather than a full-time one because a lot of the work around here is seasonal."

The conversation about Joan was quickly forgotten as we dug into our lobsters. Carl expertly cracked the shell for me and pointed out the best parts to eat. We laughed and talked so long, we were one of the last groups to leave. The evening was one of the nicest I'd spent in a long time and I didn't want it to end. Faye gave me a huge hug before she walked back to her car. She didn't say anything; the hug said it all.

Even though it was late when we got back to my place, I invited Carl inside. Tonight was the first one I hadn't spent alone since moving to the East Coast. I couldn't think of a better way to celebrate.

20 CHAPTER TWENTY

*W*e'd finished breakfast and were enjoying our third cup of coffee when the conversation turned to Carl's work. This was my chance to ask if Toby's father was in the RCMP. Carl wasn't sure and asked why I wanted to know.

For a second, I thought about telling him the truth. I had a ghost named Nicholas Denyes who might be Toby's long-lost relative. I decided our relationship wasn't ready for that yet. Instead, I told him about my trip to Kilbride and how a friend's family was connected to some Eisners. I wondered if maybe it was Toby's family.

Carl laughed. "It's a common name, but you never know." He rubbed his chin and looked as if he was debating whether or not to say something. I asked him what he was holding back. For a second I was worried that he was going to tell me he was married. My thoughts must've showed on my face because he said quickly, "It's nothing really. It's just, the gallery where you sold your painting?"

I nodded.

"Well, Beatrice is Toby's aunt. Bit of a coincidence, eh? That's how come he knows so much about art." He chuckled, "He's even been to New York a couple of times to go to the museums and galleries."

I raised my eyebrows. Somehow I'd never pictured Toby Eisner spending time at an art gallery. He mistook my expression at his laughter as criticism of Toby's choices.

"No, no. I'm not saying going to art galleries is a bad thing, or New York, either."

Now it was my turn to laugh. "I wasn't thinking of that at all. I was just thinking how you can't judge someone by first impressions. I never pictured Toby as an art expert."

Carl snorted. "I wouldn't call him an expert, though he may think of himself that way."

After lunch, we decided to get out of the house. As I locked the door, Carl said, "I guess now you can go ahead and get that alarm system. Let me know if you see any more suspicious footprints around."

Carl took me to a flea market in the parking lot of the local grocery store. We were too late to get any of the real finds, Carl informed me. One of the stalls had old bottles along with plates and kerosene lamps. I scanned the display for a bottle like the one I'd found at the beach. The owner sat in a metal-framed lawn chair with sagging plastic webbing and watched me for a few minutes. I guess he decided I might be a serious buyer because he slowly stood up and ambled over to Carl and me.

"Are you lookin' for anything special?"

I described the medicine bottle.

He shook his head. "Nope, nothin' like that today. Usually I have a few of 'em, though. If you want, I kin give you a call?"

I shook my head, and thanked him for his time.

A few tables down I found an old wooden crate. I wasn't sure what I could use it for, but I wanted to buy something for the house to mark the special occasion of it being my place now.

The drive home was magical. My spirits were as high as the

seagulls that soared above us and my heart quickened with each glimpse of the water through the trees. My cheek muscles hurt from smiling so much.

My spirits fell a little when Carl kissed me good-bye. He said he'd be hard to reach for a couple of days. He and Toby had another lead on the lobster thefts.

"I thought the season was done."

He shook his head. "There's still stuff going on." He gave me another kiss then said, "Good luck with the painting. See you in a couple of days."

* * *

Mr. Morris called back the next morning.

"Alma? I got your message."

"Mr. Morris, I sold a painting." My heart thumped in my chest and my hands shook with excitement.

"That's wonderful news. Congratulations. Your grandmother would be pleased. Send me the information on the bill of sale from the gallery and I'll get the necessary paperwork done to transfer the house into your name."

Before he hung I asked him for a favour. "Mr. Morris, would you mind calling my mother and telling her?" It was so quiet at the other end I thought maybe he'd hung up. "It's just that it would sound more official coming from you. I guess you'll need to speak to her anyway, seeing as she's the executor."

He cleared his throat. "I'll give your mother the news."

It took me an hour to get the cheque from Beatrice and bring it over to the lawyer's office. I don't think he expected to see me so quickly, judging by the look of surprise on his face when I walked into his office. He promised to get the paperwork done and ready for me to sign by the end of the week at the latest. Then I stopped back at home, grabbed my camera and sketchbook, and drove out to the lighthouse. My sketchbook was full by the end of the day. My creative muse was back! I was ready to tackle the seascape again.

I spent the following morning working on the seascape.

Around lunchtime, Mr. Morris called and asked me to drop by his office at the end of the day.

21 CHAPTER TWENTY-ONE

*T*he lawyer's secretary knew my grandmother and we chatted about her for a few minutes while I waited for the lawyer to see me. There was a pause in the conversation and she glanced over at the closed door. Then she leaned toward me and whispered, "These cafés and galleries are very popular. Mr. Morris had another inquiry." She nodded sagely. "Apparently, they're popular with young people. My Bart is always looking for a good investment." She tittered, "Maybe this is the next thing." She quickly turned back to her keyboard as Mr. Morris's office door opened.

Mr. Morris ushered me into his office and sat behind his desk. He gestured for me to take one of the chairs opposite. He cleared his throat and looked down at the papers in front of him. "Thank you for coming in. I wanted to talk to you in person rather than over the phone. I've established the credentials of the café cum gallery." He shuffled a few papers around and continued. "The will specifically stipulates a gallery."

I interrupted him. "But it is a gallery."

He shook his head. "Beatrice Eisner is a well-respected

supporter of artists." He cleared his throat. "However, I've checked and her business is registered as a café only." His voice grew stronger. "Not an art gallery."

"But…"

His voice softened. "I know that this comes as disappointing news, but it is my duty to follow the directions in your grandmother's will so that all her heirs are protected. I would be negligent in my duties if I didn't do so."

"But…" I tried to interrupt.

"Now, Ms. Sinclair. If the shoe were on the other foot, wouldn't you expect that I was diligent in protecting your inheritance?"

"But…" I said again.

He got up and perched on the edge of his desk near me. "I do have another matter to discuss." He cleared his throat. "Ms. Stokes informed me that she has an interested buyer for your aunt's house."

I jumped up. "She can't do that!"

He moved his hands in a calming motion. "Hush, Ms. Sinclair. No one said that the house is sold. I wanted to inform you that there was a potential buyer. Ms. Stokes has told them that the house would not be available for sale until August first."

I was so angry I couldn't speak. I *knew* Erin Stokes had a buyer lined up when she came to the house.

"Would you like a glass of water?"

I shook my head and headed for the door. I couldn't stay in the office a second longer. The secretary's cheerful good-bye was drowned out by the door slamming closed behind me.

* * *

The drive home was a blur. As soon as I got in the door I called Faye. Thank goodness she was home.

"It was Joan. I'm sure of it."

"You don't know that. Besides, even if she did, it doesn't change the fact that Beatrice's place isn't a gallery.

"You didn't see her face at the restaurant. She pretended to be all happy about it. She smiled, but her eyes…her eyes were cold. Even if going to the lawyer's office didn't change anything, it was still a mean and spiteful thing for her to do."

Faye sighed. "Well, now you know the Nauglers."

"And there's something else." I paced back and forth, trying to remember where I'd put the photograph. I'd show it to Faye next time we were together. "The picture of Rose Cottage…the writing on the back was crossed out and the word 'thieves' was written in big, red letters. The original words were scribbled out so hard the lines almost went right through to the front of the photograph. Joan was pretty angry."

Faye's voice grew sharper. "Well, you have to get over it and decide what you're going to do next. You don't have much time left. How's the seascape going? You said the trip with Carl and Toby was helpful."

I left Carl a message to tell him the news but he didn't call back before I went to bed. Then I remembered that he and Toby were following up on some leads and he said he'd be hard to reach.

22 CHAPTER TWENTY-TWO

*F*aye was right. The first thing to do was to finish the seascape. The second thing was to paint a few more pictures so that I'd have a collection. I could use several of the pictures I'd taken the other day of the lighthouse from different angles. I thought about the winery and how the collection of paintings could be displayed to the greatest effect. At first, the looming deadline made me hesitant. Then I reminded myself that if I could sell one painting, then I could certainly sell another one. There were loads of tourists wanting to spend money on seascapes.

Nicholas appeared after I'd made several attempts at trying to get the water just right. The pallet was full of so many shades of blue, it was ridiculous. He held out his hand. In his palm was the piece of sea glass Carl had given me. "Hold it up to the light," he commanded. "See the colours. Think about the power it took to make something so beautiful. Think about how long she worked to make it. Close your eyes and picture the waves."

He spoke to me about the different moods of the sea and

how he felt connected to her. The rise and fall of his words was like the ebb and flow of the waves. His love of the sea was evident in every word he spoke. I stopped worrying about making the painting perfect and lost myself in his stories.

I remembered what Faye said to me about not being afraid of colour. I worked steadily for the next few hours. When I finished, the water danced, the clouds floated, and the moonlight beckoned. I signed my name and stood back.

The painting had depth. Warmth. Movement.

"Well done!" Nicholas smiled at me warmly. "I knew you could do it."

I stared at the painting. Then I looked over at Nicholas. My eyes inexplicably filled with tears. My throat tightened. "I couldn't have done it without your help." He took my hand. His grip was strong, his skin rough. He gazed down at me and said, "You're welcome." He nodded at the painting. "But you did all the work."

I laughed. "And I have the stiff shoulders to prove it."

* * *

The next morning, the first thing I saw when I woke up was a necklace made of sea glass draped over the lamp shade beside my bed. The bits of sea glass were different colours than the piece Carl gave me. I lay in bed mesmerized by the colours reflected in the sun's rays. The phone ringing startled me. I thought it was Carl finally calling back.

I was surprised to hear Faye's voice. "Alma, sorry to call you so early. Have you heard about the fire?"

I wiped the sleep from my eyes. "What fire?" Why was Faye calling me about a fire? "You had a fire?"

"No, at Carl's place. The one you were at when you went sailing with Harry and Theresa."

My brain was still foggy with sleep and it was hard to follow what she was saying. What she said finally struck home. "Carl's place? Is he all right?"

"Yes, he wasn't there, thank goodness. I have to go, but I

thought you'd like to know."

It was still early enough in the morning to catch the local news broadcast. The fire at Carl's place replaced the lobster thefts as the top news story. The news reporter said, "No one was hurt in the fire, but the building was destroyed." The picture showed Carl's home, except now yellow tape fluttered from the deck railing; and exposed beams, charred by the fire, protruded from the collapsed roof. The reporter looked grim, as if her house was the one on the screen. "Police are investigating the cause, but initial reports call the fire 'suspicious'."

The camera panned over the scene, and I jumped in surprise. There was Carl. He looked as grim as the reporter, only he had reason to be. I thought about his childhood memories. Destroyed. I watched him on the television, hands shoved in his pockets, staring up at the roof. I wondered if anything survived the fire.

The phone rang a few times before it clicked to voice mail. After the beep I rushed through my message. "Hi, Carl. I just saw the news. Are you all right? I'm so sorry to hear about the house." I paused. "Please call me as soon as you can." Then I called Theresa but she didn't have any more information than what the news had reported. I couldn't sit around waiting for Carl to phone so I went back out to the lighthouse and took some more pictures.

Carl was sitting in the rocking chair on the front porch when I got home. He stood up to greet me. "Hi. I got your message.

23 CHAPTER TWENTY-THREE

*H*is face was drawn and his chin was covered in a dark smear of two-day-old stubble. When he hugged me I sensed how exhausted he was. His bristles brushed against my chin when I kissed him. "Are you all right?"

Rather than meeting my gaze, he stared out over the front lawn toward the road. He seemed to be struggling with something. He sighed and rubbed his hand over his face. "Did you mean it when you offered to help?"

"Come on in. Would you like a beer, or are you on duty?"

He followed me into the kitchen saying, "A beer'd be great. Thanks." He sat down, stretched his legs out under the table and closed his eyes. He heard me set the bottle down on the table, and his eyes flew open. "Sorry. I haven't had much sleep." He took a long swallow of the cold beer.

I sat down across from him. "I'm sorry about your place."

"Yeah. It's pretty much a write-off." He swallowed another mouthful of beer then said, "Not that there was much in there of value. I kept it mostly as a place to get away." He smiled. "But it was a nice place to go and relax. My job can be a bit rough sometimes."

"What are you going to do?"

He shrugged. "Wait for the insurance before I can do anything." He sat up and leaned across the table. "But that's not what I'm worried about." He paused. "I've been around a few fires in my time. I know when a fire is an accident and when one gets started on purpose." He shook his head. "You could almost smell the gasoline."

I sat back in surprise. "The fire was started on purpose? Who would do something like that?" It took me a minute to understand what he was saying. "Surely they can't think you did it."

"They have to cover all the bases."

I was as indignant as if I'd been accused of the crime. "Why would anybody think you'd do something like that? You've owned the place for years."

He twisted his bottle around in his hands. "Remember when I checked out the trail, did you see anyone besides us, or any sign that someone else was around? I shook my head. "Remember you took a picture of me in the clearing near the path. Do you mind if I see it?"

"Sure." I got up and dug my phone out of my purse and handed it to him. "What are you looking for?"

"Evidence." He scrolled through the camera roll and found the picture he was looking for. He stared at it for a moment then scrolled back and forth between the different pictures. "Is this all you took?" I nodded. "You didn't trash any?"

I couldn't remember. "I don't think so."

He sighed and handed the phone back to me. "Thanks."

"What were you hoping to find?"

"It doesn't matter. It was a long shot anyway."

I stood behind him and wrapped my arms around him. He smelled of smoke and sweat. "I'm sure everything will be okay."

"Yah, right," he said without conviction.

"Would you like another beer?"

"No, I better be going. I don't need to add a DUI to the list." He shoved his chair back so hard the legs scraped the hardwood floor. I knew there was more to the story but figured it had to do with confidential information. "Listen, I'll give you a call in a couple of days. Things are crazy with work right now."

"I'm sorry the pictures weren't of more help."

"Don't worry about it." He rubbed his bloodshot eyes.

"Sure you don't want to stay here tonight or rest for a bit while I make you something to eat?" He barely had enough energy to shake his head. When I opened the door, a strong gust of wind blew the knob out of my hand and the door slammed against the wall. Carl jumped back, startled.

"Whoa! It's dangerous around here," he joked. At least he hadn't lost his sense of humour. When he stepped outside, the wind blew the door closed and it hit him in the back of the legs, making him stumble. He gave an absent-minded wave as he drove away. I forgot to tell him about the footprints I'd seen underneath the window to the sunroom.

* * *

"The man's an idiot."

Nicholas's eyes were fixed on Carl's receding taillights.

"Why are you calling him an idiot? You don't even know him."

"Oh, but there's where you're wrong. I may not have known him, but I knew his father. The apple doesn't fall far from the tree. Carl might not have burned his house down, but he's mixed up in it somehow. The Brennans weren't known for being smart."

He pointed in the direction of the driveway. "That boy is trouble."

"He's an RCMP officer."

"You can paint a skunk black and call it a cat, but it's still a skunk."

I stomped into the kitchen, yanked the fridge door open,

and grabbed the jug of water. "What do you want, Nicholas?"

He rubbed his hands over his face. "I want you to be safe. I want you to live happily-ever-after in your grandmother's home." His voice softened. "I'm sorry if I was too strong."

I sighed. "I know you're only trying to help, but you need to back off. Let me make my own decisions." I took a sip of water. "And you're wrong about Carl."

He shook his head. "Trust me, both Carl and the Nauglers are up to no good. I'm certain of it." His face darkened, and the temperature in the room dropped. It was so cold I could see my breath. Tiny threads of frost climbed up the sides of the water glass. "Don't say I didn't warn you."

A flash of blue light blinded me for an instant. By the time I could see again, Nicholas was gone. Being stuck with a ghost was becoming more of a nuisance than a help.

24 Chapter Twenty-Four

*T*he winery parking lot was more crowded than the last time I'd been there and I had to navigate between the cars with my painting. I looked around to see if any tourists were trying to readjust their suitcases to fit a painting into their already jammed trunk. After what happened with Beatrice's place, I wanted to make sure the gallery was legitimate before I gave them my seascape to sell. The owner assured me they had the proper licensing.

She leaned my seascape against the wall and stood back a few paces. "This is lovely." Her praise sounded genuine. "As soon as you bring us a couple more we can put your work over there on that wall." She pointed to a spot over in the corner. "Along with your work, we'd like to have a few words about you as well, and a photograph. The tourists like to read a little bit about you; nothing much, just a few sentences."

She walked over to one of the more prominent displays and showed me a laminated artist bio complete with a striking photograph of the artist. I promised I'd get the rest of the paintings and the bio to her soon.

On the way back to my car, I heard a familiar voice call out from behind me. Joan quickly covered the distance between us. She wore a wide brimmed hat and huge sunglasses. I couldn't tell what colour her hair was underneath the hat. Her shirt covered her right shoulder, leaving the left exposed. As she drew closer, I could see more of the tattoo below her collar bone. *Love* was written after the word *Confuses*. She was chewing the ever-present wad of gum.

"So, how's the painting coming along?"

Her eyes were hidden behind the huge sunglasses. It put me at a disadvantage. You can tell so much about a person by their eyes. I didn't answer. The space between us was filled with the sound of gum snapping.

"You must be running out of time. You have until the end of July right?" She nodded back in the direction of the gallery. "I didn't see any paintings with your name."

"Did you get in touch with my grandmother's lawyer about Beatrice's place?"

Joan shrugged but remained silent.

I took a step closer. "Did you tell Erin Stokes you want to buy my house?"

She slid her sunglasses down so that she could look me in the eye. "Why are you entitled to the house any more than I am? What makes you more deserving? My family lived there long before yours." She pointed her finger at me and stabbed the air near my chest. "If your great-grandfather hadn't taken advantage of my family at a time when everyone was having trouble paying their mortgage, then we'd still be living in our house today." She didn't bother to look at my reaction.

"I've sacrificed everything to live here." It took every ounce of control not to show Joan how angry her words made me.

Joan leaned close enough that I could smell the sickly, sweet strawberry scent of her gum. "You don't know what real sacrifice is all about. You aren't the only one who's ever suffered, who's been treated unfairly. Nobody made you be an accountant. You've had lots of chances to live your dream.

You're just too scared to take them."

I was so stunned by her words the only thing I could do was watch her saunter back to the car. I knew a good rebuttal would come to me later. She took a few steps and called back over her shoulder, "By the way, are you sure this is a 'real' art gallery?" She laughed. "You wouldn't want to lose your house over a technicality, would you?"

* * *

Faye's place was on the way home from the winery. On the spur of the moment, I decided to see if she was home. She took one look at my face and ushered me inside. "What happened? Is it Carl?"

"No, it's Joan. You wouldn't believe what she said. She's going to buy my house."

"Come in and sit down. I'll put the kettle on and you can tell me all about it."

I paced around the room, clenching and unclenching my hands. Faye came in a few moments later carrying a tray with tea and some cookies. "I met her at the winery by accident. I just have to sell the seascape."

Faye frowned. "How is Joan going to get the money to buy the house? It doesn't make any sense."

I shrugged. "I don't know, I didn't ask her, but she seemed sure of herself." My hand shook and tea spilled down the front of my shirt. Faye handed me a napkin. "There's no way the Nauglers should live in my grandma's house. I can't let that happen."

"Can't your mother do something? After all, she's the executor."

"My mother wouldn't care as long as they paid a good price. She doesn't understand about the Nauglers, and even if she did, it wouldn't make any difference." My eyes filled with tears. "But I couldn't do that to Grandma. I even planted some new rose bushes. I wanted to bring the garden back to the way it was before she got sick and couldn't take care of things the way she used to. The Nauglers would probably tear them out and…and…" I thought about what Erin Stokes told me. "Put in a swimming pool or something."

She got up and handed me a list with names and phone numbers. "After Beatrice agreed to display *Rose Cottage* I didn't think you needed these contacts. Once you've finished the seascape, give these galleries a call. They know all about you." She rested her hand on my shoulder. "I'm so sorry, Alma. You must be so disappointed."

The tinkle of chimes erupted from her phone. She glanced down at the screen. "It's Theresa. She might have news about Carl's place." I nodded and got up to refill our cups. "What?" There was a pause. "When?" Another pause. "I know he was getting on, but still…" I hovered, waiting for Faye to tell me the news.

She put down the phone, blinking back tears. "Martin… Martin's dead." Her face crumpled and a sob escaped from her lips. For the first time I noticed the all wrinkles around her eyes. Her distress was disquieting. She'd introduced Martin as an old friend, but I got the sense that he was much more than that.

"I'm so sorry, Faye. What happened? Was he ill?"

The cheerful, tinkling sound of Faye's earrings was a sharp contrast to her sorrow. Her voice was pinched. "They aren't sure yet. The RCMP found him when they were investigating the fire at Carl's place. Martin's boat was tied up around the other side of the island."

"At Carl's place?"

Faye shrugged. "He's known the Brennans for years. He probably heard about the fire and went to check it out. He knew the island like the back of his hand. Martin was always one to help, that's just…" She couldn't finish the sentence. "He was a good soul. I'm going to…" She twisted the tissue like a tourniquet around her finger. "I'm going to miss him deeply."

"Faye, I didn't know. I am so sorry."

I bent down and wrapped my arms around her. A few

moments later, she pushed me away and stood. She straightened her shoulders, set our cups back on the tray, and carried everything into the kitchen.

"Can I help you clean up?"

"No, thank you. I can manage." She sniffed. "I'm all right. I just need some time alone." She walked me to the door saying, "You're a good artist, Alma. One of the galleries will sell your work."

"Thanks." I paused then said, "Faye, I am so sorry about Martin. Please call if there is anything I can do to help." She softly closed the door behind me.

It was hard waiting for Carl to call. I picked up the phone and started to dial, then disconnected. *What really happened over on the island?*

25 CHAPTER TWENTY-FIVE

*O*ne minute Nicholas stood at the top of the stairs, the next minute he was beside me. "Martin Keaton is dead!" His voice thundered through the house. The temperature dropped so quickly, my breath hung in the air like a cloud.

"Nicholas, why are you so upset about Martin Keaton?"

Nicholas snapped at me. "Martin was a good kid. He was always one to help people out." Nicholas used almost the same words as Faye. "I was a teenager when he was born. We didn't have much contact with each other when he was growing up. I was already working full time on the boats, helping my father. Later on, when Martin got older, our paths would cross from time to time. He was dependable and he didn't drink too much, like some of the others. He was a hard worker."

"So he was a friend of yours?"

Nicholas shook his head. "I wasn't so keen on him at first, he used to hang around with Stephen Naugler and that crowd. Lots of young guys figured they were tough if they hung around Naugler. I thought Martin was one of those types. Remember, he was still a youngster to me. Then I got to know him some. Everyone liked Martin. He kept to himself, helped out when he could." Nicholas smiled. "Wasn't averse to making some extra money in…" Nicholas chuckled, "…in less than legal ways, if his family was in need." Nicholas waved his finger. "But not like Stephen Naugler."

"Why are you so upset about his death?"

Nicholas's was silent for several moments. Then he quietly said, "He tried to save my life. Martin told me to stay clear of Stephen Naugler. Martin could let things go. He was smarter than me." He shook his head, "If I'd listened to him, my family wouldn't have been left to starve."

"Nicholas, you don't know that." I wasn't going to say anything about what I'd found out in Kilbride until I was more certain, but this seemed like a good time to tell him. Before I could say anything we heard the sound of a car coming up the driveway. I went to the front door to see who it was and when I turned around, Nicholas was gone. The smell of Old Spice lingered in the air.

* * *

Toby Eisner was out of uniform, but he still wore his signature sunglasses. He was alone. "Alma."

"Toby, where's Carl? Is he okay?"

Toby nodded. "He's busy dealing with some other stuff, but he's all right. He'll call as soon as he can. Things are busy right now. I'm sure you can understand that." He shoved his hands into his back pockets. It made his elbows stick out like chicken wings. "Carl mentioned that the two of you went out to the island?" He said it more like a question than a statement.

Why was he asking about that? "That was almost a month ago."

"Yes, I'm aware of that. Still, I was wondering if you saw anything unusual."

I shook my head. "Carl asked me the same thing."

"Carl? When?" He pulled his hands out of his back pockets. He wasn't acting so laid back anymore.

"He came by a few days ago, he asked to see some pictures I'd taken." Quickly, I added, "He didn't find anything. I don't know what he was looking for. He wouldn't tell me."

"Do you mind if I take a look at them?" He scrolled through the photographs but seemed as disappointed as Carl. "Was anyone else around the place?" he asked.

I tried to remember if there was any sign that someone else was around. "No. We didn't go inside." I shrugged. "There might have been."

He eagerly said, "So someone else could've been there?"

"No, I'm just saying that I don't know. We were hardly around the house. We walked up the trail. Carl wanted to show me the clearing. He told me it was a good place to paint."

"Well, if you think of anything give me a call? Okay?" He reached into his breast pocket, pulled out a card, and scribbled something on the back. "Get ahold of me at this number. Okay?" He slid his sunglasses a little lower down his nose and peered at me over the top. "You'd be surprised how many witnesses remember stuff later on. Don't worry about whether or not you think it's important, let me be the judge. Okay?" He started to turn toward his car then he quickly swung back around like he'd caught sight of something. Then he frowned. *Could he have seen Nicholas?* In a suspicious voice he asked, "There's no one else here with you?" He stared at me for a moment as if willing me to confess to a crime. Unblinking, I met his gaze. *Was he going to ask to check inside the house?* I stepped forward into his space. He didn't move. It was a standoff. His eyes scanned the house once more. Then he seemed to make up his mind. He nodded at the card in my hand. "Be sure to give me a call if you remember anything." He casually slid his sunglasses into place with his middle finger then leisurely returned to his car. He backed out of the driveway slower than molasses in January.

* * *

Faye's call woke me up. "Have you heard the news?"

I remembered the uneasy feeling last night when I'd woken up halfway through the evening news. "No." I sat up and swung my feet over the edge of the bed.

"It's Martin." For a second I foolishly thought she'd tell me there'd been a mistake. He wasn't dead at all. "He died of a heart attack. The RCMP are releasing the body." She sniffed. "The funeral will be in a few days." Another sniff. "I thought you'd like to know." I walked over to the window and pulled the curtain back a fraction. I let it fall back into place. "Is there anything I can do to help with Martin's funeral? Or help you?"

"Theresa will be along after church. I'll know better then what the plans are for the funeral and…and afterward." She gave a small sniff. I pictured the kitchen table littered with tissues, a contrast to her perfectly organized household. She was about to hang up when I added, "And, Faye, don't hesitate to call if you need anything."

Now that the cause of Martin's death was solved, surely Carl would phone. It was impossible to concentrate on my painting wondering if he was all right. Maybe I wasn't cut out to date a police officer.

26 CHAPTER TWENTY-SIX

Raindrops bounced off the pavement, it was coming down so hard. It was perfect weather for visiting dead people. The funeral home was an old Victorian house tucked away from the road. The front lawn was already a green carpet. Neatly clipped bushes lined the long driveway. A parking lot was hidden from view at the back of the house. Several people were clustered in small groups spread about on the covered porch.

A sign inside the entrance indicated Martin was resting in the Arbour Room, which turned out to be the house's original living room. Beautiful crown moulding decorated the border of the high ceilings. The coffin was placed in the small bay window. Opposite the coffin was a large archway that opened to an adjoining room, probably the original dining room. Coffee and a few trays of sweets were set up in there on a long table. The funeral home seemed too ornate for a simple fisherman.

A gentleman wearing a dark suit, white shirt, and black tie

stood inconspicuously off to the side. The blue, plush-covered kneeler in front of the coffin was empty of mourners. Everyone in the room must have already paid their respects. Their duty done, they were now free to socialize with their neighbours. The room hummed with gossip and the occasional burst of laughter. Faye, Theresa, and Harry stood over by the coffin, greeting new arrivals. It was disturbing to see such a vibrant lady change in such a short time to a frail, stooped older lady. Her handshake lacked its usual strength. There was no sign of Carl.

Bev and Gwen were among the jovial group of people that stood off to one side of the room. I said a quick prayer and made my way over to them. She made exaggerated gestures with her arms as she shared some exciting gossip with the group.

Bev's shrill voice carried over the din of the crowd. She caught sight of me and waved. They were deep in conversation about the fire at Carl's house.

"Hi, Alma," said Bev. She turned to the man next to her and said, "Honey, this is Alma. She's one of the painters from my group. She comes from away. Ontario?" She cocked her head to one side and I nodded in agreement. "Alma, this is my husband, Homer."

Homer nodded and stuck out his hand. "Pleased to meet you."

Her face lit up as she said, "I hear you were at Carl's place right before the fire." She leaned forward, eyes full of curiosity.

I shook my head. "I was there, but it was at least a month ago. It must be devastating for Carl. I think his family owned the place for years."

Gwen smiled and nodded. "I've just been to the beach. If you're lucky, you can find some nice sea glass. And that Devil's Hole played a role in many young men's tales—true or otherwise." That got a good chuckle from everyone in the group. Everyone knew Martin and they were keen to share stories about his colourful past.

Homer said, "He was quite a character. Yes, siree, he liked

his drink." That wasn't what Nicholas told me. Maybe Martin took to drinking later in life, after Nicholas was dead.

Gwen's husband, Charlie, nodded. "Same as a few others I could name." His comment elicited a polite round of laughter. "Remember when he climbed into the fountain in front of city hall and did a great version of 'Singing In the Rain'?" Charlie demonstrated a couple of dance steps. "Even drunk, Martin could carry a tune."

"He was a good soul. Nothin' ol' Martin wouldn't do to help out a friend," said Homer.

"Or make a buck or two," said Charlie. The men glanced over at me.

"What the government doesn't know won't hurt 'em." Homer winked.

That story aligned with what Nicholas had said. I was curious to find out more about Stephen Naugler. I figured this would be a good group to ask. "Oh? I heard he sometimes helped out Stephen Naugler." I gave a nervous laugh. "I suppose he sometimes crossed the line." To soften the comment I quickly added, "Not that he ever did any harm." There was an uncomfortable silence.

Gwen cleared her throat. "Stephen Naugler was a completely different kettle of fish." She glanced over at the coffin. "Martin wouldn't hurt a fly. If he sometimes helped out a friend or two by doing something the government might frown on, what's the harm in that? The government makes it hard enough for fishermen to make an honest living."

The group nodded.

Homer said, "Thems lettin' the big guys buy up the quotas so's none of the little guys can stay in business."

Charlie scowled. "I remember buyin' my quota years ago. It cost me $25.00. My son'll have to inherit it, 'cause there's no way he could make enough money to buy it from me now."

Homer said, "Except the government will still get their share with that capital gains tax, don't you worry none. They don't miss a thing. Nothing more certain than death and taxes." The group nodded in agreement.

Bev said, "Isaac Schnare sold his quota and now he and his wife Betty spend every winter down in Florida." An undercurrent of jealousy ran beneath the words.

This was not the first time she'd made the comment because her husband, Homer, bristled. "You'd be bored down there, Bev. What with missin' the grandchildren and such." As way of reply, Bev stuffed a whole coconut-raspberry square into her mouth. She took a long time chewing before she swallowed.

The group shuffled a few steps back to make room for another gentleman. Everyone seemed to know him except me. I gathered from the conversation that the new addition to the group was an old fishing buddy of Martin's.

He said, "Martin could safely land a boat anywhere 'round heres even if the fog was so thick you couldn't see your hand in front of your face." He spoke with some reverence. "I gots over ten thousand dollars' worth of equipment on my boat and I bet it's no better than what Martin coulda done gettin' me out o' the harbour." The group laughed. "I remember my dad could get out to his pots using just a watch and a compass. Never hit nothin' all the years he fished."

"Not many around that can still do that," said Charlie.

All the talk of fishing made me wonder if any of them knew Nicholas, or at least his family. The first time I spoke my voice was drowned out by laughter from a nearby group. I tried again.

"Did any of you know Nicholas Denyes?"

"Denyes?" asked Bev.

I repeated my question. I could tell by their faces each of them was trying to place the name. I added, "He was a fisherman who drowned out near the lighthouse around 1960. His widow and children moved out to Kilbride after he died."

"How did you hear about him?" asked Gwen.

I hadn't thought that far ahead. I shrugged. "I was painting out at the lighthouse and someone stopped to talk with me. They told me the story, but they didn't know many of the details."

Charlie brushed his thinning hair back from his forehead. "That spot's not so bad. Out near the reef, now that's where she can get you."

Homer piped up. "I recall a fella who died when I was a teenager. They never found the body. It was probably washed out to sea. I'm not sure if his name was Denyes or not."

Bev added. "I think that might have been his name. It was so long ago, I can't remember."

Gwen smiled. "You could always check the memorial. The town paid to have a monument resurrected in town to commemorate all the people lost at sea."

"Thanks, I checked, and his name's there." What I really wanted was to find someone who knew Nicholas's family and what happened to them. I'd have to ask Toby Eisner, but I wasn't sure how to explain why I was interested in his ancestors. If it didn't pan out, I shuddered at the thought about how many Eisners there were in the phone book and how many awkward calls I'd have to make.

* * *

Faye was clearly shaken by Martin's death. Her loss was etched in every line on her face. I wished there was something I could do for her. I thought back to the evening I'd met him at her house. No wonder he'd seemed so at home. I shouldn't have been all that surprised. Based on the information about him at the funeral home, I calculated that he was thirteen years older than Faye, not that much more than between me and Carl. Then I remembered the picture I'd taken of him out on the boat. I'd shown it to Faye and she said it looked like a painting from a calendar. It would make a perfect remembrance for Faye.

I grabbed my sketchpad and spread my pencils out on the kitchen table. I moved the picture around on the screen trying to decide the area of focus. I enlarged Martin's face, then zoomed in on the boat. Inside the cockpit was a bedraggled teddy bear. I zoomed in closer. A huge rip in the bear's stomach had been clumsily repaired with white thread. The stitches stood out starkly from the brown fur. It made the toy look like something Frankenstein might have owned. What was Martin doing with Joan's teddy bear?

I turned on the evening news before going to bed. "The RCMP have arrested two men in connection with the recent lobster thefts. We'll keep you up to date with any new developments."

Carl phoned the next morning.

* * *

"Morning. I didn't want to call too early. Did I wake you? Have you heard about the arrests?"

"Was one of them Lonny Naugler?" I asked.

He sighed. "No, that's what kept me tied up. I can't tell you much about it because the investigation isn't closed yet. We're pretty sure that he's the one responsible for the fire at my place. It was touch and go with the insurance company at first, but it was clear that I had nothing to do with it."

"Is that why you asked to see the pictures on my phone?"

"Yeah, I don't know what I was looking for. I guess I was hoping there'd be some evidence he'd been there." He grunted. "It was a long shot, but you never know, right?" He paused for a moment. "Remember I told you Toby and I had some information about the lobster thefts? It was from Martin. I couldn't say anything, but now that he's dead…" I could hear the anger in his voice. "When he died, I was sure Lonny was responsible. The information led us to the two guys we arrested, but so far they aren't saying much about Lonny or his whereabouts."

"But I thought Martin died of a heart attack."

"Yes, but I'm sure somehow Lonny was responsible."

"Are you going to Martin's funeral?"

"Yah, with the arrests and Lonny gone underground, things are quiet. Sorry I haven't been around." His voice caught. "Martin was a good guy. I owed him a lot. I wanted to make things right."

"It's okay. You said you'd be out of reach for a few of days." It seemed like he'd been away forever.

"Toby said he talked to you and told you I was okay. I didn't want you to worry."

"I got your message. What did you want to talk to me about?" The shambles with the sale of *Rose Cottage* seemed so long ago now.

"It's okay, I'll tell you about it later. Do you want to come over for some breakfast?"

27 CHAPTER TWENTY-SEVEN

A week after Martin's funeral, I gave the sketch to Faye. It gave me a good excuse to check on her.

Her eyes welled with tears when she looked at it. "Thank you so much, Alma. It's funny, but I don't have many pictures of him."

"I didn't know him very well, but everyone said he was a great guy. He will be missed."

She brought a pitcher of ice tea out to the café table in her garden. It was so secluded it made me think of being hidden away in a secret garden.

"That sketch was kind of you." She watched a bee hovering around the potted plants for a moment. "Not too many people knew about Martin and me." She laughed. "There wasn't any need to keep it secret after my father died. He was the only one who cared about the age difference." She shrugged, "But it was kind of fun to keep it our secret."

I'm sure my surprise at the news showed on my face .

"Thirteen years isn't too bad; it's almost the same as Carl and me."

Faye barely shook her head. "Not when you're barely eighteen and he's thirty-one." She gazed off into the distance. "He was a handsome lad, you know. We met at a dance. I was there with my friends. He seemed so mature." She laughed. "I guess he was, compared to the other fellows my age." She ran her hand down the sides of her glass but didn't take a drink. "My father never liked him. He said he was too old for me. I think it was because he didn't want me to marry a fisherman." She pursed her lips. "My father was a bit of a snob."

"What about your mother?"

"She never crossed him. Besides, I think she agreed with him. Martin and I met in secret for a while, but then that wasn't enough for him. He wanted our relationship to be out in the open. I wanted to run away. I was old enough, but Martin wouldn't let me. He said he wouldn't make me choose between him and my family."

"He sounds like a very special man."

Faye nodded. "We went our separate ways; I went away to art school, and he kept on fishing. After my father died, I came home." She smiled, "And we picked right back up again as if there'd never been any time away. I was divorced and he'd never married. We were too old to start a family and both of us were happy with our lives the way they were." Her eyes filled with tears. "I will miss him deeply." She dabbed her eyes with a tissue. "Thank you so much for the sketch. It's more than a likeness; it captures his spirit, too. You have a real gift. You should do more of them. "

"No, seascapes are what sells, not portraits." We walked back to my car and I finally got up the courage to ask her the question I'd wanted to since I got there.

"Faye, I was wondering... There was a bear in the photograph I took of Martin that day out on the water." She frowned. "I think it might belong to Joan."

"Why do you say that?" she asked.

"Because Joan told me a story about Lonny cutting open

the stomach of the bear she had when she was a kid. This bear's stomach was stitched up like the one she told me about." I licked my lips. "Martin said he had a soft spot for her. Did he ever say anything to you?" I could feel my stomach tighten as I waited for her to answer.

Faye chuckled. "He called the bear his lucky charm. Sailors can be a very superstitious bunch." She shook her head as if to say Martin's beliefs were childish, but she would indulge him. "He kept it on the boat. I asked him about it once. He said it reminded him about what happens when you look the other way." She gazed off in the distance and her voice grew softer. "I always thought it was a strange answer because if there was one thing about Martin Keaton, he could always be counted on to help you out." Her eyes filled with tears and she blinked them back.

It bothered me that the conversation was upsetting her. I quickly asked the question I'd been waiting to say. "What happened to the bear?"

Faye shrugged. "I imagine it's still there. He left the boat to me." She grinned. "I don't know what he was thinking. What am I going to do with a fishing boat?" It was a relief to hear the sound of her earrings jingle as she laughed.

* * *

The sketch of Martin gave me an idea of how I could repay Nicholas for his help with the seascape. I invited both Carl and Toby over for dinner. They'd been working hard on the lobster thefts and deserved a break. I purposely left my work on display, including a sketch of Nicholas. While Carl was outside grilling the steaks, I showed Toby my paintings. The collection was almost ready for the gallery at the winery. He was immediately drawn to the sketch of Nicholas.

"Who's this?" he asked.

"I was down in Kilbride and I saw some old photographs at the museum. There was something about him that caught my eye. I've been back a couple of times but I haven't been able to find out much about him." Toby bent down and stared at the sketch.

"You don't know the ten-foot rule." I laughed. He looked at me puzzled. "My work always looks better from a distance."

Toby rubbed his chin. "What's his name?"

"Nicholas Denyes." My heart was thumping, but I tried to make my voice sound indifferent.

He laughed. "What a coincidence, that was my grandfather's name." He peered closer at the sketch. "I never met him. My dad used to carry around a family picture, but I don't know where it is now." The smell of barbequed steaks drifted in from the kitchen and that was the end of the conversation.

Toby glanced over at the sunroom a few times during the evening. Before he left he asked to see the sketch one more time. Jokingly, he said, "I'll give you a few bucks for it if you ever want to sell it."

I shook my head. "It isn't for sale."

He pointed at the rest of the paintings and said, "Very nice. I'm sure you'll get a few tourists interested in these."

He didn't know how much I depended on it. The beginning of July was only a couple of days away.

28 Chapter Twenty-Eight

*T*oby dropped by a couple of days later. He stood in the front hall, his weight shifting from one leg to the other. He wiped his palms on his pants. It was the first time I'd seen Toby Eisner anything less than oozing with confidence.

"I have something to show you. I found the photograph." He took a black and white photograph from his pocket. The father had his arm loosely around the mother's shoulders. The mother held a baby and two young boys stood in front of the couple. In the background was the lighthouse. He pointed to the man and woman. "These are my grandparents, Nicholas and Violet Denyes." Then he pointed to each of the children. "This is my father, Nick Jr., my Uncle Marcus, and my other uncle, Tobias." He handed me the photograph so that I could take a closer look. It was unsettling to see a younger Nicholas staring back at me. "I never met Uncle Tobias. He died before I was born. I was named after him. If he hadn't died then my name would have been Nicholas, the same as my dad and my grandpa.

"My grandmother remarried and her husband wanted them to all have the same last name. My Aunt Bea was born a year later."

I handed the photograph back to him. "It sounds like they had a good life–your grandmother and the children."

Toby nodded. "My dad became an RCMP officer." He stared down at the photograph. "His mother made all the kids promise they'd never become fishermen, but Tobias couldn't help it. The draw of the sea was too strong. When he drowned, I think that was the end for her. She died soon after." He said hesitantly, "Do you mind if I take another look at the sketch? I think it might be my grandfather. There aren't too many pictures of him around." He held the photograph up to the sketch and compared the two. "It sure looks like the same guy to me, especially around the eyes." He slipped the photograph back in his pocket. My grandmother died never knowing what happened to her first husband." His eyes pleaded with me. "When you were doing your research down in Kilbride did you find out anything about him?"

I never said that I was doing research. He made that assumption, but I wasn't about to correct him. It was much easier than having to explain a ghost. "It was a random picture. I don't even remember where I saw it. I'm sorry." I felt so guilty lying to him, but I couldn't very well tell him the truth.

He sighed, "My Aunt Bea tried but she couldn't find anything. It was like the ocean swallowed him up." He cleared his throat then said, "My dad told me that not knowing what happened to his father was the hardest part for them."

He followed me back out to the front hall. Just as he opened the door, a blue light appeared at the top of the stairs. Toby looked up at it, his hand resting on the doorknob.

"What's that?" I held my breath, hoping Nicholas would appear. The light flickered a few times, but nothing else happened. Toby walked up the steps one at a time, his eyes never leaving the blue light. He was drawn to it like a moth to a flame. Suddenly, there was a loud bang and the door slammed shut. The light got brighter for an instant, then went out.

In the moments before the light disappeared, I'd seen Nicholas with his hand stretched out toward Toby; their fingers almost touching. The look of anguish on Nicholas's face was painful to witness.

Toby stretched out his hand toward the spot where the light had been and said again, "What was that?"

"Come on into the kitchen and I'll get you a beer. This is going to take a while." I pulled out the medicine bottle, willing either Nicholas or the blue light to appear. It was a bit of a letdown when neither occurred.

Toby reached for the bottle.

"No, don't do that. Sometimes it can give you a shock."

He grabbed the bottle anyway, as if daring something to happen. When nothing did, he laughed and set the bottle back down on the table. Then he took a long swig of beer. "You had me there for a second."

I'd tried my best, but I wasn't sure whether or not he was convinced about his grandfather being a ghost by the time he left.

I waited all evening for Nicholas to appear. Finally, just as I was at that place between sleep and wakefulness, I heard him call my name.

He sat down on the edge of the bed. I couldn't see his face but his voice was full of sorrow. "I was so close, but something held me back." The light around him grew brighter and I saw him smile. "But I saw him. Alma, I saw my grandson." The light faded and the weight on the edge of the bed lessened. His voice floated through the darkness, "Thank you."

* * *

July 1st, Canada Day, was humid and sunny by nine o'clock in the morning. Picnics, outdoor shows, and of course fireworks, were being held in every community across the country. The last thing I felt like doing was celebrating. I flipped the page in the calendar and took another sip of coffee. Carl brought it over this morning from the gourmet place in town. He also brought a box of donuts. Perfect. I drowned my sorrows with my second chocolate glazed.

Carl was taking me to the best place on the South Shore for a BBQ chicken dinner—the legion in Martha's Point. He'd offered to take an extra shift for a colleague so that he could go to the fireworks down at the harbour with his family. Carl asked me if I minded before he offered. I knew I wouldn't enjoy myself because I'd be worried about work. The collection of seascapes was almost finished, but I didn't think they were as good as the first one I'd done with Nicholas's help.

The sound of creaking floorboards woke me up. It was still dark outside.

"Nicholas?" I whispered.

The bedside lamp cast a warm glow around the bed making me feel safe. More sounds came from downstairs.

"Nicholas?" I said a little louder.

I stopped at the top of the stairs and peered over the banister for any sign of the blue light. The grandfather clock struck four, masking the sound of groaning steps as I crept downstairs.

Someone was in the sunroom.

The man stepped into the pool of moonlight. It was Lonny Naugler. His face was twisted in rage, squishing his eyes into little black slits. The window was open and a cold draft circled around my bare feet. I needed to run back upstairs and get my phone.

He saw me.

My brain focused on bits and pieces rather than the whole scene—an outstretched arm, an accusatory finger as he said, "You bitch! Your family stole this house from us. Now we're taking it back."

Lonny drew a knife from his jacket and lunged at the painting of the lighthouse. It was as if he'd been waiting for me to witness the destruction. The sound of tearing canvas set every nerve in my body on fire. His face turned from anger to glee with each slash of the knife. The disfigured painting crashed to the floor.

Suddenly, a brilliant blue light flooded the room. Nicholas towered over Lonny.

"Go ahead, old man. I'm not scared of you." Lonny snarled. He was so consumed with anger he didn't question Nicholas's appearance. He stabbed Nicholas. The blade sank into his chest, but no blood appeared. Startled, Lonny swung it in a wide arc. The blade glinted in the light. Nicholas didn't flinch. He tackled Lonny. The men fell to the floor, a tangle of arms and legs. I stepped back toward the doorway into the kitchen. Suddenly, a wave of water came out of nowhere and crashed into the two men. It sucked them under. The water churned. A glimpse of an arm. The blur of a leg. The wind pulled at my clothes. My hair whipped across my face.

As quickly as it started, the wind stopped. When I opened my eyes, the men were gone. The easel lay on the floor, one wooden leg twisted at an odd angle—my masterpiece in tatters. The rest of the collection was scattered around the room, some of them laid face down in small puddles of water.

* * *

"You're going to think I'm crazy." I rubbed my palms on my thighs. Carl began to protest, but I interrupted him. "Listen to what I have to say first, then you can decide."

He straightened his shoulders and gave me a salute. "Okay. Got it."

I said it quickly before I could change my mind. "It was a ghost."

"A ghost? Are you serious?" He laughed so hard tears streamed down his cheeks. He brushed them away with his sleeve. "Oh god, I haven't laughed like that in years."

I crossed my arms over my chest. "I knew you wouldn't believe me. Faye does, you know."

"Faye?" He smiled. "She's seen this ghost."

"No. But she's heard him."

"Him? He has a name?"

I nodded. "Nicholas Denyes. He knew your father."

He came and stood beside me, all business now. "The name doesn't sound familiar." He cleared his throat. "So, how did you meet this ghost?" The corners of his mouth twitched.

"He appeared when I found the bottle."

"Bottle? What bottle?"

"I found it washed up on the beach. The same night I found Joan. Nicholas was a lobster fisherman. Joan's father killed him."

"What? Stephen Naugler? That man was always no good. I'm not surprised he's managed to cause trouble even though he's been dead for years." His attitude became more intense at the mention of Stephen Naugler's name. "So, what's the story?"

I quickly told Carl about what happened to Nicholas and the reason he wanted revenge on the Nauglers. He listened without interruption.

When I was finished he said, "Well, I've come across some strange things in my life. Who's to say Nicholas's story isn't true. The facts add up." He rubbed his chin. "So, what happened to Lonny?" He glanced around the room. "And how do we get ahold of Nicholas?"

"That's just it. I don't know. I think they may both be gone—for good."

29 CHAPTER TWENTY-NINE

*C*arl pretended to believe my story, but I could tell by the way he dealt with the investigation that he'd dismissed the whole thing as the overstimulated imagination of a distraught woman. He didn't even bother to take fingerprints and no one from the detachment followed up.

I couldn't blame him, but it was like a big elephant in the room. *How could I be with someone who didn't believe me and couldn't be honest enough to tell me?* I buried myself in my work and Carl buried himself in his. We didn't talk about it, we just drifted apart.

For days, I expected to see Nicholas around every corner, to be waiting for me on the front porch when I got home. I couldn't stop thinking about him. I couldn't bear to throw away the easel. It was my last connection to Nicholas. I propped it up in the corner of the room. Every time I picked up my paintbrush I imagined the ocean breeze on my face, the rolling waves under my feet. Each brush stroke was a tribute to

Nicholas's memory. But in my heart, I knew none of the paintings were as good as the one he'd inspired me to paint. The one that Lonny destroyed.

* * *

It was more with a sense of relief than pride that I stood back to view my collection of seascapes on display at the winery. The photograph posted beside my work showed a sad, middle-aged women. I barely recognized myself.

I didn't feel like going home, so I drove into town and stopped at the local coffee spot. It was the kind of place where if you sat there long enough, you'd see everyone in town. I wasn't surprised to see Bev and her husband at one of the tables near the door.

She gave me a cheerful wave and motioned for me to join them. It was rude not to, though I was tempted. The ever-present line-up for coffee moved quickly and it was sooner than I'd liked when I sat down at their table.

"It's so good to see you," Bev gushed. She re-introduced me to her husband, Homer, even though he told her he remembered meeting me at the funeral home. A box of assorted donuts sat in the middle of their table. Bev noticed me looking. "It's much cheaper to get a dozen. We take the leftovers home."

"I guess the last time I saw you was at Martin's funeral."

She nodded enthusiastically. "It was a marvelous turn-out." She looked over at her husband for confirmation. "Wasn't it?"

Homer stuffed half a donut into his mouth. I think it was to avoid having to answer, or to make it obvious that his participation wasn't needed.

"We've missed you at the art meetings." She turned to her husband, who was still chewing a wad of chocolate-glazed donut. "We have such a great time. Alma is one of our star painters." I think she batted her eyelashes at me.

Flustered, I said, "Well, I wouldn't say that. We're all good. Faye's a great teacher."

Bev nodded. "Oh, I agree. I wouldn't be nearly as good if it wasn't for Faye's help." She lowered her eyes. "Although

192

Homer tells me I have an artist's eye."

I wondered what an artist's eye looked like. I said, "Yes, you're a natural."

Bev tittered. "Thank you. It's so kind of you to say." She took a sip of her coffee. "Faye's been busy, too. She seemed a little distracted last class." She lowered her voice, "I hope everything's okay?"

She looked at me as if I had some sort of secret knowledge about Faye and she was hoping I'd part with it here and now, in the coffee shop with her husband loudly chewing a second donut.

I shrugged. "As far as I know, everything's fine. I haven't had much chance to talk with her. I've been busy." I ripped the donut into even smaller pieces. "In fact, I've just come back from the winery down by the lighthouse. They've put some of my paintings on display."

Bev's hands fluttered to her heart. "Oh my goodness! That's quite a coup." I got the impression that Bev had tried to have some of her work shown there. "Is it the seascape?"

"Sort of." My donut was a pile of bite-sized pieces. I popped one into my mouth and washed it down with a mouthful of tepid coffee. Nobody said anything. We watched the line at the counter for a moment, chewing donuts and swallowing coffee. I searched for something else to say. Then it dawned on me.

"Bev?" She smiled at me waiting. "This may sound a bit strange, but Faye told me…" I ripped apart a small piece of my glazed donut and repeated, "Faye told me…"

"Yes?"

I lowered my voice. "She said you have a special gift."

"Oh?" She flushed and I realized she thought I was talking about painting.

"It's not about painting." Her smile faltered. "I mean, she says you're a great painter," I lied. Faye would never comment on Bev's talent, or lack of it. "This isn't to do with painting." I glanced over at Homer. He was polishing off a third donut. I marvelled at the capacity of his gut to withstand such abuse.

"She said it runs in your family."

She leaned forward and winked. "Oh, you mean the Gift." She giggled. "Like in that movie? I can talk to dead people."

She said it so matter of fact, like it wasn't a bizarre thing to say—never mind in the local coffee shop where everyone paid attention to everyone else's conversation. I looked around. No one was paying attention to us.

"How do you do it? I mean, do you need something from the dead person, or…"

She reached for another donut. At this rate, they wouldn't have any left to take home. "You've seen too many movies." She took a bite and chewed saying, "It's not that complicated. I just get my head in the right place and wait." She shrugged. "Sometimes it helps to be in a place where the ghost appeared, but it doesn't have to."

I stretched my legs out and leaned back, hoping that it would make me appear nonchalant about the whole thing. "Wow. That sounds interesting." I tore at the lip of my paper cup with my fingernail. "I think I might have a ghost at my place." Her eyes lit up. "Nothing scary or anything." I glanced over at Homer. He'd stopped eating and now his attention was focused on the cars in the parking lot. "I was wondering if you'd be able to come by sometime and see if you could, you know—"

She finished my sentence. "Make contact?"

I squirmed in my seat. "Yes."

"We could come by tomorrow afternoon, after Homer's doctor's appointment." Her husband tore his gaze away from the parking lot at the mention of his name. "Couldn't we?" He stared at her blankly. "Come by Alma's place tomorrow after your doctor's appointment." He nodded. "I'd come by earlier, but I have a hair appointment, and I can't guarantee how long I'll be." She leaned forward in a conspiratorial way, her hand against her lips. "My hairdresser can be a bit of a talker. She tells you everything that's going on, whether you need to hear it or not."

She stood and folded the top down on the box containing

the last four donuts. Her husband got the signal and stood, too. "Is three o'clock too late?"

"That'd be great. Thank you."

"No problem." She pushed in her chair and squeezed between the tables. "Glad to help."

Homer nodded good-bye and sauntered over to the glass door. He held it open for his wife and followed her out to the parking lot. I watched him open the car door for her, too.

I bought a box of donuts in preparation for their visit the next day.

* * *

It was a perfect afternoon for ghost hunting. Fog crept low to the ground and shrouded everything in a grey cocoon. Homer dropped Bev off right on time. I opened the door before she could ring the bell.

"Homer's welcome to stay," I said.

Bev shook her head. "It's easier for me to concentrate without any distractions. He's off to the hardware store." She smiled and handed me her jacket. "He's happy puttering around there."

"Would you like a coffee?" The donuts were already out on a platter in the centre of the kitchen table."

"No, thanks. It's better if I get right to work." She eyed the donuts. "We can relax later." She waved her finger at me. "No promises, though."

"I understand." I crossed my arms and leaned against the counter. "I've seen Nicholas in a few different rooms. I'm not sure where we should start."

"Nicholas?" She frowned. "I've heard that name before." Then it dawned on her. "So that's why you were asking about him at the funeral home."

Flustered, I pulled at the collar of my shirt as if it was choking me. "He told me his name."

Bev's eyes opened wide in astonishment. "He spoke to you?"

By her reaction I wondered if this was unusual. Perhaps I should be more vague. "A couple of times." I mumbled. "He was lost at sea."

Bev nodded sagely. She must have encountered lots of drowned fishermen. "So sad." I could have sworn her eyes filled with tears. She missed her calling. She should have been an actress, not an artist. "So many bodies aren't recovered."

"I think that's what happened to Nicholas."

"Well…" She rubbed her hands together. "Let's get started. How about you give me a tour of the house. If I get any feelings, we'll stop and see what happens."

Bev followed me upstairs. Our first stop was the guest room. Bev walked into the room and closed her eyes. I stood just outside the room, not wanting to interfere. She stood still for a few seconds. Her chest rose and fell as she breathed deeply. Bev opened her eyes slowly and turned toward me. "I don't know…" She walked over to the closet and peered inside. "Hmm…" She reached for the string attached to the bulb in the centre of the ceiling. The closet flooded with light for a moment. Then, we heard a loud pop and the closet plunged back into darkness.

"The bulb must've burst. I can go down and get another one," I said to Bev.

"No need, dear. I'm done in this room. Just remember to put a new one in before you have any guests."

I smiled tightly. "The other place I've seen him is my room, down here at the end of the hall."

Bev followed me. When we reached the door, I stepped aside and let her enter. "What a lovely room. This furniture looks expensive."

I wasn't sure how to reply. "Thank you."

She spun around on her heel, arms stretched out as if in prayer, her eyes closed. I worried that she might get dizzy. If she fell, I'd have a hard time helping her up. "Nothing here." She saw my expression and said, "You look surprised."

"Well, it's just that…" How could I explain Nicholas had often appeared in this room? "Let's go downstairs to the sunroom."

She pointed to the broken easel leaning up against the wall. "What happened?"

"I was clumsy and I tripped. Those legs stick out. They should have that bright orange tape on them." She didn't mention the bottle. My heart sank. If she didn't zero in on that, then the likelihood of success was low.

"I hope you didn't hurt yourself." Her eyes scanned the room. The old medicine bottle went unnoticed. I placed it there in hopes that it would draw her attention without my leading her to it.

"No, the easel took most of the damage."

Bev closed her eyes. She didn't appear to have heard me. She stiffened. Hands tightened into fists. Jaw clenched. Her eyes flew open. Her face white. "Oh…" She gasped. Her hands flew to her heart. "Oh my!" She wrinkled her nose as if she'd smelled something noxious. The colour drained from her face. *Maybe something would come of this after all.*

I took her elbow and guided her back into the kitchen. She sat with her hands flat on the table while I made the coffee. "Here." I held the steaming mug out to her.

She wrapped her hands around it not seeming to notice the heat. "Thank you."

We both sat quietly for a few moments, me sipping my coffee, Bev staring at hers. Finally, she raised the mug to her lips and took a careful sip. Then she took another. Soon, her cheeks filled with blotches of pink. Now it seemed safe to ask what she'd seen.

"It was something terrible. I can feel the…the evil." She squeezed her eyes shut and shivered. "That's the only word I can use to describe it. I don't always get a feeling, but when I do, it's rarely wrong." She picked up her mug and said, "This time it's a bit muddled. I get the feeling there were two men, one older than the other." She stared at the easel. "I'm surprised you haven't felt something. It's very strong." She finished the last of her coffee. "There's nothing more you can tell me?"

"Two men?"

"Well…" She reached for a donut, took a bite, and chewed for a few moments before she answered. "I can't quite figure out what happened in that room. There were two, but I only get the feeling one is there. He might be…stuck?" She shook her head. "No, that isn't the right word." She frowned. "Maybe waiting?" She said it more like a question.

I refilled our mugs. "Is he all right?"

"Hmm. I'm not sure. There was so much anger." She shook her head. "Sorry I can't be of more help."

"Don't apologize. You've helped a great deal."

"Really, I don't feel like I have." She pointed at my necklace. "That's lovely. Where did you get it?"

"A friend." I took it off and handed it to her. "Here, why don't you take it over to the window? You can see the sea glass better there."

Even in the grey afternoon light the colours glowed. She twisted and turned the beads. "Your friend is very generous. You must be very special to him." I don't know if she even realized what she'd said. She gently curled the necklace up like a snake in the palm of her hand. Then she tightened her hand around the stones. "This necklace is full of love." She smiled and held the necklace out for me to take. "Well," she said, business-like. "Homer will be here soon. I don't want to keep him waiting." She struggled into her jacket.

We talked for a few minutes about the weather until we heard a car door slam.

"Homer must be here," she said brightly.

When we got outside, Homer was coming up the steps. He waved and turned back to the car when he saw us. He had Bev's door open for her by the time she reached the car.

"Don't hesitate to call if you see any more ghosts," she yelled.

Homer waited until she was safely in the car before he shut the door.

I stood on the front porch and watched them drive away. The air was heavy with the smell of rain—not Old Spice.

* * *

The house was so quiet after Bev left. The weather had finally committed and huge drops of water dashed against the window. I curled up in the chair and watched the rivulets run down the glass, disappearing into the earth or being carried away on the wind, back up into the atmosphere, ready to start the cycle all over again.

I came to a decision. It was time for me to let go.

My tires crunched loudly on the gravel as I turned into the parking lot. There wasn't even enough of a breeze to wave a few strands of hair across my face. I carried the bag in one hand and my flashlight in the other. Carefully, I picked my way through the grass and over to the path that led down to the beach. The ocean stretched out before me and the surface of the water was so calm it looked like plastic stretched tightly over a bowl. A multitude of stars twinkled far above.

The waves barely made a whisper as they rolled onto the beach. I opened the bag and tentatively touched the neck of the bottle with the tip of my finger. I wished for a shock, even the slightest tingle to run through my body. Nicholas was gone. I knew it in my heart. He'd done what he set out to do.

"Your family is safe. Rest in peace." I said. Strands of hair softly tickled my cheek as the wind whispered in reply. Then I threw the bottle as hard as I could. The glass caught bits of moonlight as it spun through the air. I thought I saw a glimmer of blue light through my tears.

The beam from the lighthouse was reflected in my rearview mirror as I drove away. On. Off. On. Off. Nicholas had been my guide, now I was truly on my own.

30 CHAPTER THIRTY

*T*he seascapes were up in the gallery, but I couldn't afford to take a break. I scrolled through my selection of pictures, wondering what to paint next. Nothing caught my interest. I was frustrated and out of sorts. Then the sea glass necklace caught my eye and I knew exactly what my next project would be.

Each day was the same. Paint until my arms were exhausted, my fingers cramped, and my shoulder muscles in knots. Slowly Nicholas began to take shape before me—his dark eyes, curly hair, and strong jaw. I struggled to remember his eyebrows. Were they thick? Did they meet at the bridge of his nose? I stood back and stared at the painting. Something wasn't right. I made his eyebrows a millimetre or two wider apart.

The rim of his sou'wester sat low over his forehead. Deep wrinkles were carved into the corners of his tired eyes, giving him a serious, brooding look. In contrast, his mouth was ready to break into a smile. Nicholas's strength was evident in his wide shoulders and burly chest; his gentleness in the calloused hands that rested relaxed and open on his knees; and, his humility in the simple gumboots that covered his legs almost up to his knees.

The portrait was completed in a few days. I left it resting on the easel so it felt like he was still with me.

* * *

I sat in the rocking chair out on the front porch and waited for Faye to arrive. We hadn't seen each other in almost a month. We'd both aged in that short time. She slowly climbed the stairs, and I pushed myself out of the rocking chair. We hugged each other tight. It was a few minutes before either of us let go.

She stood in front of the portrait. "Are you certain he's gone?"

I ran my fingers lightly over Nicholas's face. "As sure as I can be." I felt my face grow warm. "I took your suggestion. Bev didn't exactly get in touch with Nicholas. She came here into the sunroom and…" I shrugged. "She made a pretty good guess about what happened."

Faye rested her hand lightly on my arm. "I'm sorry about Nicholas and the painting." She stood in front of the easel. "I know how important the seascape was to you, but this one of Nicholas is extraordinary. You might consider taking it to one of the galleries that I told you about. I'm certain one of them would show it."

"I don't know if I could part with it."

"Even if it meant keeping your house?" She pursed her lips. "I guess you haven't heard anything from the gallery at the winery?"

Tears that I'd held back for days broke free and streamed down my cheeks. She handed me a box of tissues and told me to sit down. Then she put the kettle on. It was a relief to talk to someone about the night Lonny Naugler destroyed my life. I never mentioned Carl's name and she didn't ask.

As she was leaving she said, "Don't give up. You're very talented. Maybe you could try doing landscapes." My dislike of the idea must have shown on my face because she quickly added, "Or maybe something else."

* * *

The boulder had a smooth edge carved at just the right height for a seat. For all I knew it was the same one where I'd found Joan. The ocean spread out before me, vast and uninhabited, all the way to the horizon. The emptiness fooled me into thinking I was the only person around for miles, but off in the distance a figure walked toward me. As they drew nearer I recognized the familiar combination of aviator sunglasses and Boston ball cap.

It was Carl. We hadn't seen each other since the night Lonny destroyed my painting.

He stopped a few feet away, his hands shoved in his pockets. Carl nodded. "Alma, it's good to see you."

"What brings you out here?" My fingers wrapped around the piece of sea glass in my pocket and squeezed.

"It's a good place to come and think." He gestured to the large boulders. "Do you mind if I join you?" He turned and gazed out at the water. "Nothing like watching the waves and letting your mind drift. It reenergizes you."

I nodded. He nudged the pebbles with the toe of his boot. The soothing sound of the waves lulled us into a relaxed, companionable silence. It was easy to forget your troubles. We sat side by side, not touching. I could tell Carl was struggling to make a decision. Seagulls had spotted us as a potential source of food. They circled and squawked around us.

Finally, he said, "It's too bad Joan got dragged into Lonny's mess. The poor kid's been through enough."

His blindness at Joan's true nature annoyed me. My temper flared and I said harshly, "She isn't exactly blameless." Carl's jaw tightened. I softened my voice. "I don't know if 'poor kid' is exactly the right term. She's an adult now. She knew what she was doing. She's responsible for her own decisions."

"You don't know what her home life was like. Her mother left when she was a baby and her father was a miserable SOB. It made my skin crawl just being around him." He kicked at the pebbles so hard they tumbled down into the ocean. The tiny pebbles were magnified by the water.

His sympathy was annoying me. "But she's grown up now, free to make her own choices, and I've seen enough to know she can't be trusted." I snapped. "Why are you so obsessed with Lonny Naugler and so protective of Joan?

"Because of my father." He strode over to the edge of the water. The waves washed over his shoes, but he didn't move. His body was rigid, his shoulders squared against the breeze. After a few minutes, his shoulders slumped and he wearily made his way back to the boulder. "I don't know why my dad was friends with him. I know times were tough, but making a deal with the devil never turns out right. The only one who wins is the devil himself."

"Tough times bring out the worst in some people…" I said.

Carl interrupted. "And the best in others." He shook his head. "Stephen Naugler didn't need tough times to bring out the worst. He was an evil man, even when times were good." His voice barely carried above the sound of the waves. "I'd been away on a training course. By the time I found out about what my father had done, it was too late. There was nothing I could do." He rubbed the back of his neck. "He'd aged a lifetime in a few months. He was haggard. He'd lost weight." He stared at me, his eyes pleading. "My father tried to make things right."

"I'm sure he did." My words sounded hollow and condescending. He didn't seem to notice. I wanted to ask exactly what had his father done, but I kept quiet and let him continue uninterrupted. Carl's words were full of hurt and anger. They sounded choppy and unrehearsed, as if it was the first time he'd ever told this story.

"I tried to get him to talk to me, but he'd always say there was nothing wrong. Finally I got him drunk enough and he broke down." He took off his cap, ran his fingers through his hair, and yanked the cap back on. "My dad was helping Stephen unload a shipment of lobster. Stephen suddenly collapsed and hit his head on a rock. There was so much blood. My father panicked. He…" The words stuck in his throat. "He…my father…he tossed the body into the water." The last few words came out in a rush, like a dam bursting.

"Does anyone else know?" I resisted the urge to reach out to him.

He hunched his shoulders. "I always got the impression that Martin knew something, but he never let on. Maybe he figured out that anything connected to Naugler would lead to trouble. Martin was never part of that crowd. He stayed his own man." His voice tightened. "He wasn't weak like my father." He sounded so sad and defeated. I reached out to him. He squeezed my hand in response then let go.

"So your father was responsible for Stephen Naugler's disappearance?"

Carl leaned so close his breath was hot on my cheek. "He didn't kill him. I'm sure of that." He was so intense that I leaned away from him. Carl stood. "Sorry."

I waved a hand in dismissal. "It's okay. What happened next?"

"I convinced my parents to get Joan in to foster care. She was running wild." He shrugged. "I don't know what they told social services but it worked." He shook his head in disgust. "Lonny was a lost cause. He'd spent too much time around his father."

He paced back and forth in front of me. "I never should've gone along with Dad's plan to keep the whole thing quiet, but it would've been the death of my mother. I couldn't do that to her."

"What happened to Lonny?"

"He went out west for a while. When he came back, I heard some rumours about what he was up to, but the RCMP never had any evidence. I tried talking to Joan, but Lonny fed her a bunch of lies about not trusting us and how their lives had been stolen from them."

"What does that mean?"

"I wasn't sure until all that happened with your house." His jaw tightened. "Once, I heard Stephen Naugler talk about the house he lived in when he was a child, but it didn't sound like your place. His version made it sound like the Taj Mahal. He was a kid when his family moved. I guess to a child the house looked bigger than it actually was."

"So the RCMP has never been able to prove Stephen or Lonny's role in the lobster thefts?"

"Over the years, the fishermen took care of the smaller robberies themselves."

I smiled. "I heard them referred to as cowboys on the water."

He shook his head. "These bigger jobs are something new. Most likely, it has to do with the price of lobsters. From the start, I had my suspicions that Lonny had something to do with them. I saw footprints the day we were up at the clearing. I waited around for a few days, but no one showed up." He smiled. "But we got them eventually—except Lonny."

"And your place catching fire wasn't a coincidence."

We walked side by side back toward the path, our steps in time with each other, our arms close but not touching.

"Why was Martin on the island? I know his death wasn't suspicious…"

Carl snorted. "I still think Lonny had something to do with it. Nobody knew the water better'n Martin. He could guide a boat into the Devil's Hole in the worst of storms." He shook his head. "Back in Stephen Naugler's time he'd get the lobsters over to Dad's place. My father never told me, but that's my guess." He shrugged. "I don't think he was ever party to the actual thefts. Martin wouldn't do that, but a little extra cash always came in handy." He shrugged. "Times were tough." He cleared his throat. "He might've been doing the same thing for Lonny and that's why his boat was tied up around the other side of the island."

He took off his sunglasses and turned to me. "Alma, I'm

sorry about the painting, really I am. I know how much it meant to you. It's just hard to believe that a ghost would be responsible for catching Lonny."

I nodded. "I know. I guess I just wanted you to be honest with me. I didn't need you to believe in ghosts. And I'm sorry, too. I didn't realize how important Lonny Naugler's arrest was to you."

* * *

Before I'd finished my breakfast the doorbell rang. Toby Eisner's face stared back at me through the window in the front door. He nodded in greeting, the aviator sunglasses firmly planted in place. He didn't take them off when he stepped inside.

"Morning. I have some news. Lonny's body was found washed up on the shore below the lighthouse." He saw my look of surprise. "I thought you'd like to know."

Had Carl told him what happened?

"Where did you say the body was found?"

"At the lighthouse." He frowned. "You look a little pale. Do you need to sit?" He led me into the kitchen and poured a glass of water.

"We know Lonny wasn't working alone." He handed me the glass. "Maybe some of the others will wash up farther down the beach. It's hard to tell what the currents will do."

"He drowned?"

Toby nodded. "That's the official cause of death."

"You sound like you don't believe it." My hand trembled and a few drops of water splashed onto the table.

"We were closing in on him and he knew it."

"Where's Carl?" I asked.

"He's taking some holidays." His response was abrupt. Toby leaned against the counter and folded his arms. "Are you sure you're all right?"

"I'm fine," I said.

He wandered over to the doorway between the kitchen and

the sunroom saying, "What are you working on?" He caught sight of the portrait. He stared at it for several seconds. Then he said, "Would you be interested in selling it?"

"No, not right now." I turned and walked back into the kitchen.

He didn't try to persuade me. He put on his sunglasses before he'd reached the front door. Instead of taking the steps two at a time as usual, he walked over to the rocking chair and pushed the arm. He watched the chair rock back and forth for a moment, then he slowly walked down the steps to his car. He paused, his hand on the door handle, and glanced up at the front bedroom. I thought he was going to say something, but instead he climbed into his car and carefully backed out of the driveway.

31 CHAPTER THIRTY-ONE

*F*or the last week, every time the phone rang my heart leapt in anticipation, hoping it was the gallery to tell me one of my paintings had sold. It didn't happen. Mr. Morris was dropping by to get the paperwork in order.

When the doorbell rang, I was surprised to see someone else standing on the front porch. I opened the door a few inches, just enough to be polite.

"Yes?"

The man was about my age. His khaki pants were neatly pressed. The navy polo horse stood out on the breast of his crisp beige shirt. His hair was grey at the temples. His tanned skin crinkled around his eyes when he smiled. He held out his hand. His grip was firm, confident.

"Good morning. Sorry to bother you. I'm Alan Boutilier, from Boutilier's Gallery. Perhaps you've heard of us? I hope you don't mind, but a friend asked me to come by and see a painting of yours? A portrait?" He politely cleared his throat.

"May I come in? It'll only take a moment." He paused for a

moment then smiled. "If you prefer, you could come by the gallery." He reached into his breast pocket and held out a business card.

I automatically took it. The heavy cream-coloured cardstock felt expensive, the black calligraphy lettering indicated this was indeed *Alan Boutilier Jr.—Owner.* I opened the door wider.

"No, it's fine. Come in."

I led the way into the sunroom. The portrait of Nicholas was still on the easel. I couldn't bear to remove it. He stood back and turned his head to one side then the other. He didn't say a word for a few moments.

"Do you have any other paintings?"

My heart dropped. He didn't like it. "I'm working on a landscape at the moment. I sold a painting of this house at the café on the old highway earlier this summer."

He raised his eyebrows. "Beatrice's place?" He sounded impressed.

I pulled the landscape from the pile of canvases leaning against the side of the sofa. "It isn't finished yet."

He reached for the painting. "Yes, I can see that." He nodded toward the portrait of Nicholas. "Would you be interested in having that one for sale in our gallery? No guarantees, mind you."

I was loath to let it go, but then I thought about Mr. Morris's upcoming visit. "You know what? Please, take it before I change my mind."

Once it was safely wrapped and stored in his trunk, I let the tears fall. It was done. In a way, Nicholas was truly gone now. I'd done everything I could to get the house. Now it was up to fate.

When Mr. Boutilier told me the picture would be hung in the gallery by the end of the week I panicked. "Could you hang it sooner?" I wrung my hands. "I'm in a bit of a time crunch."

He must be used to starving artists because he smiled and said, "Sure. I think that can be arranged."

When Mr. Morris arrived a short time later, I told him about the potential sale. I hoped it would buy me a little more time.

"Well, just before I left the office Ms. Stokes informed me that the buyer she had lined up had backed out for financial reasons."

I couldn't believe my luck. "That's wonderful news." My spirits lifted. Could it mean that because of Lonny's death Joan no longer had the money to buy the house? I hoped so.

He frowned and my moment of happiness shriveled up inside me. "Still, I want to proceed with the paperwork to be prepared for the end of the month when the estate will be inherited by its heirs according to your grandmother's will." He closed up his briefcase. "However, you still have until the end of the month." He shook my hand. "Best of luck to you, my dear."

* * *

The area around the lighthouse felt so different than a few weeks ago. Clouds decorated the blue sky with a white swirl. Sunshine warmed me as I descended the cliff to the beach. The lighthouse was the only thing that broke the long stretch of horizon. Waves sloshed back and forth against the large boulders piled at the foot of the cliff. Bits of twisted seaweed clung to larger stones and made a line along the beach—dry sand on one side, wet sand on the other. Water-logged wood was woven haphazardly amongst the seaweed barrier. The blue sky and sunshine filled me with optimism. Maybe luck would finally be on my side.

* * *

For those of us not party to the local gossip chain, we heard about Lonny's funeral arrangements on the local radio station. Margie, my favourite cashier, did share the rumour that there was seaweed found in his hair—which made sense since the official cause of death was drowning. No one seemed to know what happened—at least not officially. A few disgruntled mourners complained the RCMP hadn't done much of an investigation. They were in the minority.

I remember what Nicholas had told me. "If the sea wants you, she'll have you." I guess she wanted Lonny Naugler, Nicholas, and Nicholas's youngest son, among others.

Joan sat in the front pew. Her head was held high and even though there were other people with her in the pew, there was a distance between them, which made it appear like she was alone. I felt some sympathy toward her, but there was also a perverse sense of satisfaction knowing that neither of us might own the house.

Faye and Carl sat a few rows behind Joan. I hadn't talked to Carl since we'd met on the beach. The talk had helped clear the air but we still weren't back to the way things had been before.

The eulogies made Lonny sound like a god-fearing man who died in the prime of his life. I wondered how often eulogies told the truth. There were several dry eyes in the crowd. I guess people weren't that sorry Lonny was gone.

"Are you going to the hall for sandwiches?" asked Carl.

"I don't think so. I didn't know Lonny. His connection to Nicholas is why I came." I shrugged. "I guess I wanted some sort of closure."

"I need to go to the church hall," said Carl. "Everyone knows about my father's relationship with Stephen Naugler. If I don't go, they'll resurrect the tales about the family feud."

Faye chuckled. "Whether you go or not, they'll gossip about you. It can't be helped. The joys of living in a small town."

Neither of them acknowledged this was the end of the month or brought up the sale of the house, and I didn't tell them about the portrait at Boutilier's Gallery. I didn't want to jinx the sale, even though I was pretty sure Faye was the one who'd told Alan Boutilier about the portrait.

I watched Faye and Carl cross the parking lot to the church hall. The men who stood outside smoking, nodded to them as they approached. Most of the attendees were staying for the food so it didn't take long for me to get out of the parking lot, unlike many masses that I'd attended in my youth. When I switched my phone on, I noticed I'd missed a call.

* * *

I yanked open the door to the gallery with so much force it swung back and hit the wall. The receptionist glared at me as I entered.

"Sorry," I mouthed. I was in such a panic I couldn't focus on any one piece of art. I counted to ten and methodically walked along the perimeter of the room, scouring the walls for my painting. It wasn't there. I went around a second time. I asked the receptionist if they had a second floor. She shook her head. Finally, I gave up. My heels echoed on the stone floor as I crossed the reception area. I gave the receptionist my name and asked where my painting was hung.

She consulted her binder and frowned. "I don't have any record of a painting by that artist." She saw my distress and said, "Just a minute. Let me check with Mr. Boutilier."

A few minutes later, an elderly gentleman entered the reception area. He slowly walked across the room toward me. His cane tapped like a third leg with each step. Beads of sweat rolled down my sides. My breath came in short gasps. This wasn't the man who took my painting. What had I done?

"Hello, young lady. I'm Mr. Boutilier, the owner." He steadied himself and held out his hand. "I understand you're looking for a particular piece." He directed his comment to the receptionist. "Who was the artist, Genevieve?"

She repeated my name. It sounded strange on her tongue. "Alma Sinclair, sir."

"Well…" He stretched out the word for an imaginably long time. It sounded more like a sigh than a word. "I'm sorry, I'm not familiar with that artist. What was the painting of?"

"It was a portrait of a fisherman." I answered trying to keep the panic from my voice.

"A portrait you say?" He chuckled. "Not our sort of thing. He gave a small wave of his arm, gesturing to the artwork around him. "As you can see, most of our collections are seascapes." He raised one hand to his mouth and gave a small cough, then quickly placed both hands securely on the handle of his cane. "Lighthouses are particularly popular. Our clients are mostly tourists rather than local residents."

I heard the door open just as he finished speaking. Someone walked up behind me. I turned around. It was the man who'd taken my painting. "Mr. Boutilier, where is my painting?" I demanded.

"Ah, Ms. Sinclair. It's good to see you again." He either chose to ignore my distress or was oblivious to it. He reached out to shake my hand as if nothing unusual had happened.

The elderly gentleman smiled. "Alan, do you know this young lady?"

"Yes, Father. We just sold one of her paintings. We only had it up for one afternoon before it was sold."

"Pardon me?" I squeaked.

"Really." Mr. Boutilier Sr. beamed. "Well, young lady, that must be a record." He shook his head. "Sold in an afternoon. Not many of our artists can say that." He leaned forward precariously on his cane and extended his hand. "Congratulations. I hope you've brought more of your work for us to sell."

Alan Boutilier nodded. "When I didn't hear back from you, I was about to send the paperwork to you by registered mail." He lowered his voice. "You expressed some urgency about the sale. I wasn't sure how you wanted to be paid. I didn't get any banking information from you when we met." He looked embarrassed. "Actually, I wasn't sure we'd have much luck selling it." He gestured to the artwork lining the walls. "As you can see, it was a little different from our usual pieces."

Genevieve had watched the interaction without comment. Alan Boutilier turned to her and explained. "Yesterday was your day off. The portrait was sold before you even saw it." He turned to me. "A marvelous piece."

"Who bought it?" I asked.

Alan Boutilier looked embarrassed. "I'm not at liberty to say. The buyer wished to remain anonymous."

"Could you at least tell me if it was someone from away?" I asked. The thought of Nicholas hanging in some strange home far from the sea upset me.

"I'm sorry, Alma." He turned and held out his hand in the direction of the door through which he'd entered the reception area. "If you'd like to come into my office, we can finish up the paperwork."

Before we exited the reception area he asked, "Would you like a tea or coffee?"

Genevieve disappeared to get me a glass of water while Alan Boutilier led me through the reception area to his office. The room was furnished with a sleek, teak desk, tubular metal chairs, and track lighting. The lights were hardly needed, as two walls were floor-to-ceiling windows. Sunlight flooded the room. Works of modern art decorated the remaining walls. I sat down in the chair he indicated, opposite his desk. It was surprisingly comfortable. The phone rang and he got up to answer it. I wandered over to the window to give him some privacy.

He disconnected and called out to me. "My apologies. They've been trying to reach me. I was in another part of the building and the cell reception is terrible. He sat down beside me, rather than behind his desk. He crossed his leg and folded his hands in his lap. "Your water will be along in a moment." He smiled. He indicated the surroundings. "So, not what you expected?"

"Was I that obvious?"

He laughed. "I'm used to it. Most people expect something more traditional." He shrugged. "I enjoy the Scandinavian countries and this is my way of bringing some of it back here." He smiled. "Congratulations on the sale of your painting." I couldn't find the words to reply. I was still in shock. He laughed. "Artists give us their work to sell and when we do, they're surprised. But, I must confess, your portrait wasn't a piece I thought we'd sell so quickly." He smiled, "It goes to show that just because we're a gallery on the East Coast, it doesn't mean every piece of artwork has to be a lighthouse or a sailboat…"

"Or a stormy ocean." I laughed.

"Exactly."

Genevieve quietly entered the room and set a glass on the small table beside me. She left without making a sound.

Alan uncrossed his legs and leaned forward. "Would you like a cheque or would you like us to deposit the money directly into your account?"

I debated my options. "A cheque, please." If I could get it over to the lawyer's office in time, the sale of my home might be averted. I crossed my fingers and prayed.

Cheque in hand, I practically ran out of the gallery. When I got to my car I took out my phone to call the lawyer. I noticed I'd missed a couple of calls. The number was Mr. Morris's office.

When I called back the automated message told me the office was closed for the day. I left a message. Actually, I left three. Mr. Morris called back the next morning.

"I had until midnight," I practically shouted into the phone.

"Ms. Sinclair. As I said, my duty is to *all* the heirs." He sniffed. "You know how long it can take to sell property here. I would be remiss if I didn't take that into consideration. We were very fortunate to have a second interested buyer with a solid offer. I tried to reach you, but you were unavailable." I was so angry I couldn't speak. "The buyers have paid the deposit and it is my understanding the sale of their current home is now closed. If this sale doesn't go through they will be without a place to live. You are welcome to fight this, but it would be long and costly. Is that something you are prepared to do?"

I thought about my mother and brother. Was it worth ripping the family apart? Was it worth forcing a family to find another home? Is it worth the time and expense of a legal battle? "No." I said dejectedly.

"You had two years in which to fulfill your grandmother's stipulations. Leaving it until a couple of hours before the deadline isn't fair to the other people involved." He sighed.

"Ms. Sinclair. I'm truly sorry. I wish it had worked out differently for you." He sounded sincere.

The house wasn't mine. It now belonged to strangers.

* * *

If it was too late to save my house, then selling the portrait of Nicholas was a useless sacrifice. I knew Boutilier wouldn't tell me who'd bought it, they'd made that clear. If it was a random tourist, then I was out of luck, but something told me that tourists weren't Boutiliers' regular customers. *Would Faye have bought it?* I immediately discounted the idea. She told them about the painting, I was certain of that, but I didn't think she'd buy it. *Why would she have waited until now? Who else could it be?*

I wasn't sure how Toby would've known the portrait was at the gallery, but it was worth giving him a call. Faye didn't know his connection to Nicholas, so she wouldn't have told him. Maybe Alan Boutilier did. I tried to remember if I'd told Alan that it was a portrait of a drowned fisherman named Nicholas Denyes. It was likely that Alan and Toby knew each other. This was a small place and everyone knew everyone else. They were close in age and could have gone to school together; or their paths may have crossed through work, community events, or maybe both.

"What's up?" He sounded curious.

"You know the portrait of your grandfather? The one you saw when you came to tell me about Lonny."

"What about it?" I could hear traffic in the background. He must be at work.

"Did you buy it?"

"I thought it wasn't for sale." His voice was curt.

"Did you tell Alan Boutilier about it?"

"Who?" I heard a car door slam and the traffic noise decreased.

I sighed. Clearly, he wasn't the one who'd purchased the painting. "I guess I've got my wires crossed." Then another thought occurred to me. "Did you mention the portrait to your aunt?"

"Nope." His answer sucked all the air out of the room. I knew it had been a long shot, but I'd dared to hope.

"Okay. Thanks anyway."

I was about to hang up when he said, "Wait. Does this mean you've changed your mind about selling the portrait?"

I didn't want to have to explain, so I pretended I didn't hear his question. "You must have to get back to work. Sorry I bothered you."

"No problem." I could hear the disappointment in his voice. "Take care."

Nicholas was gone. The house was gone. I'd risked everything and lost. I hung my head in shame. "I'm sorry, Grandma," I whispered. "I let you down."

I dragged myself out onto the porch and collapsed into the rocking chair. As soon as my bottom hit the seat a flood of tears streamed down my face. I let them slide down my cheeks, crawl down my neck and pool in the collar of my shirt. The morning turned into afternoon, the afternoon turned into dusk, and still I sat, sometimes rocking back and forth and sometimes so still I could barely feel my chest rise. It was time to go back to the city, but right now, I didn't even have enough energy to get out of the chair.

The mosquitos pestered me enough that I finally went inside and made the phone call I'd been dreading.

"Hello, Mom? I heard from Mr. Morris that Grandma's house is sold." This is the first time I'd said it out loud. My throat tightened.

"I'm so sorry. You must be so disappointed. Alma, you may not believe this, but I had hoped it would turn out differently. You wanted it so badly." She sounded genuinely concerned.

I thought I had no more tears left to cry, but I was wrong. After I hung up, I cried myself to sleep.

* * *

It was the August long weekend and the highway had more cars on it than the whole of February. Seeing the parking lot at the lighthouse full of cars was annoying. There are so few people most of the year, you get used to the idea of having the whole place to yourself. I'd brought my easel and painting gear, but the idea of strangers watching me work was unsettling. I hoped all the tourists were at the lighthouse and the beach wasn't too crowded. I walked over to the edge of the cliff to check it out. Small children, dogs, and teenagers were spread out along the shore like a field full of dandelions. I gave up on the idea of painting and stomped back to the car.

Faye wasn't expecting me for a couple of hours but I hoped she wouldn't mind if I showed up a little early. The sold sign had only been up a few hours before I called asking if I could come over. Plus, I wanted to tell her about what happened with Nicholas's portrait. I was certain she'd had a hand in getting Boutilier to come to the house.

She was weeding the garden at the side of her house. A neat row of begonias poked their pink heads up from freshly turned soil. Beside her was a large turquoise plastic tub, piled with weeds. She turned at the sound of my car. When she realized it was me, she smiled and waved.

"Alma, it's good to see you." She walked toward the car.

"I'm sorry I'm a little early, but the beach was a zoo. I should've known better. Can I help you with the garden?"

"No, you've given me a good excuse to quit for today. Can I interest you in a glass of lemonade on the back patio?"

Faye's garden was a magical place. Nestled in the centre among the vines, shrubs, and hanging baskets was a wrought iron table and chairs. The colourful cushions competed with the flowers. A small pond with a waterfall was off to one side. The soothing sound of the water drowned out any traffic noise. A bird feeder hung from a nearby branch. Across the pond, a hummingbird feeder hung from the roof of the garden shed.

Faye returned with a pitcher and plastic glasses. She filled a glass to the brim and handed it to me. We sat for a few moments, watching the birds and sipping lemonade.

"I'm not sure if you've seen the sold sign yet." I sighed. "It turns out that Erin Stokes had an offer ready and sitting on the lawyer's desk a couple of days before the end of the month. I guess she had a back-up plan when things fell through with the Nauglers."

Faye raised her eyebrows. "That's a bit much, isn't it?" I set down the glass and wiped beads of condensation off the side. The disappointment at losing the house was still fresh. "You know, the worst part is, I sold Nicholas's portrait to a gallery in Lunenburg that afternoon." I blinked back the tears. "But I was too late." I swirled the lemonade around. "Thanks for trying to help."

Faye acted surprised. "What do you mean?"

She was a good actress. She made me wonder if I'd guessed wrong. "When Mr. Boutilier came to my place he mentioned a woman had told him to come and see Nicholas's portrait."

She reached out and took my hand. "I'm sorry it didn't work out. I hope you don't mind that I interfered. I know you said that you didn't want to sell the portrait, but I didn't want to see you lose the house." She patted my hand. "You're a very good artist, you know. Alan wouldn't have taken your painting if he didn't think it was good enough."

She took a sip of her lemonade and carefully set her glass down on a folded napkin. "Alan must be getting on. He must be almost eighty." She paused then said, "And he came to your place?" She sounded surprised.

"No, his son."

"So they sold your painting?"

"Uh huh." I studied my toenails. They were still polish free this late in the summer. I cleared my throat.

"So, do you know of some good, out of the way places to paint? Ones that aren't overrun by tourists?"

Faye laughed as she refilled my glass. "Remember, they're our bread and butter around here."

I sighed. "I know. I was at the lighthouse before coming

here. You get so spoiled having the place to yourself."

"The painting group is over for the summer, but why don't you and I get together? I'll think of a place and let you know when we can meet."

When it was time to go, Faye walked with me out to my car. "When do you need to be out of…" She paused. "The place you are now?"

32 Chapter Thirty-Two

*Th*e new people took possession of the house at the end of September so I was determined to make the most of my remaining time in Nova Scotia. I was on the beach taking photographs when I heard a dog barking at the top of the cliff. Moments later, a figure appeared. Blond hair whipped around her face. A bright red knapsack clung to her back like a hump. She managed the path down to the beach in a few easy strides. At one point she bent to navigate a particularly tricky section. The rhinestones on her back pants pockets glistened in the sun.

I froze.

The two navigated the path down to the beach. The dog raced back and forth, covering enough distance to climb the path up and back twice before its owner safely made it to the beach.

The dog raced up to me and stopped a few feet away. It appeared to be a mix of at least three different breeds. It was the size of a German Shepherd, with black and white colouring like a Border collie, and hair like a poodle. The combination resulted in one of the oddest-looking dogs I'd ever seen. It barked a few times then ran back to its owner.

I put the lens cover on and stowed the camera in its case while she approached.

"Hey," said Joan as she came up to me.

"Hey back at you," I said cautiously. The dog danced around between us.

Joan smiled. "This is Xena." She bent down and petted the dog. "Good girl." The dog wagged her tail and gazed up at Joan. There was a connection between them that almost made me jealous.

"I didn't know you had a dog."

"Yeah, like, some idiot kept her tied to a post for two years." She grinned. "They think she's run off." She pulled a treat from her pocket and the dog obediently sat down.

The waves crashed on the beach behind us. We stood unmoving, like two figures in a tableau.

I broke the tension. "How are you?"

"Good." She hooked her thumbs under the straps of her knapsack. Joan gazed out at the water, her voice barely audible above the waves. "That house stuff." She shrugged. "Lonny always talked about that place, your place." She laughed. "He couldn't believe, like, how you found me. He said it was some kind of sign." She snorted. "He kept saying this was the chance to get our house back. He was obsessed. I'm surprised you didn't see him peering in your windows or something." *That explained the footprints under the window and in the garden.* Joan picked up a stick and threw it into the water. The dog happily raced after it. "When I told him the deal about the painting we figured it'd be easy." The dog shook itself off, spraying us with water. "No one thought you'd, like, be able to sell a painting." She had the grace to look a little uncomfortable.

My shoulders tensed. "Yeah, lots of people thought that." I picked up a stone and threw it in the water. "Except my grandma. So why were you looking for me?"

"My brother..." She shook her head. "My brother and dad

fed me so many lies. It was stupid to believe them." She brushed the hair back from her face. "I knew, it wouldn't work. The house—your house—was gone years ago." She stared down at her feet. "My grandfather died, and my grandmother, she, like, she couldn't pay the taxes, so she and my dad moved back to Cape Island to stay with family." She stared out at the waves. Her voice softened. "My dad always talked about the place where he lived. When he was, like, a kid? In Pleasant Cove?" She laughed. "He called it a mansion." She grinned. "I pictured a much bigger place, like…"

"Like Tara in *Gone With the Wind*?" I suggested.

She gave me a blank look.

"Forget it," I said.

Joan shrugged. "Anyways, I guess, like, little kids remember things much bigger than they really are." She shrugged. "Maybe that's why things are, like, such a let-down when you get older. You know?" She held out her hand to me. "No hard feelings?" *Was she here to apologize?*

Her grip was strong and confident. "It's okay," I said. "I'm sorry about Lonny."

Joan hung her head and kicked at the wet sand with the toe of her shoe, making a horseshoe-shaped indent. "I'm tired of, like, living my life the way other people think I should." It sounded as if she was repeating something someone else had told her. "I shouldn't have listened to him. I shoulda done my own thing." Joan picked up another stone and threw it, harder this time. "Now he's gone and I'm free to do what I want."

"Family can really mess you up sometimes, can't it?" The dog watched with interest as I picked up a stone and tried to make it skip across the waves. It sank near the shore with a loud plop.

Joan said, "Lonny took too many chances." She shook her head in disgust. "There wasn't enough places to keep, like, that many lobsters. A few people owed Lonny favours. He stored most of the haul with friends, waiting for the prices to go up?" She snorted. "He ran out of places, that's why he was on the island. He knew Carl never went there until, like, later. No one else'd come by, neither." Joan's voice grew hard. "I think Martin... Well...he told Carl."

"Carl knew Lonny was at his house?" I said, surprised.

Joan looked at me as if I'd said something stupid. "No, Martin wouldn't have said that. He'd, like, never say Lonny's name." She shielded her eyes from the sun with her hand. "He probably told Carl to just, like, check his property. Maybe he said he saw something." She grinned. "You know, something suspicious." She dragged out the word suspicious like it was a toffee and she was trying to make it last. "Carl's a good guy." Joan stuffed a piece of gum in her mouth and asked, "So, you guys still together?" I shouldn't have been surprised that she knew about us, but I was. "He's the one who got me into, like, foster care? When I was a teenager. Faye said she was too old and besides, she was afraid of my dad. Faye got the Boutiliers to take me."

"Faye?" Faye's role in Joan's care was news to me. She'd never let on she'd tried to help Joan. I wondered if Martin had something to do with it.

"I guess Theresa showed her some of my sketches. She thought I had 'talent'." Her fingers made air quotations when she said talent. "She figured the Boutiliers would be good for me."

"Joan, can I ask you a question?"

She nodded, a wary expression on her face. I took out my phone and showed her the picture I'd taken of Martin the day Carl and I went up to the house. I zoomed in and showed her the bear.

"How did your old bear end up on Martin's boat?"

She grinned and pulled the knapsack off her back. The neck of her shirt opened, revealing the whole tattoo. *Lust Confuses Love* stretched from one collarbone to the other as she bent down to undo the string. I caught sight of some ragged, brown fur peeking out of the open knapsack.

Even though the white stitches were grimy with age, they caught the sunlight as she pulled the stuffed animal out of the bag. "You mean this guy?" she said proudly. She held the teddy bear out toward me. "Alma, meet Freddy." She said it like a formal introduction. Then Joan cradled Freddy in one arm and ran her fingertips lightly over the stitches. She looked at me and her face clouded. "It was so long ago. I thought I'd lost him forever." She rubbed a worn patch of fur on his ear between her thumb and forefinger. *She must've done that a thousand times when she was a kid.* "Faye gave him back to me." Her eyes glistened with tears. "I never knew Martin kept my bear safe all these years. Faye told me he like, called it his lucky charm." I doubted Faye told her the part about the bear being Martin's reminder to help others.

"I remember you told me the story about Lonny cutting his stomach open. When I saw it in the picture, I guessed it might be yours. It was a bit of a stretch but…"

Joan smiled. "I wondered how she knew it was mine. I figured Martin must've like, told her. I used to bring Freddy with me everywhere when I was a kid. When I got older, sometimes he'd be the only thing… like, when I was upset…" She shrugged. "I wondered what'd happened to him."

"How did Martin get hold of him?"

She shrugged. "Don't know. Sometimes Martin went fishing with my dad. I remember one night my dad was in one of his drunken fits. He like, dragged me and Lonny out of bed to go fishing."

"That must've been scary."

"We were used to it. 'Cept this time Martin got my dad to let me stay home."

"Martin stopped him?"

Joan nodded. "Yup. But dad grabbed Freddy on his way out. He knew just how to get me. Dad was always mean but he was real nasty when he was drunk. Said he was gonna like, toss Freddy into the water and watch him sink." She lowered her voice and imitated the sound of her father's voice. "If you're old enough to stay home you don't need a damn baby toy anymore." She gazed down at Freddy. "I went to the foster home like, after that." She wrapped her arms around the bear so tightly, his tummy squished in like the middle of an hourglass. "I guess Martin must've saved him somehow."

I said, "Faye and Martin were good friends. She knew he would have wanted you to have it."

"They were, like, together?" She grinned. "I kinda figured as much."

"Not too many people knew about it. He was quite a bit older than her."

Joan got defensive. "So? Like, what does that have to do with it?"

Her comment flustered me. "I don't know. It's just that he was pretty old when they met. It was sort of like robbing the cradle."

"My dad was fifty-seven and my mom was eighteen when they met." She glared at me. Her hands clenched. "Now that's robbing the cradle." She pulled back the collar of her shirt to expose her tattoo. "This is to remind me, so I won't end up like my dad," she said fiercely.

Her intensity made me uncomfortable so I moved the conversation in a different direction. "What are you going to do now?" I said as I watched her close up the knapsack.

"I'm going to look for my mom." She bit her lower lip. "Theresa's been, like, a big help."

"Theresa?"

Joan nodded. "My mom was one of Theresa's students." She grinned. "A long time ago." She shrugged. "They kept in touch for a while after my mom left town." She laughed. "Who would've guessed, a teacher was, like, her only friend?"

I smiled, thinking of Nicholas. "Help sometimes comes from the strangest places."

"Theresa said it was my mom's way of staying close to us." Joan kicked at the sand some more. The wet sand sprayed onto the dry white sand, leaving pockmarks. Her voice tightened. "Then my mom stopped writing." She pushed at the sand with her toe, making the horseshoe deeper. "Theresa gave me the last address she had for my mom, from ten years ago." Joan picked up her knapsack and slid her arms through the straps. "Anyway, I've, like, got a place to start. I'll wait tables or whatever and I'll be doing what I want, not what somebody else thinks I should do."

"Good luck, Joan." I thought about the teddy bear stuffed in her backpack. "If there's anything I can do to help, let me know." I wasn't sure what help I could give, but it felt like the right thing to say.

She picked up an unremarkable stone and turned it over to reveal an intricate pattern of crystals. She smiled and handed me the stone. "Thanks for the memories, kid." She didn't bother trying to say it with a Bogie accent.

Her childhood must've been a real patchwork of experiences that included Humphrey Bogart but not Clark Gable. I rubbed the stone's surface, smooth on one side and rough on the other, as I watched her and Xena walk away. The dog raced ahead but every few seconds she'd turn around to make sure Joan was still right behind her.

* * *

When I got home from the beach, I walked around to the backyard. The first star of the evening twinkled high above me. At the same time, red and orange ribbons stretched across the horizon. The air was filled with the sweet fragrance of roses. I breathed in their fragrance. I loved this place so much. I was going to miss it more than I'd ever imagined. I didn't regret my decision to risk everything to come out here on a whim. No, I thought. Not a whim. To live my dream.

I thought about Nicholas. He'd risked his life to do what he loved. It had cost him the chance to see his children grow up and to grow old with the woman he loved. I thought about what I'd lost. A house. That's what I'd lost—a roof, windows, a garden. It suddenly dawned on me that my loss was nothing compared to the sacrifice Nicholas had made. My spirits lifted.

"Thank you, Nicholas," I yelled up at the first star of the evening. Then I cupped a rose in my hand, its soft petals caressed my palm. "Thank you, Grandma," I whispered.

My dream could still come true.

* * *

My hand shook as I dialed. I thought about my conversation with Joan on the beach and my hand became steadier. I didn't waste time with pleasantries. I launched right into what I wanted to say.

"Mom, I've decided that I'm staying here. I mean, not in this house. In Nova Scotia. I'm not moving back to the city. This is what I've always wanted to do."

She started off calm but as she continued to speak her voice became terse. "You tried. Nobody can say you didn't, but you need to think of your future. The best thing for you to do is to come back home." I imagined her face getting redder, her mouth tightening. "Where will you live?"

"There are plenty of other places to live out here," I reasoned. My free hand waved around like I was being attacked by a swarm of mosquitoes. Joan's words ran through my head, and I said, "All my life I've done what everyone else thought I should do, but not anymore. I should have stood up for myself years ago." I resisted the urge to stomp my foot. "It is time I lived my life, not the life others expect me to live."

Now my mother sounded like she was speaking to a small child. "I know this is your life, and you've done very well. You're an excellent accountant." I almost expected her to say, *"Why don't you fix yourself a nice cup of hot chocolate. And we can talk about it again in the morning."*

"Yes, being an accountant was fine. I'm not saying that."

My mother sounded exasperated. "Then I don't understand. Why can't you paint in your spare time? You could travel. Maybe you could take painting classes in Greece, or somewhere." She sounded proud of her idea, as if no one else had ever thought of taking art classes in foreign countries.

"Because I want to live here, not Greece." I sighed. "Life is about taking risks. I need to do this. I'm using my inheritance money to help buy a small house here." I suppressed the yell building deep inside me. "And I'm going to spend my time painting. I've sold two paintings. *Two!* I don't care if I sell my paintings at galleries or cafés or on the side of the road." Okay, the side of the road was a little extreme, but I was trying to make a point. The urge to scream grew. My chest threatened to explode if I held it in much longer. "I don't care if I sell a damn thing. You keep saying you want what's best for me. Well, this is what's best."

"If you say so, dear," she said condescendingly.

I wanted to throw the phone across the room. Instead, I gripped it tighter. "Mom, I'm a good artist. I know I am. I don't need to sell something at an art gallery to tell me that." I took a breath. "And I don't need to hear it from strangers, or family…or…anyone." After I ended the call I sat down for a few moments. Was I scared? Yes. Was I pumped? Yes. Was I happy? Yes!

I dug the bottle of champagne out of the back of the fridge that I'd been saving for a special occasion. It was the best champagne I'd ever tasted.

* * *

Beatrice's café was busy, but Faye and I managed to find a table by the window. The place wasn't air conditioned so this was a real stroke of luck. We commented on the different paintings as we waited for the waitress to take our order. A different woman than the one I'd met earlier in the season came over to serve us. Beatrice didn't seem to be around.

"So, what's the special occasion?" asked Faye. Her hair was held back with a bright red scarf, and earrings with little beads clanked every time she moved her head. It was nice to see her back to normal. She hadn't been the same since Martin's death.

I slapped my hands on the tabletop in a drum roll. "I'm going to live here and be an artist. So I'm in the market for a house. Do you know of any places on the water?"

She frowned. "Those are harder to come by, and more expensive. Let me ask around."

"I have my share of the sale of the house and I have the

money from selling my condo. I used some of it to live on these past couple of years, but I was pretty careful." I grinned. "Sticking to a budget is something I'm very good at."

She nodded. "That's good. Lots of places come up for sale at the end of the season, especially ones on the water. The owners get one last summer in before they're ready to sell."

"Well, I'll tell you one person I won't be dealing with, Erin Stokes." Just saying her name made me angry. "I'm sure she had a buyer all lined up that day she came to measure the rooms. She looked me right in the eye and lied to me. She said she was there just in case she had to list the place." I thought I was over the whole thing, but my eyes welled up with tears.

We were finishing up our dessert—we'd split a cinnamon bun—when I remembered something else I'd wanted to say to Faye. "That was kind of you to give Joan back the teddy bear."

Now it was Faye's turn to get teary eyed. "Martin would have wanted her to have it."

On the way out, I noticed a small watercolour of a cottage. It had a small deck and you could just see the water peeking through the trees. It was exactly the sort of house I'd imagined buying. I looked at the card stapled below the painting but there was no mention of where the place was, just the title *Blue Shutters* and the artist's name. Faye didn't know the artist but she recognized the cottage. I went back to the counter and bought it.

33 CHAPTER THIRTY-THREE

*A*ugust was proving to be hotter than normal. I had all the windows open, hoping a breeze would cool the house down. Every ceiling fan had been working overtime to keep the air moving. As she'd promised, Faye called and we set up a time to go painting. It would be a nice break from packing.

"How do you feel about painting up at the clearing at Carl's house?" She said cautiously. "We won't be bothered by a lot of tourists there." I'd told her a bit about what happened between us. She wouldn't take sides.

"Won't it be busy, with all the workmen rebuilding his house?" I hadn't seen Carl since Martin's funeral. He'd called and left a couple of messages, but the sale of the house had been such an emotional roller coaster, I just didn't have the energy to spend on a relationship. I knew it wasn't right, but I hadn't returned his calls.

"I'm not sure what's happening with that. We can ask him when we see him."

I assumed Theresa and Harry would take us or another of Faye's friends. "He's coming with us?" The ceiling fan above me began to rattle and vibrate. I half-listened to Faye's answer as I pulled the chain. The fan stopped. I had to pull the chain a second time to get it moving at the slowest speed. "How will we fit all of our stuff into his boat?"

"He bought Martin's boat." Faye's laughter told me that I hadn't been successful in hiding my feeling of surprise at her news.

Flustered, I switched topics. "And he's okay with us going over there to paint?"

She grinned. "Of course he's okay. We're bringing lunch."

I hated turning on the oven, it was so hot, but I'd promised Faye I'd bring the dessert. Chocolate chip cookies were quick, easy, and I had all the ingredients. As the kitchen warmed up, I regretted my decision. I should've made the trip into town to buy some brownies at the bakery. I justified the decision by telling myself that this might be the last time I baked something in this kitchen.

My parents were coming next week to help go through my grandmother's things. I didn't want to think about the mammoth task involved in distributing all the doilies fairly among the heirs. The upside was that their visit would give me a chance to show them my new home.

* * *

Faye was already down at the dock when I pulled up. She had on a wide-brimmed hat with a colourful scarf tied around it like a sash. Pink and purple silk fluttered in the breeze. Every once in a while her earrings caught the sun's rays and glittered like stars. I remembered to bring my sunglasses with me this time. I forgot a hat.

In one hand we gripped the handle of the large cooler Faye had brought. It was so heavy I don't know how she managed to get it in the car by herself. In the other hand, we each carried our bag of painting supplies. We lugged the cooler over to a bench near the dock. My painting bag banged against my leg with every other step. When we reached the bench we dropped the cooler onto the grass with a loud thump. My hairline was soaked with perspiration. I wiped it off with my arm as we sat down on the bench to wait for Carl. All the time I'd spent styling my hair and putting on makeup, wasted.

Faye said, "I heard from Joan. She hasn't found her mom yet. She has a waitressing job and she's sharing a place with a couple of the other girls from work." We both turned at the sound of an approaching car. It wasn't Carl's. Faye continued. "I told her your place was sold. She sounded surprised." Faye shrugged. "I guess she didn't know about Ms. Stokes's back-up plan."

My shirt stuck to my body. I pulled it away from my skin in an attempt to create a pocket of cooler air between the fabric and my body. Although we were the only people in sight, Faye stood and waved when Carl pulled into the parking lot.

He whistled as he approached. "Morning, ladies." He easily picked up the cooler and without another word, walked down to his boat. Faye and I traipsed along behind him. He said over his shoulder, "I haven't had a chance to clean the boat out." He grinned. "It isn't like sailing on the *Hail Terry*."

He was right. The boat smelled of fish and cleaner. Carl had tried to get rid of the smell, but I think every crevice was subjected to ocean life for too many years. The trip over to the island was much louder in the motorboat. Instead of talking, Faye and I sat back and enjoyed the scenery.

Carl led the way. He carried the cooler. Faye had a blanket tucked under her arm. And I brought the folding camp chairs.

The rebuilding of Carl's house was finally underway. The new house was using the existing foundation. The wooden skeleton had holes for doors and windows. The openings were in different locations than the original structure. We stopped to inspect the progress.

"You've made some changes," I said.

Carl nodded. "Figured I'd take the opportunity to improve the layout. Bigger windows and the floor plan is open-concept. I had to move the front door to accommodate the change."

Faye nodded approvingly. "I love open concept homes. It

makes the rooms feel so airy." Her eyes scanned the area. "This is such a beautiful spot, you want to make the most of it. Limit the barriers to the outdoors."

Carl agreed. "It'll be a great place to spend my retirement years—fishing, reading, and cooking." He grinned and set the cooler down in the dirt so he could point out where the new deck would go. "I even bought myself a smoker. I'm going to set it up over there. And everything is going to be energy efficient and maintenance free. I'm putting solar panels on the roof." He picked the cooler up and headed toward the path that led to the clearing.

"Wow, it sounds like it'll be quite the place." I said.

His head was turned in the direction we were walking so it was difficult to hear his response. "Not too modern, though. There'll be a wrap-around porch with a porch swing."

We climbed the rest of the way in silence. I wasn't sure what the other two were thinking about, but was I picturing Carl's new home. Maybe he'd be interested in some of my decorating magazines.

By the time we reached the clearing, my forehead and the back of my neck were drenched in sweat. My chest was tight and I was gulping down lungfuls of air. The other two didn't appear to be bothered by the walk up the hill. I tried to get my breathing back to normal without anyone noticing how out of shape I was.

My heartbeat slowed to a mild thump as I looked around. The view was as spectacular as the first time I'd been there. Faye dropped her blanket on one of the camp chairs and wandered off to find a spot to paint.

I took a slug of water. It dribbled down my chin. I was tempted to splash some on the back of my neck but I wasn't sure I had enough water to waste.

Carl walked over to the edge of the clearing. He stood, legs apart, hands on hips and stared out to sea. The breeze ruffled his grey hair. It was much longer than when I first met him.

I opened the cooler. A large jug of lemonade was propped in one corner and held in place with ice packs. Faye had packed plastic cups. I poured lemonade into one and carried it over to Carl.

He turned and smiled as I handed him the glass. "Thanks." He drained half the glass in one swallow. We watched the seagulls swooping and circling down at the base of the cliff. Keeping his eyes on the birds, he said, "Sorry to hear about your place." He frowned. "I thought you had until the end of the month?"

I nodded. "Yeah, well, things didn't go as planned. If I'd known how it would turn out, I never would've sold the portrait." My hands clenched in anger.

Carl shuffled from foot to foot. He seemed nervous. "That night…" He cleared his throat then continued, "You're lucky Nicholas was there. Lonny wouldn't have hesitated to hurt you, or worse. He was an angry SOB. I don't care what the people at church said, the world's a better place without him." I looked at Carl, surprised. *What made him change his mind about Nicholas?*

Faye sat quietly and listened to the exchange between Carl and me. Then she cleared her throat and said, "I don't like to speak ill of the dead, but I agree with Carl."

Carl seemed to have said what he needed to. He turned and pointed near the edge of the cliff. "Do you want to set up over there?"

I pointed to a spot with a view of the water. "It's a bit in the shade, but there's still lots of sunlight."

Carl walked over and picked up my bag. "Do you want a chair, too?"

Once he'd helped me set up, Carl wandered off into the bush while Faye and I painted for a couple of hours. When he reappeared, he spread out the blanket and anchored the corners with nearby stones. "Lunch is ready," he called.

I stretched out on the blanket beside Carl. Faye set the other folding chair next to the cooler. She filled her plate then used the lid of the cooler as a side table. After we finished eating we flipped through the pages of our watercolour pads and compared paintings. I wasn't used to watercolour, but painting outdoor with acrylic was a challenge because the paint dried so quickly. The soft watercolours were a nice change from the bright acrylic paints.

Faye closed her pad of paper and said, "Tell Carl about your new place."

I grinned. "You're not the only one who's going to have a house on the water."

He turned to me surprised, "Really? That's great. Where?"

"Well, the place isn't exactly on the water, but you can see the ocean from the deck. It's near the lighthouse. It isn't as big as my grandmother's house, but it's perfect for me. I don't need all that room. It's just more to clean and fill with clutter. It doesn't need much work, but I want to paint the shutters blue." Faye and I looked at each other and smiled.

"When do you move in?"

I drained my water bottle. "In the fall. The lawyer negotiated sixty days before I need to move out of my grandmother's house. He wanted to make sure I had time to find a new place." I got up and refilled the bottle with the last of the lemonade. "A friend of Faye's is selling. It just came on the market."

"You're lucky," said Carl.

Faye shook her head. "No, it's a sign that it was meant to be."

34 CHAPTER THIRTY-FOUR

I phoned Toby to invite him to my housewarming party. I was about to hang up when he answered. "Alma? I've been meaning to call you." He paused. "If you're interested, my grandmother had a tombstone engraved for Nicholas, even though there wasn't a body. It's in the cemetery in Kilbride." He hesitated, then said, "Anyway, I have the spot. I can send you the information." He sounded a little embarrassed. "I don't know…if…if you're interested?"

* * *

Although the rose bushes were picked over this late in the season, I managed to find one shoved over in the corner of the local nursery. It was a little worse for wear. A few tiny, white blossoms clung to dropping branches. I had the store give it a good dose of water. I was careful not to get my necklace caught as I pushed the shovel aside and lined my trunk with some plastic.

The cemetery was shaded by large trees. Birds chirped as I navigated my way through the rows and rows of tombstones. Nicholas's marker was more of a memorial than a gravestone. The marker was a simple white stone, curved at the top.

Nicholas Denyes
1910-1960
"I will always be a fisherman
It's not something I do
It is who I am."
—*Unknown*

I carefully cleared a patch of dirt at the base of the stone and planted the tiny rose bush. Since being watered at the nursery, the leaves already looked greener and the tiny blossoms were pointing up to the sun. As I stood, a white feather brushed my cheek and landed on my shoulder. The sea glass necklace twinkled in the sunlight as I moved to pick it off my sweater.

I held the tiny feather in the palm of my hand. It reminded me of sleepovers at my grandmother's. I'd often find a feather lying on the pillow beside me when I woke up in the morning. I'd gently place it in the palm of my hand and walk downstairs slowly, so the air wouldn't make it blow away. I'd hold it up to her. She'd smile and say, "An angel watched over you while you were sleeping." I never thought anything of it until I was older. My grandmother was allergic to feathers. All her pillows were made of foam.

I carefully placed the feather in my wallet. The singing of the birds accompanied me back to my car.

* * *

I'd moved into my new place. My parents were gone. Grandma's belongings were distributed, sold, or given to charity. A few friends were coming over for a sort of housewarming party. My grandparents' set of champagne glasses sparkled on the small kitchen island. Carl was the first to arrive. He had a large gift wrapped in brown paper with a big bow. His eyes widened in surprise. "Nice dress. You look good in red."

My cheek muscles hurt my grin was so wide. "Thank you. I know it's a little fancy, but I've been saving it for a special occasion."

He walked into the small living room and searched for somewhere to put the package down. He couldn't seem to find a suitable spot, so he shoved it toward me, as if he couldn't wait to get rid of it.

"This is for you." He shuffled from foot to foot. "Open it." He realized his words sounded like a command. He spoke quickly as I unwrapped the package. "Before everyone comes, if that's okay." He watched intently as the last of the wrapping fell to the ground. I gasped. Tears sprung to my eyes. Carl's words jumbled together. "When Faye mentioned she'd told Alan Boutilier about the portrait of Nicholas, I called the gallery and…"

"And you bought the painting." I couldn't believe it. I thought I'd never see it again. I'd tried to replicate it, but none of my attempts ever turned out as good as the original. "You? You had it all this time. Why didn't you tell me?" The portrait blurred as my eyes filled with tears.

Carl took a step toward me then stopped, his arms limp at his sides, his face full of concern. "I'm sorry I didn't buy it in time to save your grandmother's home. I wasn't sure what to do. Then, when I heard about your new place, I thought I'd wait and surprise you. If I'd known how upset you'd be, I would've given it to you sooner."

I picked up the portrait and placed it on the mantle. Selling the portrait had been my only regret. Now, seeing it framed on either side by windows that looked out toward the ocean, I was glad I'd taken the risk to live my dream. The portrait of Nicholas looked right at home.

I turned to Carl and hugged him. "Thank you."

"I'm forgiven?" He took a step back, keeping hold of my

hands. He grew serious. "I know what it feels like to lose your home."

I smiled up at him. "No, this is what it feels like to come home."

Tendrils

A Blue Portal Novel

Read ahead for a sneak peek from another title in the Blue Portal series to find out about the mysterious blue bottle's new adventure.

Tendrils

A Blue Portal Novel

V.A. Purcell

CHAPTER ONE

*I*t was sad and ugly, but it was mine.

I had high hopes for the house, but now the challenges it presented overwhelmed me. The mountain of boxes—all labelled with my name, *Kate Armsworthy,* in thick black marker—were piled haphazardly in the centre of the room and looked as daunting as Mt. Everest. This would take a lifetime to organize. My chest tightened as I looked at my watch. I couldn't believe it had only been an hour since I'd started to unpack. Every muscle in my body ached as if I'd worked all day. My fists were clenched so tightly I had to concentrate to uncurl my fingers.

The furniture was shoved up against the walls. I grabbed one of the wing-back chairs and pushed it over to the window. I sat down for a second, then got up and turned the chair around so my back was to the stack of boxes. It unsettled me to see familiar pieces of furniture in such unfamiliar surroundings. The chaos created by things out of place made me anxious.

Twisted, naked branches tapped at the window with every gust of wind. Leaves that used to be bright orange and red were now a brown mush that blanketed the lawn. The once neatly-clipped shrubs that dotted the edge of the driveway sported spindly branches that grew out in different directions. Their shape was reminiscent of bushes in a forgotten cemetery, rather than those of a well-maintained country home. The few dry leaves left this late in the fall swirled and spun around the lawn in crazy dance steps, their random movements reminding me of how I'd ended up right here, right now.

It was always supposed to be the two of us, and instead it was just me…alone. Lonely Widow Armsworthy. It bothered me to abandon my unpacking, but the walls were closing in and I needed to escape.

In my rush to leave, I almost closed the door on Kelowna's tail. My golden retriever stuck closer to me than my own shadow. The two of us headed across the weed-choked lawn and down toward the beach. I carefully navigated the steep bank while my sure-footed dog reached the bottom well ahead of me. I envied his ability to leap over the tall weeds and scramble down toward the boulders that protected my property from the waves that eroded the fragile shoreline. I reached the edge of the yard and looked back at the house once more. The second story and the steep roof, capped with a widow's walk, was the only thing in sight. A shiver crawled up my spine and raised goose bumps on my arms. If only Alfred Hitchcock could see this place.

We'd bought my husband's family home from his mother after his father passed away, and used it as our vacation home for the past two years. We were the third generation of Armsworthys to live in the house. It had been built at a time when people appreciated being closer to the road rather than the water. The garage was set behind the house, which gave it the best view of the ocean. The house was clad in weathered, mud-brown siding with a covered porch that extended across the front and wrapped around one side. Additions, which started off as porches and were later made into rooms, clung precariously to the other side and the back of the house.

But for all its ugliness, there was something comfortable about the old place, too. The house sat snugly on a hill—the old highway in front and the ocean behind. It felt solid, like it could withstand the tornado from the Wizard of Oz. It had roots and by association, anyone who lived in it had roots, too.

Off in the distance, white-steepled churches dotted the shoreline. Nearer, boats bobbed in the water, their sails wrapped tightly to their masts. They were anchored just offshore to avoid the ebb and flow of the tidal waters. Once, Graham and I saw a couple of seals far out in the water, but that was a long time ago.

Beside me, Kelowna was busy digging in the neglected garden that ran along the edge of the boulders. The weeds were particularly tall and green here, and the boulders provided shelter from the ocean breeze. It was an ideal spot. I'd planned to walk down to the shore, but the look in his eyes begged me to stay and help. Certain it was a rotten shoe or something worse, I pretended to help by shuffling the dirt around with the toe of my shoe. I didn't want to take the chance of my hands smelling like dead fish—not even for my best friend. Soon we unearthed a bit of glass. At first I thought it was just a shard, but as we continued to dig, I saw that it was a bottle. Intrigued, I bent down to help him.

I created a trench with my fingers and pried the bottle out of the dirt. I cleaned it off as best as I could with the sleeve of my shirt. The glass was thick and the top of the bottle was chipped. The bottle was shaped like an old liquor flask with an elongated neck, and embossed letters rose through the dirt still caked to its front. It looked quite old, and maybe valuable. I shook out as much of the soil as I could, and took it with me. Then we walked along the small beach to search for more treasures.

We walked a short distance until the beach narrowed to a small strip of sand, and then we turned back toward the house. The tide was coming in and the wind picked up as we walked. It whipped at my pant legs and found all sorts of cracks in my jacket. I shivered as the chill wormed its way down my arms and back.

At first I blamed the weather for my discomfort, but as I walked along I realized it was my hand—the one that held the bottle—that bothered me the most. Not only was it warm, but it throbbed in time to the beat of my heart. I held the bottle up to my face and tried to peer inside, but the glass was too thick. Thoughts of poisonous creatures and strange, toxic plants popped into my head and I dropped the bottle. It didn't break as it hit the soft sand, but even so, I expected something to scuttle out of it. I held my breath and waited, but nothing moved except the waves as they hit the narrow beach.

I kicked the bottle a few times, just to make sure there wasn't anything that clung to its insides. I stared at my hand. I couldn't see any mark and it didn't hurt. My palm still felt warm, but the pulsing had stopped as soon as I'd let go of the bottle.

Carefully, I picked it up to see if it felt warm. *Nothing.* I thought maybe I'd gripped the bottle too tightly. I switched hands and held it loosely by its long neck. By the time I reached the house, the hand that held the bottle was warm and my arm throbbed. But I wasn't quite ready to give up my treasure.

In my haste to let go of the bottle, I didn't even bother to take off my coat. I carried it through the kitchen and into the room which doubled as both a pantry and laundry room.

I dropped it into a plastic basin, then I set the basin in the old porcelain sink and watched little air bubbles escape from its mouth as it filled with water. Some of the dirt started to loosen and swirl around. Once I felt sure nothing would crawl out, I turned off the tap and left the bottle to soak.

I put on the kettle, then sat at the kitchen table to wait for it to boil. The room was depressing. The décor hadn't changed in forty years: painted cupboards that didn't close any more, fake wood grain counter tops chipped along the edges, and one electrical outlet for the whole kitchen.

Memories rose like bubbles in a pot of boiling water. I remembered Graham leaning over the blueprints of the renovations we'd planned, pointing out to friends and family the "great room" complete with a beamed ceiling, and the kitchen redesigned to include an island. His glasses had slipped down his nose as he bent over the pages. He'd absent-mindedly pushed them back up with the tip of his finger, only to have them slip down again a few minutes later. The memory was so clear I could almost reach out and touch him.

I reached for the pile of mail on the table beside me. The letter on top was addressed to Mrs. Kate Armsworthy, not Mr. and Mrs. I picked it up and then tossed it back on top of the pile unopened. I left the rest of the mail untouched.

My reflection in the window stared back at me. I was pleased to see my shoulder-length hair looked respectable. At least my grey roots were covered thanks to a recent trip to the hairdresser—the second one I'd tried in town. The dye job from the first hairdresser I'd used had left a dark stripe right down the centre of my head. But I'd never dyed my own hair and I was determined not to start now. My bangs were shorter than I'd wanted, but they'd grow back. At least I didn't look like a punk rocker.

Restless, I surveyed the bare walls in the sunroom that adjoined the kitchen. Maybe if I hung a few pictures it would make the room feel more like home. We hadn't bothered to move any of our paintings while it was just our vacation home. All I needed was the hammer and some picture hooks.

I kept all the tools in a drawer in the pantry just so I wouldn't have to go down to the basement. The stairs were steep and it was damp and full of cobwebs. Graham always teased me about it, but I didn't care. I hated it and made any excuse not to go down there.

I left the cup half-full and went to get the hammer and picture hooks. The first thing I did when I stepped into the pantry was glance over at the sink. Brown squiggly lines covered the bottom of the basin. Puzzled, I stepped a little closer. At first I thought it was worms, but as I moved closer I realized the brown squiggles looked like letters. The way they were shaped reminded me of the letters in the "secret code" you get when you order tickets on-line. It looked like the letters *p,i,v,n,o,u,t,g,e,d.*

I reached for my phone and snapped a picture of the "message"; then checked to make sure the letters were clear enough to read. While in the pantry, I grabbed the hammer and hooks.

The appearance of the squiggle-type letters rattled me. The whole time I worked, I couldn't stop thinking about the bottle and the crazy letters in the bottom of the sink. My hands tingled just thinking about the bottle. I knew my imagination was getting the better of me, but I decided the sooner I got it out of my house the better. I didn't care if it was valuable or not.

I swung open the door and marched into the pantry. Just as I reached for the basin, the water began to swirl. I watched it go faster and faster, and the bottle spun around and around. It seemed like ages, but it was probably only a few seconds before it came to a stop. The bottle's final position caught the light from the ceiling fixture in such a way that it painted a rainbow on the wall.

The dirt caked to the outside had been washed away and revealed marks etched into the surface. They appeared and reappeared as the waves rolled over the curved glass. Once the bottle stopped, the waves slowed and the surface of the water stilled. The water acted like a magnifying glass and enlarged the marks. The unfamiliar symbols looked quite different from the letters I'd seen in the bottom of the basin.

Before I could change my mind, I grabbed the edge of the basin and pulled it out of the sink. Water sloshed over the edge and spilled on the floor and down my pant legs. I rushed to toss the contents of the basin out onto the lawn. The bottle landed on a patch of brown, scraggly grass. I checked to make sure there wasn't any dirt left in the basin, then I took it back inside and put it on the kitchen counter. Even though the bottle was gone, I wasn't ready to go back into the pantry quite yet.

My hands shook as I poured myself a very large glass of wine, then gulped it down in record time. I carried a second glass into the sunroom, determined to finish the job I'd started. Besides, it would keep me busy. I put several holes in the wall before I hammered the hooks in the correct spot. At least the pictures would hide my mistakes.

Just as I was about to hang the last painting, there was a loud bang and I almost dropped it. It sounded like something had fallen in the basement. I was debating about whether or not to go investigate when the doorbell rang. I glanced through curtain at the side window. It was my neighbour, Mrs. Llewellyn. Kelowna rushed to the door in anticipation; he doesn't have any filter when it comes to people.

Everyone is a friend.

The Llewellyns had lived next door for as long as I could remember. Graham hadn't minded Mr. Llewellyn, but he called Mrs. Llewellyn an old busybody. Since there was such an age difference between us and the Llewellyns, and because we'd been seasonal residents until recently, there really hadn't been much need to interact with them beyond comments about the weather. Mrs. Llewellyn surveyed our yard, and I could tell by her stiff posture and pursed mouth that she was less than impressed. She held a casserole dish covered in foil.

Her husband, Albert, was more approachable. I'm not sure what he thought about our place. Probably the same thing as his wife, at least in public. They struck me as that sort of a couple. She definitely wore the pants in the family.

As I opened the door to let her in, she held out the dish.

"Hello, Kate. Here's a little something for you. I saw the moving trucks a while ago, but I thought you might still be busy unpacking."

She glanced at the unopened boxes visible from the mudroom. "I always find it so stressful to live out of boxes. When we moved in next door, even though I was pregnant, I had everything unpacked in no time. Albert teased me and told me to slow down. But you don't have that problem, do you?"

The smile she attempted really was more of a sneer. She shouldn't have bothered to make the effort. It only emphasized her insincerity.

"This is very kind of you." I took the casserole dish from her. "It looks delicious."

"It's my famous tuna casserole. I make my own bread crumbs for the topping."

"I was just in the middle of something. And as you noticed, I haven't really unpacked yet. Sorry I can't offer you a cup of tea."

I hoped she wouldn't notice I'd lied. As an avid tea drinker, a kettle and teapot were the first things I'd unpacked when I moved into the house. "I'd love to invite you and Mr. Llewellyn over for tea once I'm settled. It was very kind of you to drop by."

I set the casserole dish on the bench in the back hall and opened the back door, hoping Ivy would get the hint. I know she wanted to snoop around a bit, but I wasn't going to give her the satisfaction of seeing how little unpacking I'd actually done.

Just as I put the casserole into the fridge there was another knock and I heard someone come inside. I must have forgotten to lock the door when Mrs. Llewellyn left. Her shrill voice called out.

"Kate? I found this lying by your back door. It must have fallen out of one of your boxes."

She was holding the antique bottle. I grabbed it from her, afraid she might get the same tingling sensation I got when I'd first held it. I gave her the warmest smile I could.

"Thank you so much! It's a family keepsake. I would have been so upset if I'd lost it."

I don't know why I lied. I stood there for a moment not quite sure what to say next, but she saved me from any further conversation.

"I don't want to keep you from your unpacking." She turned back toward the door. "Have a lovely evening, my dear."

This time I locked the door behind her and stood looking out the window to make sure she was gone.

I really wanted to throw the bottle back outside, but I was afraid Ivy Llewellyn might be spying on me from her kitchen window. I hurried back into the pantry and set the bottle on the old tiled counter beside the sink.

I carried my mug into the sunroom and watched the last of the day's light catch the waves. This room was the one we had used the most, so there hadn't been much to do with it once all the rest of our belongings had been moved in. The furniture was arranged so Graham's big chair faced the old propane stove. The windows on either side of the stove offered a beautiful view of the water. Unlike the wing chairs in the living room, the furniture in the sunroom was so worn, it looked like it belonged in the old house.

When I set my mug down on the coffee table, I noticed all the scratches on its surface. I remembered when the first scratch was made by our daughter, Samantha, when she'd worked on a school project. After that, the rest of the marks hadn't mattered as much. It had been many years since anyone sat around it and did school work.

It made me think about what Ivy had said about being pregnant. Funny, I'd never seen any sign of children or grandchildren. I shrugged. Maybe they lived far away. I would, if I were related to her.

Graham's chair was just big enough to sit with my legs tucked under me. I was frustrated that even with all the stress involved with the move, I still hadn't lost any weight. My black yoga pants were more comfortable than my jeans, and unless I needed to dress up, they were my pants of choice. I pulled the sleeves down on my bright pink sweater to cover my cold hands. It was one of my favourite tops because it was loose enough to hide the extra pounds around my middle. I picked up my mug and wrapped my hands around it. The warmth that seeped into my fingers soothed me. Although the tingling had disappeared, I inspected my hands for any signs of swelling or redness while I sipped my tea.

I read my mystery novel until suppertime. Ivy Llewellyn's casserole was probably quite good, but it didn't appeal to me. I couldn't quite bring myself to throw it out, so I scraped it into one of my dishes and stuck it in the freezer.

Then I scrubbed the casserole dish until it sparkled and set it on the bench by the back door.

There wasn't much food to choose from. I made a peanut butter and jelly sandwich and heated up a bowl of soup in the microwave. Then I took my supper out to the living room on a tray and turned on the television. Mrs. Llewellyn's casserole might not have been so bad, I thought, as I took a spoonful of tepid soup.

That night, Kelowna followed me upstairs and curled up on the carpet at the foot of the bed. He fell asleep immediately, but I lay in bed and thought about the message in the dirt. I'd avoided the pantry, afraid of what I might find. My hands started to tingle at the thought of the strange bottle. Just as I was starting to drift off to sleep, I remembered I hadn't gone down to the basement to see if anything had fallen. I knew I wouldn't fall asleep until I checked. I'd have to go back through the pantry to get to the basement.

Tendrils

Available now in paperback and ebook.

Torn Feathers

Coming Soon

ABOUT THE AUTHOR

V.A. Purcell is the author of *Tendrils*, *Rogue Wave* and *Torn Feathers*. These novels comprise the Blue Portal series. Set on the South Shore of Nova Scotia, each story introduces readers to a new set of characters and adventures. They can be read in any order.

She has also written *Kindling Friendships*, a memoire novella.

Veronica lives on the South Shore of Nova Scotia with her husband and their standard poodle, Griffyn.

Visit her at www.vapurcell.com